# HE WAS PERFECT.

His face roared into my soul. *Imprint. Genetic imprint.*

I looked down fast. He didn't move. Someone up ahead was taking a huge amount of time stowing their luggage. *Thank you, someone!* I started to take the boy in bit by bit. I slid sly looks at his legs, jean-clad, long, muscle-defined.

My eyes moved up to his crotch and screeched past, panic-stricken. I tipped my head back just a bit, looked at his arms, chest. *Beautiful.* My eyes glided upward, reached his face again.

He was looking right at me, like he was waiting for my eyes to get to his. He was gorgeous and grinning, all sarcastic and knowing.

I went red. Hideously red. Like a boiler suddenly being turned full on.

"Seen enough?" he drawled.

## Also by Kate Cann

Grecian Holiday

Spanish Holiday

California Holiday

Diving In

In the Deep End

Sink or Swim

# Mediterranean Holiday

## Or, How I Moved to a Tiny Island and Found the Love of My Life

## KATE CANN

HARPER TEEN

*An Imprint of* HarperCollins*Publishers*

**AUTHOR'S NOTE**

The island of Caminos is my invention, but there are two
small hot rocky islands off Malta called Gozo and Comino.

HarperTeen is an imprint of HarperCollins Publishers.

Mediterranean Holiday
Copyright © 2007 by Kate Cann
All rights reserved. Printed in the United States of America.
No part of this book may be used or reproduced in any manner
whatsoever without written permission except in the case of brief
quotations embodied in critical articles and reviews. For information
address HarperCollins Children's Books, a division of HarperCollins
Publishers, 1350 Avenue of the Americas, New York, NY 10019.
www.harperteen.com

Library of Congress Catalog Card Number: 2006933589
ISBN-10: 0-06-115216-1 — ISBN-13: 978-0-06-115216-0

Typography by Andrea Vandergrift
❖
First HarperTeen edition, 2007

To Sian, Ian, Ianthe, Freya, and
Rowena, with love

## CHAPTER 1

WHEN DAVINIA MORGAN-HARWOOD was first shown
into our sixth-form common room and introduced
by our class monitor, the whole place went silent.
And not only because no one could really believe
that was her *name*.

First of all, she was looking round at the rest of
us as though we'd been dumped on the floor by an
incontinent dog. She looked like, far from hoping
she'd be accepted by her new classmates, she'd bite
your face if you came anywhere near her.

Second of all, she was gorgeous. I mean seriously, unfairly gorgeous. A mass of dead-straight,
glowing auburn hair casually caught back with a
wide black hair clip, huge fog-lamp brown eyes,
quirky but perfect face, long legs . . . the works.
And most of all, she had such *style*, such I-am-
who-I-am, screw-the-rest-of-you chutzpah.

She was in the uniform that the sad ex-prison

1

guards who've got jobs as teachers here in this godforsaken, all-girls, fee-paying ghetto made us wear, but on her, it looked *good*. The skirt was tighter than it should've been; the shirt looser and unbuttoned low, the sweater tied French-style; and her shoes must've cost ten times the whole lot of it put together.

"*Shit!*" muttered Abby, next to me. Abby, as she frequently assured me, was my best friend. "Who the hell does she think *she* is?"

I didn't answer—I was too busy ogling.

"Davinia had . . . er . . . some *problems* at her last school," barked our monitor. "And as the A level exams are upon us she'll have some catching up to do, so I want you all to help her adjust and fit in. ANY QUESTIONS?"

She glared round at us, daring anyone to say a word. Then she turned on her dumpy beer-bottle legs and marched out.

Cissie, the class captain, had already been primed to Look After the New Girl. She sashayed bossily over to her and bleated, "Hi, Davinia? Do you shorten that?"

"Do I shorten *what*?" snapped Davinia.

"Your name? I wondered if you got called Davy, or Dav, or . . . ?"

"No."

"O-*kay* . . . well, let me show you where the kettle is. So you can make coffee?"

Davinia stared at her blankly, then she said, "I don't want coffee."

"*Right.*" Cissie prided herself on her diplomacy and her ability to deal with awkward students. "So—you know where your locker is?"

"*Yes,*" snapped Davinia. She radiated boredom and irritation.

I was utterly bowled over by her arrogance. Here she was in a new school, and she was acting like a queen bitch and she just didn't care. It was suicidal and breathtakingly brilliant.

"What did you get kicked out for?" demanded Abby, hackles rising like the tough little terrier she is.

Davinia looked down and smiled with just one side of her mouth, all sneering and sexy. Then she looked up and said, "Cocaine."

It only took till lunchtime before the bullies were on to her. Marsha Hunt, big and mean, and Una Trilby, stick-thin and warped, led their nasty gang over to her as she waited in the lunch line. Marsha juggernauted her way in front and announced, "You're new."

I was sitting at a table nearby with Abby. I waited with my breath held for Davinia to react, to complain, to say something that would give Marsha's mob the excuse they needed to get verbal and sneakily physical. To give them an excuse to jump her at the end of the day.

"Yup," said Davinia, and she drew out of her pocket a tiny gray-blue mobile and started to read her texts.

"I'm talking to you," growled Marsha.

"S'OK," said Davinia, still text-checking, "I can do more than one thing at a time, I'm gifted like that."

Marsha was stunned, but you could feel her working up a head of steam as her mob shuffled balefully around her. Then, before it could all explode, Davinia looked up and gave her *the* most stunning and disarming smile and said, "Go on!"

"Go on what?" croaked Marsha. You could tell she was charmed, despite herself.

"With what you were saying."

"Are you making fun of me?"

"What? Why d'you think that?"

"You're making fun of me," Marsha repeated stolidly.

"Of course I'm not. What kind of idiot would I be to make fun of someone on my first day here?" Then she smiled brilliantly again, and said, "Tell me, is that macaroni and cheese edible?"

"It's really good actually," said Marsha. The words were out before she remembered she was trying to bully the new girl.

"I'll get some then," said Davinia, and she practically pushed by Marsha and picked up a plateful. She added a salad to her tray and sailed on to pay, then sat by herself at an empty table near the long, low windows.

"*Did you see that?*" breathed Abby.

"What?" I answered. "Nothing happened." For some reason, I didn't want to talk about Davinia to Abby. It was like I wanted to keep her to myself.

"Exactly," Abby rushed on. "She just . . . brushed Marsha aside. Look at them all . . . Una's gobsmacked. They don't know what happened. So they're pretending nothing did."

"Nothing *did*," I echoed.

"Oh, *right*!" said Abby, indignantly. She hated it when I didn't agree with everything she said. "One of their victims just . . . *danced away*. Why aren't they going after her?"

"Because . . ." I wanted to say "because of that amazing smile she gave" but I said, "She just acted like she wasn't scared of them, that's all."

"She wasn't acting, if you ask me. She actually *wasn't scared*. Trust me. She's either thick or . . . or . . ."

"Or what?" I asked, but before Abby could answer I went on, "Hey—there's Ciara. Shall we get her to come over and join us?" Abby, a bit frostily, agreed, and I waved to Ciara and the subject was dropped.

Except that, whenever I thought I could get away with it, I slid my eyes toward the window to look at Davinia. Who ate all of her salad and half her macaroni and cheese, then calmly stood up and walked, perfectly poised, out of the dining room.

As I watched her go, I wondered if I could possibly be turning into a lesbian.

## CHAPTER 2

**THREE DAYS WENT BY.** Davinia continued on her solitary path, not talking to anyone, communing a great deal with her expensive little phone. To Marsha, Una, and the Mob, she was invisible, not there. They didn't understand how she'd managed to deal with them; they felt vaguely humiliated; something in them didn't want to risk coming up against her again. To Captain Cissie, she was an ungrateful snob. To just about everyone else, including Abby, she was standoffish and up her own arse, not worth bothering about. To me . . .

Well, I continued to hover in a fog of curiosity and obsession. The thing is, I kind of wanted to be a lesbian. My experiences with heterosexuality so far had been such a turnoff I reckoned I was like Pavlov's dogs—those poor mutts who were given shocks to turn them off something otherwise nice. I wasn't technically a virgin but I considered myself a complete learner, and I thought maybe learning about sex with a girl might be better.

But Davinia wasn't making this easy. She hardly ever appeared in the sixth-form common room (where did she go?), but I was in the same class as her for history, where I had to keep reminding myself to stop staring at her.

We passed a few times in the corridor and she'd look right through me, like she looked through everyone.

And then one Friday afternoon, she spoke to me.

It was silent(ish) study period in the library. When I came through the door I saw her right away, sitting on her own at the large table by the middle window. I skirted past, walking as usual over to the end farthest from the librarian and her central control desk; then on a brave impulse I swung round and marched back to Davinia's table. She didn't look up. I pulled out the chair farthest away from her, and sat down.

The early summer sunshine was coming through the window and lighting up her arms and her hands. She had perfect hands. She didn't have nasty nail extensions or anything, just these very elegant, slightly pointy fingers with long, white-tipped nails. She kept moving them around, drumming silently on the desk, and doodling huge, weeping eyes on her notebook. The pages of the book she was supposed to be reading remained unturned. I made myself focus my eyes on my book and keep them there, halfheartedly reading, taking a few useless notes. Then I heard a hiss, and the words, "How do you *stand* it here?"

I slewed my eyes sideways. There was still no one else at the table but Davinia, so it must have been her talking.

To me.

Some instinct told me to go for it, to *seize the day*, however badly it turned out. I reckoned Davinia would either like me or she wouldn't, so there was no sense pussyfooting and being careful. "By getting regularly shit-faced," I said.

And she laughed. *She laughed.* "You mean drunk, right?" she gurgled.

"Yes. Very drunk. And counting the days till I get out of here. Every day goes by—it's one fewer."

"I don't know how any of you stand it. It's such a drab, narrow, *boring* little school. To have been here, only here, since you were five years old—"

"I haven't," I broke in, delighted to put this part of the record straight—to make this connection with her. "I've only been here since the start of the year. I did my GCSEs at Whitecourt

9

Comprehensive, but my parents split up, it was awful—we had to move, and they pushed me into coming here . . ."

"You came from the *State System*?" She said the words like they're the name of a local sewage works, and it killed me that she picked up on my comprehensive school as being the most shocking, of-concern thing out of all the stuff I've just told her.

"Yes," I say. "Thank *God.*"

"Why thank God?"

"Because if I hadn't been there first, I'd probably be as stupid and smug and *narrow* as most of the other girls here, that's why!"

Narrow—it was her word. You show someone that you like them by mirroring their bodies and using their words, and I did this, again, by instinct. She laughed, then she got to her feet and shifted round the table and sat right next to me, pulling her books and folders with her, completely confident I'd accept her. My heart was thudding with triumph and excitement. "Did you really get chucked out for cocaine?" I asked.

"No. I just said that to shut all those . . . *gonks* up. Just the usual staying out, alcohol in the dorm stuff. I was given three warnings, and I blew it."

"The dorm—you boarded?"

"Yes. God, we had such a *laugh*. We were right near the boys' school, we used to climb out of the bathroom windows. . . . They'd have cars waiting underneath. . . ."

"But a *dorm*? I couldn't stand it. The lack of privacy."

"God, it wasn't a problem. I mean—there were only two other girls in mine, and they'd get out of the way if I . . . you know . . . needed them to." She smirked. "I loved that room. We had this unutterably wonderful en suite, with a really good shower. . . ."

Normally, I'd sneer critically at a privileged setup like that, but this time I didn't.

"Anyway," she went on. "Four of us got expelled at the same time—and there were three kicked out from the boys' school. Big scandal—in the local papers and everything."

"Wow. Did you keep a copy?"

"Of course! Framed! It goes on about us being a 'fast set' like we were out of the 1920s or something—it's hilarious. My mother was *hysterical*, of course, when it all happened. She convinced herself I'd been led astray by the others—her innocent baby. She banned me from seeing them *ever* again—"

*"Girls!"* The librarian at the central control desk peered at us menacingly. "This is supposed to be a *silent study period*!"

I let a few minutes go by, then I whispered, "D'you stick to it? Not seeing your friends?"

Davinia shrugged. "No. But it's a lot of work, setting up meetings. Mummy's so neurotic about it all. Anyway, she said she wanted me at home with her, and at a nice, safe school. . . . Daddy lectured me about all the money he'd spent on me that he may as well have just poured down the drain. . . . Shit, it was all *vile*. I threw the most spectacular fits but that just convinced Mummy all the more that I was out of control and in danger. . . ."

"Blimey," I said.

*"Blimey,"* Davinia echoed, but not nastily, then she turned her amazing eyes on me and demanded, "How come you came here when you moved house? How come you didn't go to another *state* school?"

"Oh, my mum had done all this research on how it's bad news to move house when your kid is a teenager."

*"What?* Why?"

"Because at the new school, the teenager will inevitably move into a lower status group than the one they were in before and, to gain acceptance, they may drink more, do more drugs, and have loose sex."

"You sound like a sociologist," she mocked, and I didn't mind.

"Just the daughter of one."

"But . . . you've *come* to a new school. . . ."

"Yeah, but as my mother rightly spotted, it has none of the dangers of a big comprehensive. So although I had to settle for a 'lower status group' than the really, *really* great friends I had before . . ." I stopped and took a breath. I could feel her fog-lamp eyes on my face. Then I went on: ". . . I don't have to do drugs and sex to gain acceptance. I have to do pointless hanging around in the town shopping center and little trips to Pizza Hut because they all look too young to get into bars and . . . I have to do sleepovers."

"You are shitting me."

"*Sleepovers!* With lots of DVDs. *Boring* DVDs."

And we both laughed. At the central control desk, the librarian's head shot up like a missile periscope, and we both choked ourselves silent.

And I was in a state of bliss. That conversation . . . that had raced. I had taken a risk and spoken just like I felt and been bold and articulate, and Davinia had loved it.

As we pretended to read, the energy between

us hummed around us, almost as good as talking again.

I felt a bit guilty at the way I'd happily trashed my new friends, especially Abby.

But only a bit.

As Davinia saw it, she'd stepped down from the heights, and I'd been shunted up from the depths. We were both out of place and we'd found each other.

## CHAPTER 3

**WHEN I GOT BACK TO** our flat that night, Dad was there. It was obvious that he'd been crying. He does this a lot when he's on his own and he always tries to mop himself up before I get back but I can tell. No one has that many colds.

I didn't mention it, though. It makes it worse, makes it more real, if you mention it. Instead I tried to be jolly and affirmative; I made him a mug of tea and told him about my day (the lessons part, not my fixation on Davinia) and talked about what we were going to cook for supper that night. It's nearly always frozen chicken breasts or frozen cod steaks, with frozen vegetables, because we're trying to be healthy, which is a bit of a joke, isn't it, everything being frozen? We vary it with potatoes one night, rice the next, pasta after that. Or we ring for a pizza.

If I wasn't there to make sure he ate, I think

he'd just dwindle away with grief. He still hasn't got over what my mum did to us. Neither have I, but it's accepted between us that my misery is nothing compared to his.

I was nearly torn apart when my mum announced she was leaving, though. It came completely out of nowhere. One summer afternoon she sat me down all efficiently, and told me she'd "got involved with someone else" and she couldn't carry on the charade of living with my father anymore and she was moving in with her new lover. She said I wasn't a child anymore and she'd still be there for me, just not living with me. She said she knew how much she'd hurt me but we both knew it was better to be honest so she was coming right out with it.

. The thing is, she hadn't been honest, not a bit. At the start of that year she'd lied to me, lied through her teeth. She'd started going out more, staying out until late, and looking so much better . . . not just the new clothes and the different haircut, but looking better right through to the pores on her skin.

I thought she was having an affair. I'd confronted her. I'd waited until Dad was away and I'd asked her what she was up to, why she was changing.

"Oh, darling, it's just my *age*." She'd laughed. "I've realized I've got to take myself in hand now, if I don't want to turn into an old *crone*. And I want to get out more, see more of my friends. Nothing wrong with that, is there?"

Nothing at all, I replied, all shaky, and then I gulped out that I'd been afraid she'd been cheating on Dad. She burst out laughing, swore black and blue she wasn't, hugged me. . . . The *relief*, it was like her wrapping a big warm duvet round me.

My mum wouldn't lie to me, after all. She'd never lie to me. I kept telling myself that as I slogged away at my GCSEs, and all the time little doubts wriggled in, something I overheard when she was on the phone or the way she'd hide her mobile away or the row she had with my dad about spending over three hundred pounds to get her teeth bleached. . . .

And then, almost as soon as I'd finished my GCSEs, she made her dreadful announcement. She assured me we'd "get through this," we'd still be friends, it just meant a readjustment, it would take time. . . .

I asked her why she'd lied to me before. She made out that that was for my good, because she didn't want me to screw up my exams.

I couldn't shout at her; I couldn't even cry.

When you're hurt that badly, you just shut down, you withdraw.

And then she told me she'd told me first, before she'd spoken to my dad.

And after she'd told him, nothing I was feeling seemed important anymore.

It was like an avalanche; it was like disaster after disaster, and me just trying to stay alive inside it. Dad was *stricken*—it was terrifying, hearing his anger and grief. Mum moved out that evening, round to her lover's. She was crying as she hugged me good-bye, promising to see me soon. I felt like I might die of misery and rage letting go of her, but I could tell that everything in her was yearning, absolutely yearning, to escape to her new life. Then my aunt June, my dad's bossy older sister, arrived and stayed with us that night. Mum had texted her what had happened. *Texted her!* Usually I couldn't stand Aunt June but it was a relief to have her there. Dad's howling appalled me. Aunt June said no child (me) could be expected to deal with it. Aunt June stayed on for a week; she cooked large meals that we didn't eat and fed Dad whisky and slagged off my mum and talked about a fresh start. And she primed me about taking care of him. "He needs you," she said. "Think of all he's done for you in the past, and try and be strong for him now."

Within days our lovely home was put up for sale; the proceeds were to be split so Mum could buy a new home with her lover. She wanted to see me; I refused. I wouldn't talk to her on the phone. She sent me cards and messages telling me she understood how I felt and it would all take time but that I'd understand as I grew older and it would heal in the end.

I tore them up.

The house was sold for a good price, and Dad seemed to rally a little. He announced he wanted to move nearer his work; he'd had more than an hour's drive twice a day for years now, not wanting to uproot us from the family home when he switched jobs. He wanted to make a fresh start, away from where everyone knew what had happened and looked at him with pity on their faces. And it was good timing for me, he said—I could do my A levels at a school or college nearby.

Aunt June counseled me against making any kind of fuss about this. She said Dad was bound to be a bit selfish after all he'd been through. She told me lots of people made a change after GCSEs and she reminded me I'd been thinking of going to the sixth-form college in the town nearby. When I said yes, but a lot of my good friends were going to go there too, she told me starchily that I could still see them, we weren't emigrating. I'd just have the chance to make new friends, as well.

And then Mum phoned Dad and mooted the idea of paying for a private college for me, for all the sociological reasons I'd outlined to Davinia. I think she saw it as some kind of compensation for all the hurt I'd been through. I was vulnerable, she said, and I needed the kind of pastoral care that only a small, fee-paying college could give me.

And Dad agreed with her. Since this was the first thing they'd agreed on in years, and since I was past caring about anything much anymore, I went along with it, and the rest you know.

Apart from the fact that I still haven't spoken to Mum, not even on the phone.

After our grim little dinner (defrosted chicken breasts, tinned sweet corn, rice) I went up to my room and lay on my back on my bed, and let Davinia fill my mind.

She felt like freedom.

**WHEN I GOT TO SCHOOL** the next day, Abby was shirty about something. She ignored me when I said hello in the cloakroom and when I asked her if she was OK, she snapped, "Why wouldn't I be?"

"Come on, Abby, something's up," I said, and I had this sudden crazy thought that she was angry because she'd seen me in the library with Davinia. This is what comes of going to an all-girls' school. You start thinking in this neurotic, lesbian way. "What's up?" I repeated.

"Nothing!" she squawked, ramming her coat on its peg.

"What've you got first session?" I asked.

"Math," she snapped back. "It's Wednesday, so it's *math*." There was a resentful tang to her voice, like if I was a *real* friend I'd *know* she had math.

Then I remembered that she'd texted me last night, just as I was drifting off to sleep, and I hadn't replied. She took any little slight like that mega-seriously. I was just about to apologize, say something to smooth it over, when suddenly it all seemed so monumentally petty I couldn't be bothered. I was sick of the stupid sulk-game she was playing, sick of *her*. "OK, don't have too grim a time," I said, all offhand, and I slung my bag over my shoulder and walked off to my lesson.

The trouble was, I'd stopped feeling grateful to Abby. It was really damaging our friendship. She'd taken me under her wing when I first started at the school—she'd been through all the way from year zero and she knew everyone and everything and I was a nice new project for her. Because I was so grateful I went along with everything she said, just about. I was this stupid, grateful, flattering echo chamber. And she loved it; she told me I was her new best friend, and she introduced me to her old friends and took me about and invited me shopping and to sleepovers.

But you can have enough of being grateful. Plus I was getting pretty sick of how controlling she was, how opinionated. It was boring.

I didn't look for her at break, and at lunchtime I went into the dining hall on my own to queue up. Abby was already there, eating at a table with some of her "old" friends.

Now, in the unspoken rules of our friendship, eating with other people was a major betrayal. OK, it could happen, but if it did happen, the one sitting down was meant to leap to her feet and wave the other energetically over, saying something like, "Oh, *there* you are! I tried calling you—you still had your phone off!"

Abby didn't do this. Instead, she made a big show of having a good time with her old friends.

A bit of me felt upset, scared even . . . but another bit didn't. That other bit felt exhilarated, let off the hook. I joined the queue, planning to not so much as *glance* in Abby's direction until I'd completely eaten my lunch.

I didn't think about Davinia. It seemed too much to hope for, that she might turn up and eat with me. But just as I was picking up an empty plate to get it filled, she appeared on the other side of the chrome queuing bar. "Hi!" she said. "Can I join you?" Then without waiting for an answer, she limbo-danced under the bar and was standing right in front of me.

"You just have!" I said, grinning—I was feeling all kind of seized up with excitement and pleasure, really glad that everyone had seen her join me like that, that Abby had seen it. The gang of fifth-formers behind me in the line shifted indignantly and one of them said, "There's a *queue*, you know!"

"Oh, shut up," snarled Davinia. "You shouldn't be eating anything, with that arse."

The girl went scarlet, as two of her friends suppressed smirks.

"What're you going to have?" I asked.

"It all looks like it's already been digested," moaned Davinia. "Salad, I guess. Soup and salad."

I'd been planning to get chips, but I found myself getting soup and salad too, and then we paid and, without discussing it, headed for a small empty table at the far side of the hall.

"God, this is so *scuzzy*!" she wailed.

"What, the soup?"

"This *dining room*! It's got absolutely no *style*. . . . At my old school, we had this gorgeous sunken lighting, and proper padded seats, not these cheap things. . . ." I started to gurgle, and she shot an indignant glance at my face. "What're you laughing at?"

"I'm thinking what you'd say if you could see the dining room at *my* old school. Strip lighting, metal benches, cracked Formica tables, grease . . ."

"Oh, *yuck*."

"It was like something out of *Prisoner Cell Block H*. Especially the fights."

"The *fights*—oh, God, of course—you had

boys too, didn't you?"

"Yeah. Really, really hard boys. But the girls used to fight too. There were loads of fights—we used to love 'em. Rival gangs. Vendettas. People got suspended every week for bringing in knives. . . ."

Davinia was lapping this up, and I rambled on happily, exaggerating its roughness, and then she told me absurd things about the rarefied setup she'd come from, exaggerating its privilege, and we were both laughing at each other, and I was feeling wild, out of my rut. It was . . . I dunno. I can't explain it. It was just this huge buzz to be so different, to have come from such different places, and yet get on so well. It was like the places we'd come from weren't real, like most of the things people went on about were just surface stuff.

I completely forgot about Abby until I glanced up and saw her marching out of the dining door with one of her old friends on either side of her, like moral supports.

I looked back at Davinia; she was smiling at me. "Are you up to anything on Saturday?" she asked.

CHAPTER 5

I SHOULD'VE BEEN MORE suspicious. I should've taken it more slowly—not got so carried away. Davinia had been banned from seeing all her old friends—the friends that her mother insisted had "led her astray." Davinia despised everyone she'd met at her new school. So it wasn't exactly a compliment that she'd picked me out. I was just a bit less awful than all the other girls, that was all. She was stranded on a desert island and I'd turned up. I was the only girl she *had*.

But I was still practically delirious with triumph and happiness, when she invited me over to her house that Saturday.

"We can just . . . I dunno, hang out for a bit," she'd said, "and then maybe go into town, get a latte or something. I have to warn you Mummy'll be there. She *watches* me. Honestly, the last time she went away with Daddy . . . one of their gruesome little romantic weekends away . . . she got this *employee* to move in with me."

"Employee?" I echo.

"I dunno, some unspeakably boring woman who works for Daddy. She spent all her time in the Jacuzzi or with her head in the fridge."

She told me the address and instructed me to come "anytime after twelve" because she couldn't guarantee to be up before then. I turned up at twenty past. The house just about blew me away when I found it. It was ultramodern and even larger and more expensive than I'd expected. I walked on past it at first, checking the number, checking the name of the street, because I just couldn't summon the courage to turn onto the wide drive.

Then I came back and walked through the huge desert plants and sculptural path-lights up to the door. Her mother opened it. I could see Davinia in her. She was a *Desperate Housewife* type—hair sleek, shiny jewelry, clothes far too good for slobbing around in the house. She was the sort my mum would despise for not earning a penny piece since the day she got married.

But I warmed to her. She gave me a really welcoming smile, asked me to call her Cassie, told me she'd heard all about me (which I knew was a lie, but a nice one), and told me she'd fixed lunch for us both.

And she was *there*, wasn't she? She was still at home.

She shouted for Davinia, and got a kind of impatient bellow in reply. "She's just got out of the shower," Cassie said. "Why don't you go on up? Second door on the right."

I crept up the stairs, practically sinking into the deep-pile dusty-blue carpet. The second door on the right was ajar, and I could hear the sound of a hair dryer going in the room. I called, "Hey, Davinia, it's me!" pushed the door open, and went in.

Davinia was sitting at her many-mirrored dressing table drying her hair in nothing but a pair of silky turquoise pants. "Sorry!" I gasped, and ducked out again. I was reeling. I'd seen about fifty reflections of her perfect tits. I thought I probably couldn't be a lesbian after all, not to be more pleased about this.

"What're you sorry for?" she cried. "Come in!" I went back in. "I forgot you've never boarded," she said, completely unabashed, hooking up a matching turquoise bra. "We get used to each other's bodies."

"S'OK," I muttered. I went and sat on the edge of her huge, lilac-draped bed, feeling all clunky and unsophisticated, and studied her room intently so I wouldn't watch her getting dressed. It was amazing—all fitted out in blond wood, with floor-length lilac curtains. Two shelves with nothing on them but beautiful bags, lined up like books. Three chairs, mounded up with clothes. An open door to the side of the bed told me she had her own en suite bathroom. *Of course.* There was even a balcony—I could see it beyond the huge, steel-framed windows—a modern metal balcony with spiky plants lined up in steel tubs. I could feel myself kind of pulsing with longing and envy, just looking at it all.

Davinia had put on a cashmere sweater, and now she was shimmying into jeans so far away from the jeans I wear that they should have a different name.

"Where shall we go?" she said. "Into town? Or is there a film you wanted to see?"

A film? I didn't want to waste time with her watching a film. I wanted to talk, find out who she was, how she felt, what she thought . . . and I wanted her to want that with me.

There was a musical shout from downstairs. Davinia groaned. "Lunch," she said. "Mummy's very happy I've made a *new friend* at the shithole, so she's making an *effort*. Are you hungry?"

I smiled, shrugged, nodded. *Brilliant*, Chloe. Why couldn't I think of something sharp to say?

I was thrown, that was the problem—upset at the sarcasm she'd laid on the words *new friend*. Plus there was something wrong—we weren't sparking like we had before. The energy between us was sluggish, awkward. It was my fault, it had to be my fault.

We made our way out of the bedroom, and down the stairs to the enormous kitchen. Cassie had vanished; a long chrome bar had bright dishes with salad, bread, and deli-type meat laid out.

"Tuck in," said Davinia gloomily, and we sat on the hi-tech stools and started piling up our plates.

"This looks *wonderful*," I gushed.

"So come on, what shall we do? I can't shop. I've spent all my allowance for this month."

"Let's window shop," I said eagerly. "Let's just go into town, like you said, and wander about and get a coffee and see who we see and . . . stuff."

"Did I say that? God, boring of me. D'you want some wine with this?"

"OK," I said unhappily, and she leaped up from her stool and went over to a huge steel wine rack in the corner and pulled out a bottle of white wine. Then she went over to the fridge and swapped it for another bottle from there. "Finish your water," she said, unscrewing the cap from the wine. I drained my glass and she filled both our glasses, then slid the bottle under her stool where it would be hidden by her legs. It all looked like a very practiced habit.

"Does your mum get mad if you drink?" I asked.

She shrugged, swallowing down big gulps of wine. "No big deal. I can do without the boring lecture about *bingeing* if she catches me at it. If she comes in, put your hand round the glass so she can't see what's in it." She drained her glass—I'd barely started mine—and pulled the bottle out from under her chair and refilled it.

Then she leaned across and chinked her glass against mine. "Cheers," she said, her eyes dancing into mine. "Glad you're here."

And suddenly, everything was glowing again. "*I'm* glad I'm here," I squeaked. "You have . . . God, your house is *amazing*."

"It's OK. Like the vino?"

I took a sip and, this time, tasted it. "It's fantastic."

"It should be. It costs about thirty quid a bottle."

"You are *kidding*."

"Daddy gets it cheaper of course, buying cases of it at a time."

"Won't he mind you drinking it?"

Davinia tossed her shiny auburn hair back. "He won't notice it's gone. And anyway, he's always wittering on about wine and trying to teach me to appreciate it. . . . 'This one, Davinia, has a hint of gooseberry, with undercurrents of mown grass and a tang of cat pee. . . .'"

I laughed, and she joined in, then she filled my glass almost to the brim. "Come on, drink up," she said. "And *eat* something." She pushed a fat green olive in my mouth. I chewed it, smiling. "And then let's go moneyless shopping."

## CHAPTER 6

WE WERE REVVING AS WE swung along the road and jumped on the first bus heading for town. Davinia kept going on about how it was the *frigging pits* to have to take a bus, and somehow, from her mouth, *frigging* sounded cool and not embarrassing. She was acting loud and outrageous and everyone was staring at her. I knew she was pretty pissed, but I didn't care—we were getting on great again. We were cracking up laughing.

We went to the big, new, seriously posh shopping hall in the center of town and breezed through, arm in arm. Davinia could pull off going into the most expensive shops and trying stuff on; she made the assistants jump for her. They must've thought, with her clothes and cut-glass accent, that she was loaded. "I can't wait for the summer, can you?" she said, as we trawled through a rack of bikinis. "Where you going, somewhere good?"

. A thump of despair interrupted my good feeling. These summer holidays would be the first ones since Mum left. "I haven't even thought about it," I said truthfully. "You know I told you my parents split up. . . ."

"Did you? Oh, God, yes."

"Well, it wasn't mutual. Mum left to move in with someone else. Dad's still really cut up about it. . . ."

"God—you won't have to go away with just your *dad* will you?" The way she said it, a two-week stay in a slaughterhouse would be more fun.

"I don't know. He'll be feeling pretty lonely. . . ."

"Well, he must have friends."

"Not really. When Mum left, she seemed to take all their friends with her. I mean—I thought they were *their* friends, but they were really hers. They phoned for a bit to see if he was OK and then . . ."

Davinia huffed impatiently. "Look, this is all *not* your concern. You can't start propping him up, I mean *yuck*, it would be like you're a substitute *wife* or something. . . ."

I laughed. I wanted to think she was right.

". . . plus you wouldn't be doing *him* any favors, letting him lean on you," she went on piously. "I mean—he's got to start getting over it. You can't be around forever, can you?"

I thought of my sad dad, I thought of how he got back from work and just seemed to *stop*, how if I wasn't there to make him eat he probably wouldn't bother. I thought of Aunt June's biweekly phone calls, checking that I was looking after him. "He needs you," she always said. "It's time to give something back, Chloe, after all he's done for you in the past." Oh, my selfish, survivor side wanted to think Davinia was right, all right.

"Don't look so *down*!" Davinia cried, a tang of disgust in her voice. "*Christ*, it just makes me *sick* when parents land their stupid *agendas* on you, like you have no right to lead your life the way *you* choose. Mine are always on about how *hard* I make everything for them, like I ought to be living my life in a way that gives them no grief whatsoever. Like I ought to think about them before *myself*!" Her voice rose with horror at the very thought. "We had a major row about it the other night. I said: 'The grief is your choice. If you choose to get upset about what I do, that's *your choice*.'"

"Oh, come on, Davinia! If you get arrested or take an overdose or something . . ."

"Oh, obviously not *that*! Although, frankly— it's not the end of the world, is it? I've been arrested twice in the last year, *neither* of them my fault, *all* fixable, and they just went on and on and *on. . . ."* A shop assistant was hovering near us, wanting to shift us from the rack of bikinis, but she didn't dare interrupt Davinia. "Honestly, it makes me sick. I can't *wait* to leave home, earn my own living. They've always used money as a way of controlling me. It's unspeakably sick. If I don't conform to what they want—I'm *poor.* You haven't asked me what I'm doing this summer."

"What?" I laughed, exhilarated by her barrage of words. "Oh—OK—what *are* you doing?"

*"Suffering!"* she said dramatically. "Having absolutely no fun whatsoever! After I got expelled, they canceled this fantastic trip I was going on with some of my best friends—to Thailand and on to Australia—they've literally canceled my life, I loathe them!"

"So you're not going away. . . ."

"Oh, I can go away with *them* if I want. They part-own this holiday flat in Caminos, we've been going there since I was an *embryo.*"

"Caminos?"

"A tiny island off Malta. You know—in the Mediterranean. Sweet in its way but not exactly racing with nightlife. Still, I guess I'll go. The alternative is staying at home with the frigging fridge-guzzling piggy employee moving in again. At least if I go I'll get a *tan.*"

So saying, she gathered up the armful of bikinis she'd pulled out of the rack, and signaled in an imperious fashion to the hovering shop assistant, saying "I'm gonna try these on."

Davinia summoned me a couple of times to check out the bikinis she was trying on. It was hard to be objective about them, because with her body, old sandwich wrappers would have looked divine. But the sea-green one with silver piping was the best, and I told her so. "It's *eighty pounds*," she moaned. "That's like . . . twenty pounds a square centimeter. Still, cheap bikinis are dreadful. Oh, well." And she whipped the changing room curtain shut in my face.

When we at last got outside of the shop, she nudged me very hard and pulled the fantastic seagreen bikini halfway out of her bag.

"Oh, my God!" I squawked. "You nicked it!"

"Bit louder, Chloe, yeah?" she hissed, stuffing it back in her bag. "So that security guard over there can hear?"

"Sorry!" I gulped. "But how . . . It had one of those heavy duty tags on—how the hell d'you get it off?"

She bared her sharp little white vampire teeth at me. "I made a tiny tear in the cloth but it won't matter. I can sew it. Put a brooch over it."

"What did you do with the tag?"

"Shoved it under the carpet in the changing room. There was this bit in the corner, where it was coming away. Don't look so horrified, Chloe! I *had* to have it. Didn't I?"

# CHAPTER 7

IT'S THEIR FAULT, I TOLD myself as we headed back from town. *If they didn't charge such absurd high prices for such tiny scraps of cloth, they wouldn't get them nicked. . . .* I felt kind of scared by Davinia's attitude, but excited by it too. It was like she thought the world was a great big candy box there to be plundered whenever she felt like it. I loved the way she took everyone on, shouting *me, me, me!* I wanted to be that way too.

On the bus back, though, she deflated again. She got all weary and negative, like she'd been when I'd first arrived at her house. I thought the alcohol was probably wearing off and the thought bothered me. Maybe she was really hooked on it.

She stood up to get off the bus and didn't say anything about me coming back with her, so as my stop was ten minutes farther on I just stayed put.

"See you, then," I called out to her back.

"Yeah," she said without turning round. "See you."

I spent Saturday night and all Sunday on my own, at home with Dad, trying not to obsess about the time I'd spent with Davinia, trying not to fantasize about what it would be like to *be* her. With that fabulous huge bedroom with its own bathroom, its own balcony. With those clothes, those parents indulging her all the time. With her arrogant, wonderful, shameless confidence.

She was the perfect rich wild child and I was besotted, whatever I tried to tell myself.

I thought about phoning her, or texting her. We'd swapped numbers when she'd asked me round to her place on Saturday. But I kept remembering how indifferent she'd been as she got off the bus, and I couldn't make myself do it.

So I accepted I'd be on my own. I didn't waste time wondering if Abby would phone because I knew she wouldn't. If I wanted her back as a friend I'd have to do some serious, protracted groveling first. I couldn't be bothered to even think about it.

It was Sunday afternoon before Dad noticed I hadn't left the house for nearly twenty-four hours. He rallied a bit and asked me if I was OK, and when I said yes, fine, he wondered if we should do something about having a late Sunday lunch.

"Sunday lunch?" I echoed. We never had Sunday lunch. Sundays we grazed on cereal and toast and ordered a takeaway in the evening.

"We could go to a pub," he said. "One of those gastro-pubs—they serve till all hours. Why don't we?"

"Why not?" I said back. But it felt weird and a bit sad as we both got ready to go out, and when he shouted up from the hall, "Ready, Chloe?" I wanted to call back down that I'd changed my mind.

But I couldn't do that to him. I hurried down to join him. He'd shaved and put on a dark blue sweater that I hadn't seen him wear for ages. "You look nice," I said, and then something caught in my throat and I kind of jumped at him and gave him a big hug. He hugged me back, all embarrassed, but pleased too, and we set off down the road together.

It was OK, in the pub. You think you're going to stand out as a sad, fractured family remnant but you don't, you fit in among all the other ill-matched people with their complicated lives. It's the picture-perfect couples and advert-happy families who stand out. Dad had two beers and I had a white wine spritzer, and we talked about how they'd done the pub up. He looked more relaxed than I'd seen him for ages. "This is nice," he said.

"Yeah," I agreed.

There was a long silence and I wondered if we might start talking about important things, such as Mum and how our lives were floundering without her, but we didn't. Then our food arrived and we talked about that.

But it was good to be out with him and not just closed in together inside the flat. On the way back I said, "How's work, Dad, is it going all right?"

"Yes, it is actually," he replied. "In fact—if things keep going this way I'll be up for a promotion by the end of the year."

"You're kidding me!" I'd always vaguely worried that he'd be fired for being so doomy and miserable in the office. "That's brilliant!"

"It's all right, isn't it? More money, but more interesting work too . . ." He chatted on about the promotion, and my thoughts wandered off into a happier future, where he emerged from all his grief and made a new life. . . . "And I'd really enjoy that. I haven't played golf for ages."

"Golf?" I echoed stupidly.

"I thought you'd stopped listening! Not that I blame you, love . . . Mike Harvey's planning a golf weekend, next month. You'll be OK on your own, won't you?"

I was delighted, of course I was. I wanted my dad to start living again, making a life for himself. But it scared me too. I felt like, right now, Dad was making more of a go of things than I was.

I sat up in my room and looked at my utterly inactive phone and thought about Davinia probably forgetting all about me. I thought of Abby full of rage at how I'd treated her and I thought of my old friends at Whitecourt Comprehensive, how already we'd lost touch because . . . well, you lose touch. I felt overwhelmed with tiredness and went to bed at 9:15.

On Monday morning I woke up with my stomach tight with panic and decided there and then that I had to grovel to Abby so she'd let me be her friend again. I knew she wouldn't let me be her best friend, not for a long, long while, if ever. I'd be a sort of probation friend always under the threat of being ditched. But it would be better than being all on my own.

I decided Davinia Morgan-Harwood was a loose cannon, a rogue guillemot. I had no idea what a guillemot was but I'd heard the word somewhere and it seemed to suit Davinia. However sparkling she was, I couldn't keep yearning after her. I couldn't afford to trust her. She was out of my league. I knew she'd never be a proper friend, someone you could rely on.

I had to let her go.

I made sure I bumped into Abby in the cloakroom. "Hey," I said.

There was a long, pointed pause. Then she said, "Hi," but didn't look at me.

"Good weekend?" I asked.

Abby was torn between wanting to punish me by not talking to me, or to punish me by telling me in glorious detail all about her fabulous weekend. So she compromised with a sort of tantalizing shorthand. "*Fantastic*, actually. Went to that new club on the High Street—whole crowd of us— *totally* trashed—met up with these *amazing* guys— seeing them again next week—Sunday just a *wipeout.*"

I wanted to say, *Great, the first time you go to a club* ever, *and I get left out.* But I didn't, of course.

There was a silence. Then she spat the word *"You?"* at me.

"Well . . . I saw Davinia. But only to go shopping."

"Exciting!" Abby sneered; then she swept up

her stuff and stalked out.

Davinia wasn't at school that day. Despite my decision to "let her go," I kept thinking about her, of course. I kept wondering about texting her, to check she was OK, but whenever I took out my phone I'd get an image of her reading my text, pulling a face, and pressing ERASE, and I couldn't bring myself to risk that. If I texted her and got nothing back, I'd feel even lower than I did now. So—with the logic of the miserable loner—I decided it was better to do nothing.

Abby and I were together in English Lit but she didn't sit near me or look at me. In fact no one spoke to me all day apart from a little Year Eight squeaking "sorry" when she banged into me, and even that was halfhearted.

That night, I went to bed at quarter to nine, and watched very bad, boring telly on the little portable I've got. *If I continue at this rate*, I thought, *by the end of this week I'll be in bed half an hour after I get in from school. . . .*

**THE NEXT DAY, TUESDAY,** I was in the sixth-form restroom washing my hands when Abby drew up at the basin beside mine and said, "Davinia still ill, is she?"

"I don't know," I muttered, my heart thumping with this awful degrading gratitude and *hope.* "I don't know if she *is* ill."

Abby smirked at this evidence of our lack-of-friendship, while I gazed pleadingly at her reflection in the smeary over-the-sink mirror and said, "Look, Abby, I'm sorry I pissed you off over Davinia. . . ."

Her reflection mimed disdainful surprise. "What d'you *mean*?"

"You've been pissed off with me ever since I sat with her in the dining room. . . ."

"Oh, come on. It wasn't that—it was the fact that you *ignored* me!"

"You ignored me first!"

"Hardly! I was talking and you got the hump and went and sat with Davinia. *Anyway*," she went on, before I could argue, "that's so *petty*. It isn't about that." Her reflection grew patronizing. "You've been weird for weeks, Chloe. Everyone says so."

I thought of Abby discussing me with her cronies. I wanted to slap her.

"You've been acting all . . . cut off," she went on. "Distanced, like you can't be bothered with any of us anymore."

*Well spotted*, I thought.

"And now," she continued, "there's this . . . *thing* with Davinia. . . ."

"What *thing* with Davinia?" I echoed, my voice all tiny and cracked.

In the smeary mirror, Abby was looking even more superior and now it was repulsively mixed with concern. "You know what it's all about, don't you?" she asked.

I made myself sound submissive. "What?"

"It's about your mother."

"Oh, *spare* me!"

"I'm serious. Your mother leaving created this . . . *huge* gap in your life. This *void*. And now you've got infatuated with Davinia because you want her to fill it."

"Oh, for Christ's sake, I'm not *infatuated*!"

"Well, that's the way it looks. Sasha said she saw you in the library with her, looking completely smitten."

"Sasha needs her head seen to." I spun round and faced Abby and she turned to look at me. This wonderful anger was beating away in me. Who the hell did Abby think she was, applying her flaky psychology to my *mother*?

"Chloe—admit it," she said, "you're *infatuated* with Davinia. You were just waiting for someone to come along to fill that space."

"Oh, please. If that's true, how come I didn't get 'infatuated' with *you*?"

Abby looked down. "We were talking about that. Basically, it's pretty unhealthy and whoever you got infatuated with would've had to've had that . . . *side* to them. Davinia's obviously a real ego-freak. She probably *loves* your adulation."

There was a pause. I turned and gripped the edge of the basin.

"I'm right, aren't I?" she nagged on. "It's really *sad*, honestly, Chloe. You should take a look at what's happening. It's kind of . . . *warped*. We *all* think so."

This was the crossroads. This was where I groveled and agreed and maybe got taken back on as a trainee friend. Or—

"Actually, Abby, you're right," I said. "But it's only warped if you're narrow-minded about being gay."

"*What?*"

"I'm a lesbian."

I wanted Abby to look impressed, but she didn't. She just laughed patronizingly and said, "Oh, come *on*! Don't be ridiculous, Chloe!"

Her scorn . . . it was appalling. It was all the worse because she thought she was being kind.

"What*ever*, you're right, I'm infatuated with her," I hissed. "She's great. Whereas *you*—there's absolutely nothing in you to get infatuated *about*. You're exactly like everybody else in this whole fucking *sad* small-minded bloody *boring pathetic school*."

Abby turned on her heel and stormed off.

I'd not so much burned my bridges with her as set explosives under them and blown them thirty meters out of the water.

There was no going back now.

Ever.

## CHAPTER 9

TUESDAY NIGHT, BED AT 8:30, right on schedule. I went to school on Wednesday morning thinking I was beyond caring. I was the walking undead— bleak, barely breathing, numbed to my half- existence. And as I was shuffling up to the school gates a Daimler slammed to a halt on the zigzag no-stopping lines, and Davinia leaped out and shrieked, *"Hey! Chloe!"*

I felt like I'd had a shot of something extremely powerful and probably illegal. I stopped, grinning, and she sashayed up to me, saying, "Well, *thanks* for your concern, kid! Not *one* text to check if I wasn't at death's door!"

"Were you?" I asked.

"As far as the school is concerned, yes." She linked her arm in mine and together we swaggered up the wide school drive. "Daddy's written me a note. Another of his 'this is the last note I'm ever

writing for you, I mean it this time' notes. I just—
*God*! I *needed* a couple of days off! Sunday, I visited
my friend Lizzy—one of the *few* old friends of mine
who haven't been frigging *outlawed*—and somehow forgot to come back till Monday night."

"What on earth were you up to?"

"Oh, just . . . stuff. Actually we met up with
this guy Mark and went down to the river and
stole a boat."

*"You stole a boat?"*

"It was just sitting there, tied up! We rowed
out to this little island and spent the night there.
Mark made a fire and everything . . . it was really
fantastically good, we had vodka and Cheesy
Wotsits. . . ."

"All you need." I laughed.

". . . but of course I was *wrecked* yesterday. I
slept, and then the parents went out and I took a
bottle of champagne into the jacuzzi with me. *That*
made me feel better."

"You've really got a jacuzzi?" I demanded. We
were weaving our way through the huddles of girls
by the main entrance now, and Davinia refused to
unlink from me; she was making them scatter.

"Yes, it's fabulous," she said. "Come round
after school sometime, we'll charge it up, you'll
love it, it's soooo relaxing."

I was warm, the blood in my veins was singing. "I'd love to," I said. "Hey—I'm glad you weren't really ill. I'm sorry I didn't text you, but—"

"No worries." She squeezed my arm. "I could've texted you, right? And I was a cow to you on Saturday, wasn't I? Especially at the end."

"*No*, just—"

"I just got . . . *down*. D'you ever get like that? Just unutterably . . . *down*."

"Yes," I said fervently. "Often." We advanced up the sixth-form common room steps together.

"No reason, no rhyme . . . just that everything absolutely sucks."

"Especially in this dump."

"*Right*."

Abby and Sasha were over by the kettle, sneering knowingly in our direction. I had a violent urge to sling my arm round Davinia's neck and give her a big soul kiss, all for their benefit. But right then the start-of-school buzzer went, like a nuclear attack warning. "See you later, sweetheart." Davinia sighed.

I floated over to my locker to grab the books I needed. However nervous I felt round the edges—about blasting Abby and reversing my decision to "let Davinia go"—the core of me was in heaven.

* * *

Over the next few days I decided to be brave and act as if Davinia was my friend, because I thought this might actually make her my friend. I started to text her; she texted me back. We ate lunch together. We met up in the common room and groaned over the horror of our existence in this appalling school and we completely ignored everyone else. It was delicious. She was the act and I was the audience but I didn't care. Every sign of our friendship growing—like when I made her laugh or we got deep into a good conversation or she texted me first—I seized on and treasured.

And on Friday she said, "Doing anything tonight?"

I shrugged, too hopeful to speak.

"Well, I'm broke," she said. "No—more than broke—in serious debt. I have to avoid just about everyone I owe money to. That is . . . all my friends. Except you. Don't ever lend me money, Chlo."

"Can't lend what you don't have," I said, trying to tamp down the joy I felt at being included as one of her friends. And I liked her calling me Chlo—no one else did.

"God, *what are we like*?" she mourned. "Hopeless. Look—the parents are always out on a Friday night. D'you want to come round and try out the jacuzzi?"

I arrived at her house around 8:30 that Friday, and she took me into a dark room full of wet, luxurious warmth, and pressed a couple of switches on the wall. Instantaneously, dozens of tiny lights came on, reflected into infinity in three black glass walls, and then the jacuzzi, raised on a platform in the center, growled into life. Large exotic plants stood round its sides, dipping toward the churning water. The room was decked in soft teak, like a sauna, and it gave off a faint spicy smell. "It's fantastic," I breathed.

"It should be," said Davinia, "it cost a fortune. Mummy and Daddy's twenty-fifth wedding anniversary present to themselves. Nauseating, eh?"

"Not at all," I said, ignoring the pang I felt because my parents wouldn't be celebrating theirs, not ever. "I think it's great. I mean, come on—you get to share it!"

"That's true. But they get *sooooo* pissed off with me—they keep coming down all geared up for some romantic privacy and find me in the pool! Now come on—get naked. *Completely* naked. It's completely wanky to wear anything in a jacuzzi."

She gestured toward a door next to us. "Go into the shower room if you're shy—there're robes hanging up."

I fumbled as I stripped off in the shiny shower room. The first time I'd been to her house she'd been undressed and now, out there, she was undressing again. Should I deduce something from this?

Did I want to deduce something from this?

I didn't know what I was thinking or feeling. I bundled myself into a large, white terry cloth robe, took a deep breath, and walked out.

She was naked, standing on the edge of the pool, coiling her hair on the top of her head and fixing it there with a large, tortoiseshell clip. She looked so beautiful and uninhibited it took my breath away. I didn't know what I felt, looking at her there. My eyes were feasting on her, but it didn't seem like desire or sex . . . I just thought she was perfect. I wanted to be like her, beautiful and uninhibited like her, and I felt like a sad prat in my robe. I slipped out of it and chucked it on a cane chair, then walked over to join her. I could feel her eyes on me as I moved. "You're thinner than me, you cow," she said. "I'm getting a belly."

"No, you're not!"

"I am. It's the booze. Sod it, I don't care."

"Davinia, you know you look amazing."

"Hmm. What a waste," she mock-moaned. "Two unutterably gorgeous nymphs and no gorgeous men to leer at us."

I laughed and we stepped into the water, and sat opposite each other in the softly lit cauldron. Hot-water jets pummeled us and all around steam swirled and huge green leaves dripped. "Bliss." I sighed. "This is *bliss*!"

"Isn't it?" she said, and she lifted her legs out of the water like a mermaid lifts her tail. She briefly examined her perfectly enameled toenails, and shwooshed them back down again. I realized I was staring at her, just literally ogling her face and her neck and her shoulders, and I looked away.

"These plants are amazing," I said. "They must grow like crazy in this steam."

"They do. We have to hack them back with a machete."

I laughed. "All we need are jungle drums."

"That can be arranged," she murmured, reaching out her arm to a panel on the floor behind her head. Immediately, some kind of funky blues was filling the air. "Now we just need a few monkeys swinging by," she said. "No—forget stupid *monkeys*. With their stupid *tails*. And *fur*. What I need is someone incredibly fit in one of those jungle swimsuits."

*"Whaaaat?"*

"You know—a loincloth. God, sexy name! *Loin . . . cloth.* A very small loincloth. *God*, I want a boyfriend."

I smiled, and this *relief* kind of filled me, and the water growled and swirled, and I thought: It's enough. Just being with her like this is enough, forget being a lesbian.

"A boyfriend shouldn't be a problem for someone who looks like you look," I murmured.

"I don't just want *sex*," she replied scathingly, "anyone can find just *sex*. I want someone who adores me . . . but who isn't an idiot. That's not so easy, believe me." Then she realized how her words could be taken and her eyes flew open and we both laughed. "Shit—you know what I mean!"

"Yes. Someone who adores you because he intelligently sees how fantastic and wonderful you are, not someone who adores you because he's got the personality of a puppy."

"Exactly! Hey—you're right, Chlo! Someone who fits adoring me alongside being interesting and dynamic and kind of masterful . . . but in an adoring way."

"Sure. Who can hold decent conversations and is really exciting to be with, but whose adoration is like this *undercurrent* . . ."

"This energy, always there . . ."

"Charging everything up, this energy of utter, utter . . ."

"*Adoration!*" We chanted that word together, laughing, then she said, "Shall I get something to drink?"

"Lovely," I said, trying not to squeak, trying not to show how happy I was.

She stood up, water streaming off her skin, and looked down at me and said, "You're all right, you know that, Chlo?"

I could have dissolved with sheer pleasure right there and then, and gurgled into the water overflow. I stretched out and let the water jets massage me—back, thighs, feet. I was feeling charged, turned on, but it was enough just to feel that way. I didn't want to take it further, I didn't want more of anything, I just wanted—*somehow!*—to live like this from now on.

Davinia came back with a tray laden with four clinking glasses, a jug of ice cubes and water, and a bottle of the palest amber-colored wine.

"Cheers," she said, and got in across from me again. "Life could be worse. Drink a glass of water in between the wine and you won't get a hangover."

"Is that right?"

"No. But it helps a bit. Hey—I forgot to tell you. I spoke to the parents. If you can get the airfare together, you're welcome to come to Caminos with us this summer."

THE NEXT EIGHT WEEKS or so went by very, very fast. School went into panic countdown mode about exams. Davinia and I agreed we'd do some work, and try and get through them with a bit of credit. Dad had a long phone call with Davinia's mum about the holiday—a very civilized discussion, he said, she seemed a nice woman despite being so "moneyed"—and we booked my flight.

I continued as Davinia's only friend at school, and I felt far more secure now that the holiday was going to happen, but things were kind of on hold, with the exams and her being under lock and key and everything. I hardly saw her out of school and we didn't get a lot closer and I never somehow felt sure of her. She just wasn't the sort you could be sure of. But it was so amazing being around her that I stopped worrying about it. Despite being under lock and key, Davinia escaped a few times.

We made it to a pub twice and to a party held by someone in our class (Davinia spent the night sprawled on the sofa getting drunk and being sarcastic and, to be honest, the party was so dire you couldn't blame her). And once, we went clubbing together. It was a really upmarket club; I followed in her gorgeous wake in a mixture of ecstasy and terror. She charmed the doormen into letting us jump the queue and when we were inside she said, "Chlo, I have absolutely no money—we're going to have to work the room to get drinks." Then, ignoring my yelp that I'd pay, she sailed up to two nondescript-looking guys in their twenties and within five minutes we both had a fat drink in our hands. And within ten minutes we were on our own again because Davinia had starting ignoring the guys so thoroughly they'd wandered off in shame.

"Don't they ever get nasty?" I hissed over the pulsing music. "When you treat them like that?"

"You never pick the macho ones," she said. "Just the desperate-looking ones."

"Davinia, that is cruel."

"I know. So what? It's more cruel that I've got no money. Those two have *jobs*. Come on, let's dance."

All the time, Caminos was ahead of me like the

Promised Land. Davinia showed me a couple of pictures of the apartment and some of the local beaches, and laughed half patronizing and half pleased when I enthused about them. She told me how easy life was on the island; how everyone spoke English "'cos we conquered them sometime. They even use our money." She warned me it was "heavily Catholic" so you got "little old ladies in black" crossing themselves if your tops were too low or your skirts too short. And she warned me again about the "utter, complete and total lack of any decent nightlife." But I didn't care, I was just aching to get there.

Any guilt I felt about leaving Dad on his own evaporated when he told me he'd booked up a trip with some friends to play golf in Portugal at around the same time. He seemed almost boyish with excitement at the prospect. And then he stunned me by saying, "Chloe—what about meeting up with Mum before you go?"

"*What?* Where did that come from?"

"Well . . . I had to tell her about you going away, didn't I? Naturally she wanted all the details, wanted to know who you were going with, what they were like. . . ."

"None of her bloody business."

"It is, you know it is. Chloe—it's almost a year

since you've seen her or even spoken to her. A year this summer."

"*I* know." The approach of the exams had thrown me into a really dark state, and it wasn't only because I hated exams. It was because of the memory of Mum walking out right after they'd finished last year. "You're being very forgiving all of a sudden," I muttered. Then my mind seized up with suspicion and I demanded, "Have *you* seen her?"

Dad wouldn't meet my eye. Then at last he said, "Yes, I have. I've met her a couple of times, just to talk. About you, mainly."

I felt awful when he said that. Kind of betrayed, abandoned—*weird*. Up until then, all contact between my parents had been by phone and letter. But now . . . "Didn't you think to tell *me*?" I croaked. "That you'd *seen* her?"

"Chloe, I'm telling you now. Look—I wasn't sure I was going to go through with meeting her, at first. And afterward, I felt all churned up about it. I didn't want to land that on you. But the second time . . . it was easier. I'm coming to terms with what happened. I'm trying to be a grown-up."

"Good for you."

"Don't be like that, Chloe."

"What d'you expect me to be like?"

He smiled at me, and said, "Look, darling, it's different for me—it's over between Mum and me. *Really* over, and that's still awful, but . . . I can begin to accept it. But it's not over for you, it'll never be over, she'll always be your mum. Look, one of the main reasons I agreed to meet her was because her heart is *broken* over the fact that you won't have anything to do with her."

"She should've thought about that before she lied to me," I said. "She should've thought about that before she walked out."

Dad shrugged, and the conversation was finished.

And then it was exam time, and then the exams were over, and then there were only five days to go before I got on the same flight as Davinia Morgan-Harwood and flew off for six whole weeks in the sun. *Six weeks!* It was more than a holiday, it was practically moving out there for good.

But *then* . . . something really weird happened. It was a warning and I should have heeded it. That's what you're supposed to do with warnings, isn't it? *Heed* them.

Five days before we flew out, I talked to a real, live—well, undead—doppelganger. A doppleganger, for the ignorant among you, is a ghost who stalks the earth looking like the absolute spitting image of someone already alive.

It was Davinia's doppelganger.

She was standing in front of this really stylish new silver jewelers in town, ogling through the glass, and I called out, "Oh, God—don't tell me you're that obscenely rich! Don't tell me you can afford that stuff!"

And she turned round and smiled, just like Davinia's smile . . . like her top lip's lifting in a cute snarl—and said, "No, I can't." It was Davinia's voice, I swear it.

"So," I said, breezing over to stand beside her at the window, "you been shopping? Bought anything?"

She shook her head, and her absolutely straight auburn hair just like Davinia's swished on her shoulders. "No," she said. "No money."

And it was then something crawled up my spine, and I should have known it wasn't Davinia, but I'm so paranoid all I could think was: *Why is she being weird with me? She's acting different. What's she up to?*

"Me neither," I said, all chummy. "Well, I'm not touching my holiday money. God, I sound like a little kid. *Holiday money.*"

She huffed out a little laugh. *Why is she looking*

*at me like that? Why is she being so distant?*

"Yeah. God, I can't wait, can you? It's gonna be brilliant . . . I can't wait to see the apartment. . . ." I rattled on, feeling more and more uneasy, kind of spaced out. . . . "And those photos you showed me of the beach right near it, I mean, God, what a paradise. . . ."

"I'm not who you think I am," she broke in.

I nearly freaked when she said that. It was so very *weird* and sinister. And then the penny dropped. "Oh, my God," I shrieked. "Oh, my God, you're not Davinia, are you, you're not *her*!"

Davinia's replica mouth curled with distaste at her name. "No," she said. "I'm Tasha."

"Oh, my *God*," I blustered, "you have a double. An absolute *double*, I can't tell you . . ."

"I thought you were just some nutter being ultrafriendly," she interrupted, laughing (with Davinia's laugh). "Or maybe a decoy from a gang . . . I was looking round waiting to be mugged—"

"Oh, I am *so sorry*!" I gulped out. "God, this is weird—I mean, you *sound* like her as well, you could *be* her. . . ."

"Wow, freaky," she said, and she stepped back from me a fraction. "You obviously *know* her well, too . . . If you're going on holiday with her, I mean. . . ."

There was an awkward pause then, and I knew she was thinking, like I was: *You can't know her that well, can you? Not if you've mistaken a stranger for her. . . .*

Then I muttered "sorry" again, and she laughed and said no problem, and I felt so shaken I went straight into the first little café I walked by, one filled up with grannies and girls not much older than me with toddlers crawling all over them.

"You all right, dear?" asked the thickset woman behind the counter. She had a strong accent—German or Swedish or something. "You look a bit shaken up."

"I am," I blurted out. "I've just seen my best friend's double—I mean, I really thought it was her. . . . I *talked* to her. . . . It was *mad*!"

"Ha!" huffed the woman. "Her doppelganger. That's what we call it in my country."

"A doppel—what?" I asked.

As she processed my cappuccino, she told me about the legend of the doppelgangers, and said, "Your friend will laugh when you tell her! Although—maybe you shouldn't tell her. Seeing a doppelganger is supposed to be very bad luck."

I wanted to ask, *Who for? The doppelganger person or the one who sees it?* I must have looked stricken, because the woman laughed all cozily and said, "Ach, just an old story. A load of nonsense."

But I knew from the start that I wouldn't tell Davinia, and not only because of the bad luck it was supposed to bring. It opened up too many cracks between us. I kept hearing the girl, the stranger, saying, *I'm not who you think I am.*

Like I said, it was a warning.

I should have heeded it.

## CHAPTER 11

**BUT I DIDN'T. I GOT** on the plane, almost literally beside myself with excitement. Davinia's parents had booked themselves into first class; we were in tourist. I think this was partly out of consideration for my dad's wallet; I also think Davinia had done some kind of deal whereby she got the balance between the two flight costs. I wouldn't have put it past her, anyway.

But the great thing about it was, it was like we were traveling alone.

Davinia sauntered down the narrow aisle with me following and it was like her glamour and gorgeousness was flowing back on to me, making me that way too. I tried to copy her laid-back style despite being about to combust with excitement. We found our seats, then she made everyone behind us wait as she pulled a magazine and a bottle of mineral water from her bag. A middle-aged man ahead of her helped her stow it in the overhead locker, and she acted like she was doing him a favor and not the other way round.

She was so elegantly calm and cool about everything. As we settled into our seats (naturally, she took the window seat), I hissed, "Aren't you even the slightest *bit* excited?"

"You don't have to whisper, Chlo. It's not a frigging church. And yeah—course I am." Then she opened her magazine with a sigh.

I settled back, to enjoy being excited all on my own. To my left, a troop of lads was pushing by, all loud and swaggery and macho, the way boys do when they're in new territory together. As the fourth one walked by me the troop halted, and I looked past at the fifth boy, and I absolutely knew I wasn't a lesbian, not even a little bit.

He was perfect.

His face roared into my soul. Imprint. Genetic imprint.

I wanted him.

I looked down, fast. He didn't move. Someone up ahead was taking a huge amount of time stowing their luggage. *Thank you, someone!* I started to take the boy in bit by bit. I slid sly looks at his legs, jean-clad, long, muscle-defined.

*Not only am I not a lesbian, I'm not even a girl*

*version of one of Pavlov's dogs*, I thought. All my pre-
vious aversion-therapy experiences with boys had
been wiped out at a stroke. I was *cured*.

My eyes moved up to his crotch and screeched
past, panic-stricken. I tipped my head back just a
bit, looked at his arms, chest. *Beautiful*. My eyes
glided upward, reached his face again.

He was looking right at me, like he was waiting for my eyes to get to his. He was gorgeous and
grinning, all sarcastic and knowing.

I went red. Hideously red. Like a boiler suddenly being turned full on.

"Seen enough?" he drawled, all cocksure.

I looked away, didn't answer. *I hated him*. And
then the line moved on, and he went past.

Davinia was oblivious, thank God. She wasn't
aware I was burning up with shame and hatred. I
couldn't bear it if she knew.

"Jesus," she muttered, "what a gang of yobs.
Oh, *God*—" She twisted up in her seat, glared
indignantly behind. "They're only a couple of rows
behind us. They'll start on the lagers and then
they'll start singing football songs." Then she suddenly yelped, *"Fuck off!"* and plummeted back
down into her seat.

"Davinia," I croaked, still wanting to die, "who
did you just shout *fuck off* at?"

"One of those yobs," she said. "He puckered his gob up at me. *Yuck.*"

"What did he look like?" I muttered. Even though I was all withered up with humiliation, I wanted it not to be *him* who blew her a kiss.

"What the frig does it matter what he looked like?" she snapped.

"Because one of them just did it to me too," I lied. "As he went past."

"He looked like a rat. Bad teeth and unspeakably appalling bleached hair."

Not my boy. He had great teeth and brown hair. Rich, autumn-brown hair. I hated him.

"God," groaned Davinia, "when're the *drinks* coming round?"

We were ready for takeoff. The seat beside me was still empty, so at Davinia's insistence I shifted into it and we spread ourselves out in comfort.

I turned my head on the back of the seat, straining my ears to hear what the boys were saying. All I could hear was this kind of happy rumbling, broken up regularly by the *F* word and jeering laughter. They sounded like they were having a lot better time than we were.

The drinks trolley trundled by. Davinia charmed an extra tiny bottle of Sauvignon Blanc out of the male flight attendant, who maybe wasn't as gay as he acted or maybe he just admired her chutzpah.

The man in the row behind us, the one who'd helped Davinia stow her case, turned round bravely to the boys and asked them to keep their noise down. This was met with loud indignation and then I heard a voice say, "No, you're right, mate. We'll keep it down."

And the noise level dropped.

I still hated *him*, but somehow I wanted it to be *him* who'd said that, who had that kind of maturity, who commanded the respect of the others.

Clearly, I was slipping into a deep and obsessional psychotic state. Davinia—if she found out—which I'd make damn sure she never did—would be appalled.

Lunch arrived, in a whole set of tiddly plastic boxes, then cleared. Davinia didn't want to chat much—this would've bothered me before but now I was so preoccupied I hardly noticed. I was not only preoccupied with the boy two rows back—I also needed, *badly*, to go to the toilet.

HOW PATHETIC, TO BE seventeen years old and be so embarrassed about going to the toilet you're in danger of peeing your pants. I just didn't want to stand up and be on view to *him* but there was no way round it, I'd have to walk by *him*. The alternative was heading up the plane toward the business-class restrooms and having about a million flight attendants direct me very loudly back down again.

I nudged Davinia. "Shall we go to the loo?" I muttered. I was thinking if she came too I could hide behind her.

"What's the point of going together?" She yawned. "It just lengthens the queue."

There was no point arguing. My bladder was about to explode. I got unsteadily to my feet and lurched along the tiny aisle. I could feel six pairs of male eyes on me, three pairs on each side. *Let me get past before they pass audible judgment on me*, I prayed. *Let me not trip up and land across their laps.* I lurched on as elegantly as I could and got past them, thank *God,* and reached the queue for the restrooms.

I'd only been waiting there a moment or so, when I sensed someone draw up behind me. Close behind me. I thought it was Davinia changing her mind and then the next split instant I knew it wasn't, and I had this overpowering, overwhelming sense that it was *him.*

The logical thing would've been to look behind me and *see* who it was, but that was completely out of the question in case it *was* him. *Shit, shit!* What was he up to? Had he come to jeer at me some more? Maybe he thought I might be game for a quicky in the toilets?

*Hurry up!* I screamed silently at the people ahead of me. *Calm down!* I screamed to myself.

The queue shunted forward as the two cubicle doors swung open one after the other and two people came out. As they pushed past us to get back to their seats *he* pressed right up against me. I was going to have to look. It was beyond indecent, it was—

I turned. "All right?" he smirked. Face about a millimeter from mine, breathing god-breath all over me. Body right up against me, smell of cotton and male cologne. "Sorry," he said. "Bit of a crush, innit?"

I thought I was going to die right there and then of adoration and desire. And then . . . THEN . . . "The bog's free," he announced, nodding toward the door swinging open again. Then he grinned, insultingly, suggestively. "Unless you'd sooner stay here, of course."

I waited inside the nasty toilet cubicle for absolutely sodding hours. I didn't care if they thought I had chronic diarrhea, I didn't care what they thought. Nothing could be as embarrassing as bumping into that shit again. Twice—TWICE!!!—he'd made out I was lusting after him.

How dare he.

I loathed him.

DAVINIA GROANED AS THE car swung off the main road and into a wide drive between two concrete posts with large concrete balls on the top, draped by an exuberant climbing plant with the most wonderful deep-pink flowers. "Here again." She sighed.

"I'm so excited!" I mewed encouragingly.

"I suppose since it's your first time," she allowed grudgingly.

As we'd got off the plane at Malta Airport and collected our luggage, I'd still been shaken by what I saw as my total and abject humiliation at *his* hands. I kept my eyes narrowly focused right ahead or on the ground; I didn't want to risk seeing him. And I almost made it; all I did was catch a glimpse of him as he strolled through customs with his mates. He looked equally fantastic from the side and from behind.

I'd started to feel better as we exited the airport.

The late afternoon exotic heat hit us, powerful and exciting, and the Morgan-Harwoods had everything arranged. The hire car was waiting for us at the airport; Mr. Morgan-Harwood (who had a genial wide smile and told me to call him Paul) took the wheel and pulled off confidently into the stream of traffic. Malta was very built up, with only tiny snags of green, but the sky above it was such a beautiful blue it didn't seem to matter. Paul turned into a supermarket car park, and we all went in and watched Cassie serenely transfer a vast amount of delicious food into her trolley. Meanwhile Paul studied the wine bottles lined up on the shelves and transferred a vast amount of them into his trolley. It all ran very smoothly with the ease of long practice and it was all so . . . *fantastic.* So unlike the harassed, anxious start of holidays I'd had with my mum and dad.

Then we'd driven onto the ferry that was taking us over to Caminos. The sea was so intensely blue it made the sky look weak. It was unreal. There I was, Chloe Marshall, heading for a little rocky island—you could see both ends of it—floating alone in all this blue.

"That's our flat," said Davinia, pointing. "One floor up, the one at the end with the curved balcony."

The flat was in a large apartment block that looked as though it had been put up in the 1960s. Old-fashioned modern, with flat roofs, lots of glass, and narrow balconies. It was less pretentious than I'd thought it would be and I liked it immediately. I was fizzing with excitement as I got out of the car.

"Davinia, can you go on ahead of us?" asked Paul calmly. He always seemed to be calm. "And call the lift?"

"*God!*" snarled Davinia, as though she'd just been asked to empty about fifty latrine buckets, and stomped off, empty-handed.

"She always does that!" trilled Cassie, as though it was an endearing trick Davinia pulled. "She never thinks to take a case with her!"

The apartment lobby was lined and floored in cool marble. As we walked in, a tiny lizard scooted across the wall and hid behind a fire hydrant.

"It's *here*!" Davinia shouted crossly. "I can't hold it for*ever*!"

We went up two by two with our cases in the lift. Paul let us into the flat, and then said he'd go back down for the food. "Can I help?" I asked. I didn't want to sound like a creep but I couldn't join in with Davinia in her brat-act, I just couldn't. Even though a part of me . . . I dunno. *Celebrated* her brat-act, somehow. Celebrated the way she felt so free to do it.

"Well, thank you, Chloe!" said Paul. "But Cassie and I can manage. You do the pictures with Davinia. . . ." And they went over to the lift, like a couple glad just to be alone together. Which, thinking about it, they were. Despite being middle-aged and everything.

I followed Davinia through the door of the flat. "Do the pictures . . . ?" I repeated.

"These!" said Davinia, gesturing.

The walls of the white flat were lined with monstrous paintings. Embryos crouched in pitch-black wombs, screaming. Strange, puppetlike children with dunces' caps on and despair in their eyes. And abstracts so frenetic and tortured they gave you a migraine just looking at them.

"They belong to the people who own this flat with us," said Davinia scathingly. "Their *son* does them. He's utterly frigged-up in the head."

"Have you told him that?"

"Several times. He's too frigged-up to take any notice."

I stared round at his work. "They're hideous," I breathed.

"They think he's a genius—can you imagine? He actually does sell some of them too. To other utterly frigged-up people. Mummy and Daddy are too bloody soft to tell the Winstons what disturbing crap they are so we have to do this *every* time we come—take all of them down and stow them in a big cupboard at the end of the hall."

I walked into the middle of the huge room. It was a fantastic space—completely open plan, with a kitchen area at the back and a corridor to the right. And at the far side, great glass doors led onto the balcony. The view was just of streets—but it didn't matter, they weren't English streets, they were all in this sandy-colored stone and everywhere there were tubs of glorious, tumbling flowers . . . and beyond, the rocky skyline meeting the blue. I slid one of the heavy doors open and the heat rushed in on my face.

"Any chance of you *helping*?" groaned Davinia. I turned. She'd stacked two paintings against the wall and was reaching for a third.

"Sure!" I cried. "I was just . . . admiring it all! It's fantastic!"

"Yeah, it's OK," admitted Davinia. "Or it will be when we've got these down."

Arms full of ugly paintings, we headed along the marble-floored corridor, which had a wall on one side and a series of doors on the other. "Bathroom," announced Davinia, gesturing. Then she pulled open a door right at the end and we dumped the paintings inside, next to a bucket and mop and a vacuum.

"Good." She sighed. "Now let's get our cases and I'll show you our room. And then I'll take you up on the roof. It's brilliant for sunbathing."

Our room was at the back at the flat, near the closet. It was wide, white, and plain, with twin beds and a long low dressing table and large, fitted wardrobes. "Minimalist." Davinia sneered. "Totally *basic*. But it does the job."

"Oh, it's great," I said. "Perfect." I headed for the huge window. At this end of the flat the view was wild and wonderful, out onto scruffy terraces of rampant, overgrown vines and armies of prickly pear cactuses bursting with yellow flowers. Another narrow balcony ran the length of it—it had three pots with dead plants in them, and it looked sturdy enough. "Do you use the balcony?" I asked.

Davinia, busy hanging her clothes in the wardrobe, scoffed. "*No!* I'd have to climb out of the window."

"That's not a problem, is it?" I pulled the window open and hopped out.

The late sun boomed down on me. A fabulous smell, vanillalike and sweet, drifted up from a mound of purple flowers growing wild across the open wasteland below. I kind of shivered with pleasure, and sank down, thinking I could bring a cushion out here, and just sit and *be*. . . . The wonderful loathsome boy from the plane pushed his way into my mind and I shook him out again. I focused intently on a pretty, skinny cat trotting out from behind the flowers, making its way purposefully along.

"For Christ's sake, Chlo, what are you *up* to?" Davinia's head and bare shoulders appeared in the window. She'd put a bikini on already—I recognized it as the one she stole when we first went shopping together. "You're screwing up the *air-conditioning*, with the window open like that. . . ."

"Sorry," I said, and got to my feet. "It's just—that's such a nice spot. . . ."

"If you like *thin stone shelves*, I suppose it is! Honestly, Chlo, you are weird, you can't even stretch out on it. Look—I'm gonna catch the last of the rays up on the roof. If you want to come with me, you'll have to unpack later."

CHAPTER 14

I SO MUCH WANTED TO be Davinia's perfect friend that I just allowed myself to be absorbed up into what she wanted to do. I'd have liked to have taken my time, enjoyed unpacking, relished the exoticness of everything, but I told myself she'd hardly be as blown away by the place as I was— she came here year after year, it was ordinary for her. So I stripped at top speed and put on a bikini, a safe black one, and wrapped a sarong round me and padded out after her into the main room of the flat.

Cassie and Paul were moving about the kitchen, stacking food in the fridge. "Glass of Pimm's?" asked Paul, beaming at us.

"Yeah, thanks," said Davinia begrudgingly. "We'll take ours up onto the roof."

"Well, don't be too long. We thought we'd go to The Cabin tonight, say hello. . . ."

"Oh, *God*!" groaned Davinia. "Not the boring old *Cabin* . . ."

"You can always stay here and make yourself an omelet," said Cassie.

"No, it's OK." Davinia sighed with the air of someone bestowing a massive favor. "We'll come."

We picked up our lovely frosty glasses of Pimm's and cucumber and mint, and went out into the hall. We had to walk up another two flights of stairs, then we got to a narrow iron set of steps, and then we were out on the roof.

It was very stark out there. The deep blue sky bore down oppressively—it felt weirdly bleak. Washing lines, some with clothes on, were strung across the space. Davinia headed purposefully for a line of wooden bunkers, all with numbers on, and unbolted the third one. Then she pulled two folded-up sunbeds from inside, handed one to me, unfolded hers, and lay down on it with a relieved "*Whuff!*"

I set my sunbed up beside hers and settled down on it. I was itching to explore, but I knew what kind of response I'd get from Davinia if I suggested a walk. She took cabs everywhere unless she was broke, when she just about deigned to get on a bus.

"It's too late to sunbathe," she moaned. "The sun's not even *warm.*"

She flipped grumpily onto her stomach, and I sipped my Pimm's and watched the great red ball of the sun sink lower behind the washing lines. The boy from the plane kept zipping into my head, like a computer pop-up. I blocked him hard, and stared at Davinia, trying to revive the possible-lesbian feelings. Then I had this weird thought, which was that Davinia saw the whole place, the whole holiday, on the same level as the jacuzzi at her house. I didn't quite know what it meant, that thought, but I didn't like thinking it.

Her mobile went. *"God!"* she groaned. "That'll be the call to dinner." She pulled her phone out of her bag, barked, *"What?"* into it, then said, "I'm not even hungry!" in an accusing voice, as though the state of her stomach was entirely her parents' fault. Then she groaned, "OK, *OK!* We'll be down in five." And lobbed her phone back in her bag again.

"We're going to have to *walk* there," she complained. "God! Just so they can get pissed. *So* unfair!"

My spirits hiked at the thought of walking. I wanted to experience the island, sense it, smell it— not just look out at it from the back of a car. "Never mind," I said loyally. "How long will it take?"

"At least *twenty minutes*," she said. "God. If you

walk, it's down this awful rough track, down by the shore. . . ."

"Oh, how gorgeous!" I broke in.

Davinia opened one eye and surveyed me, with her eyebrow doing that amazing cartoon zigzag thing it does. "Oh, for goodness' sake, Chloe, don't go getting all *excited*. It's this shitty little shack of a restaurant, and Mummy and Daddy get all turned on by the fact that the fish comes in straight from the boats and into the kitchen. I mean—*so what*? Who wants to see the poor things thrashing about anyway? *With their heads on?* It's frigging perverted if you ask me."

"I suppose it proves they're fresh," I said. "And—some people think if you're going to eat meat and fish, you should see where it comes from, you know, *acknowledge* it. . . ."

"Oh, *what*? So McDonald's should start slaughtering cows right behind the counter, ay? And if you have a leg of lamb on Sunday, you're supposed to have a load of *wool* on your plate to remind you where it came from. . . ."

We both got the giggles, trying to think of nastier and nastier examples, then Davinia's phone went again. She swore, blocked the call, and rolled off her sunbed. "Come on," she said, all aggrieved. "Let's go to *dinner*!"

It wasn't until we got back to our room that I remembered about phoning Dad to tell him I'd got here safely. I hopped out of the window onto the skinny balcony again, hunting for reception; he answered right away. I told him how fantastic it was here and he made a point of saying he'd let Mum know because she'd be worried. I said nothing to that, just told him I'd call again soon, and we rang off.

When I climbed back in our room, Davinia was laying full length on the bed, not moving. "Aren't you going to get ready?" I asked. "What are you wearing?"

"What d'you mean, 'what am I wearing'?" She sneered.

"Well—it's our first night here! Aren't we going to celebrate—dress up a bit?"

"Chloe, we'll be in among a load of smelly fishermen and *locals*. There is absolutely no point in putting anything *good* on. Mummy and Daddy think they're so cool 'cos they've discovered this place, they think it's all authentic and *real*—it's a *hovel*, Chlo. Trust me."

She rolled wearily off the bed and pulled on a T-shirt and shorts, and I did the same, and we both put on trainers so "We can at least try not to fall arse over tit on the death-trap path they'll be forcing us down!" as Davinia said. She vetoed me putting my hair up in this big jazzy clip I'd bought, and groaned when I slicked some lip gloss on. "Honestly, Chloe, what's the *point*? *I* wouldn't bother *going* if I wasn't so hungry. . . ."

There was an impatient shout from Paul. We hurried out to the main room, and the four of us rode down in the lift, and then out of the main doors and into the Caminos evening. A soft breeze, sweet-smelling and warm, stroked my face and lifted my hair. It was gorgeous, exotic—my skin was tingling with it. The sun was sinking fast, much faster than it does in England. And there was a whirring, chirring noise, undulating up and down. . . . It was part of the evening, it was perfect, and I knew what it was. . . . "Cicadas!" I said triumphantly.

"Yeah, bloody horrible bugs," said Davinia.

"Jesus, you *misery*!" I laughed, and she joined in.

"OK, OK," she grumbled, "I'll cheer up with a nice glass of something extremely cold in my hand. And some *food*—as long as it's stopped breathing."

It was stunning, stumbling down the steep, stony track to the beach, with the sunset and the great stretch of sea ahead of us. I kept skidding because I couldn't keep my eyes on the path, I wanted to look up and out the whole time.

Soon, we were on the beach, skirting round the rocks. The last beach I'd been on had been in Cornwall, with litter bins and notices about NO DOGS—this felt wild and free in comparison, effortlessly beautiful. "This is *so great*," I squealed. "I love it here!"

"It's lovely, isn't it?" said Paul. "It's nice someone appreciates it."

"Yeah, well, if Chloe came back *year after year after year*," moaned Davinia, "maybe she'd get a bit sick of it too!"

I wanted to say I'd never get sick of it, ever, but I had to balance being polite to Paul and Cassie with sucking up to Davinia—it was a fine line to walk down.

"There's The Cabin," said Cassie, voice soft, pointing ahead. "Isn't it sweet?"

"Gorgeous," I muttered, hoping Davinia wouldn't hear me.

The Cabin looked like a stage set for a play about trolls. It gave the impression of growing out of the sand, like some strange natural eruption. As we drew closer, I could see how it got its shape— great flowering vines, rooted in white-painted oil drums, almost covered the wooden shack underneath it. Fishing nets were draped on poles, marking out an area in the sand that was covered in rough wooden benches and tables. Candles in jam jars twinkled from the nets, in among shells and seaweed. . . . "Oh-my-*God*," said Davinia, pointing accusingly, "they've got hold of some plastic lobsters. Well, it was only a matter of time."

"Oh, shut up," said Cassie. "Hey—there's Tony!" And she danced forward into the wide embrace of a nut-brown, short-legged man who'd come out from the shack, exclaiming with joy.

Davinia nudged me. "Daddy's got his tolerant face on. Basically, Tony has got the absolute hots for my mother, but Daddy has to be tolerant about it or he'd look like a wanker. *And* get his food spat in."

We followed them inside, where candles glowed in carafes, more nets draped, and a whole series of photos formed a messy collage on the far wall. "See what I mean?" groaned Davinia. "Unspeakably naff. This is *Tony's* idea of interior design!"

I advanced toward the wall of photos; I'd seen a threesome that looked vaguely familiar. "Don't you *dare* . . . !" hissed Davinia. I ignored her.

"Me at twelve," she groaned, drawing up beside me. "*Serious* puppy fat!"

It was like seeing Davinia's face peering out

from a bowl of pudding. The gorgeous eyes were there, and the cartoon eyebrows, but the delicate nose and sexy chin were all unshaped, somehow, waiting to be formed. She was grinning cheerfully, flanked by her parents, who looked pretty much the same as they did now.

"I've *asked* Tony to take it down, and he says he wants it as a record of how long we've all been friends. *God!*" Suddenly, her hand shot out and tore it off the wall.

"You *can't*!" I gasped. "He'll be so upset!"

"Bugger him. *I'm* upset seeing what a fat ugly heifer I used to be." She wadded it up viciously, and stuffed it in her shorts pocket. "Hey—unpin that photo down there, the overlapping one. *Quick*—he'll see us. Give it here."

I did what she asked, and soon another family group was pinned where the Morgan-Harwoods used to be, and the gap at the bottom hardly noticeable at all. "Come on," she said in a satisfied voice. "Let's get a drink."

"What if Tony notices? What if he asks about it?"

"I'll say I've got a stalker who stole it. Then I'll pose for another one in which I'll look unutterably gorgeous. You can be in it too."

\* \* \*

We were shown to a table right out at the front with nothing between us and the sea. Dinner was simple, but wonderful. The other tables were filling up with holiday makers, but our table was the one getting the star treatment. Shellfish on a great platter, perfect, icy-cold wine, salad, and local bread that was out of this world. And Tony in constant attendance, checking that everything was all right.

Cassie and Paul were getting romantic with each other, holding hands across the table, softly planning the days ahead. Davinia rolled her eyes at me, and I laughed and asked, "What are we doing tomorrow?"

She looked surprised. "Sunbathing."

"On this beach?"

"If you want to. Or up on the roof again."

"Oh, let's come *here*! I love to swim in the sea."

"OK." She shrugged. "It's just so *yucky*. Fish pee in it, you know. And people."

"Dav-*in*-ia . . ."

"OK, OK. I just hate not being near a bathroom. I hate salt drying on my skin."

"But they've got a shower-thing, haven't they—I saw it as we walked across the beach."

"*That?* Queuing up behind other people to get sprayed by cold water? I don't think so. I'll just use lots of oil."

93

"What about the evening?" I laughed.

"Oh, don't worry, we'll be on our own—tonight's a one-off. In fact, after this we'll have to bully them to take us out to eat again. It can get expensive."

"But it's not just eating, is it? I mean—there must be clubs here, bars. . . ."

"Chloe, don't sound so *excited*," she groaned. "I told you—there's nothing to do here. I mean—yes, there are clubs, but I wouldn't be seen dead in them. Crap music, no style, full of naff holiday makers. There's a couple of bars, but . . . OK. OK, tomorrow night I'll take you to Hilly's. That's *just about* OK."

I grinned and peeled the last enormous prawn left on my plate. "Just about OK" by Davinia's standards had to be absolutely mind-blowing.

CHAPTER 15

THE NEXT MORNING, WE woke up to an empty flat. Davinia dispatched me to the kitchen to get orange juice ("*not* the shitty carton rubbish—Mummy'll've squeezed some—it'll be in a glass jug") and I found a note propped against the kettle.

*Didn't want to wake you—driven to the other side of the island. Back early evening. Have fun, be safe!*

As I headed back to our room, I had a mental image of the two of them creeping out of the flat like grounded teenagers, desperate not to wake their daughter in case she demanded to come along too. I showed the note to Davinia but didn't share that thought with her; she grouched about how selfish they were to have taken the car.

"But Davinia," I said, "we can't drive!"

"So? They can't give us a *lift* to anywhere now."

"Oh, right. So it's not just the car, it's the chauffeurs too."

"What's your point?" she snapped, and rolled out of bed.

We ate breakfast out on the balcony as the sun climbed the sky and the day got hotter. I was restless to get down on the beach, but Davinia wanted a second cup of coffee and more toast (which I had to make) before, finally, she agreed to move. We shed our nightclothes and put on bikinis and sarongs. I loved packing up a beach bag with just sun cream, purse, book, towel, hairbrush . . . nothing else needed. Davinia gave me a huge, striped beach umbrella to carry, she took two reed mats, and we negotiated the path we'd walked down last night to the beach.

"God, it's crowded!" she grumbled, as we reached the sand. "Where do all these *people* come from?" She made us walk right past The Cabin, right on to where great dramatic rocks jutted out into the sea, because it was a "better spot."

"Why *better*?" I demanded. "It all looks wonderful."

"Oh, just *better*," she said. "The people who go there. You know."

This didn't stop her grumbling about the distance she had to walk, though. She also complained about the stuff she had to carry with her, she complained about the rocks, she complained that we couldn't ·hire "proper sunbeds." Then, once we'd found an empty spot and settled down, she complained about the kids several meters away from us making too much noise, about the sand being too gritty, and the flies.

"What flies?" I demanded. "I haven't seen any!"

"They're not landing on you," she said darkly, as though I'd somehow engineered this. "Trust me, tonight I'll have bites all over."

But basically, I was so thrilled to be down on the beach on our own, I let all her moaning wash over me. I loved it, I loved the relaxed hippiness of it, everyone just turning up and hunkering down. We'd been to the seaside in southern Italy the year before Mum had run out on us, and I'd hated it. Everyone was so stylish and sophisticated on the beach, and I'd been absolutely crippled by inhibition. It didn't help that we'd brought our own beach umbrella and within seconds of Dad erecting it, someone had belted down from the hotel at the top of the beach and yelled at us. We had minimal Italian between us, but we'd cottoned on pretty fast that the only umbrellas allowed were the uniform hotel blue ones.

I thought about telling Davinia this but I knew she'd side with the hotel, so I didn't. Instead I looked around me, loving the heartbreakingly blue sky meeting the sea, nothing else on the horizon, and asked, "Are you coming for a swim?"

"Not yet!" she snapped indignantly. "We've hardly started sunbathing!"

I oiled up and settled down with my book. It was *The Handmaid's Tale* by Margaret Atwood, one of Mum's that she'd left behind. Davinia, peering at it disapprovingly, said, "What d'you want to read that boring old crap for?" and, when I didn't answer, went back to her copy of *Heat*.

Round the edges of all the perfection, I was feeling sad, knocked off balance, because of the way Davinia was being. It was like a rift had opened up between us. What had worked at school—us ganging up and being snide about absolutely everyone around us—well, it was just madness here. Here was paradise. But Davinia didn't seem to have spotted the difference. She wanted to carry on moaning and groaning just like before.

I read on, head and shoulders under the sunshade, legs getting brown out in the sun, mind getting lost in the terrifying world of my book. It was past midday now, and the heat was intense. I was longing to immerse myself in the waves lapping right in front of me.

"Fancy a swim now?" I said.

"*Noooo*," she grumbled. "God, Chloe, I was just dozing off then. *You* go."

But I stayed put. I felt really self-conscious about standing up in my bikini, walking away from the security of our staked-out patch. A group of teenage boys was sitting on the rocks; they were taking turns diving dramatically into the water below. They had to be locals, they knew where to dive without smashing their skulls in. They'd climb out, foot-sure and athletic on the sharp rocks, and dive back in again. I felt like such an inactive blob in comparison.

I spent some time watching where two little girls negotiated their way past the stones into the sea, then I got to my feet. I waded through the hot sand to the sea edge, longing for the cold water, then kicked off my flip-flops and waded in, following the route of the little girls. The stones hurt my feet but I kept going, trying not to wobble, arms out for balance, suspecting the eyes of the rock-diving boys were all over my arse. The water rose to my waist. I tipped forward . . . and then I was swimming.

It felt wonderful. It felt like freedom. I swam and swam out toward the horizon and I forgot about everything, all the jabber in my head, I was out of it. After a while I paused, treading water. I put my leg down, to find I was out of my depth. But I was a strong swimmer, I was all right. I stopped heading for the horizon, and swam parallel to the beach, right past the rock where the boys were, then turned around and swam back.

Davinia was sitting up, looking out at the sea. I waved to her but she didn't wave back—maybe she didn't see me. And I realized what it meant, that thought I'd had up on the roof, about the whole place, the whole holiday, being on the same level as the jacuzzi at her house. It had something to do with her being so self-centered she couldn't get out of the bounds of her own small self. I didn't know what to do with that thought. So I let it go, like it could wash away on the waves.

I SWAM BACK TO THE beach and waded out, soused in triumph and well-being. I located my flip-flops and put them back on, then, ignoring Davinia, I strode straight up to the beach shower and waited my turn behind two small Scottish boys. The shower worked by pulling a large chain and the little boys thought this was hilarious. They took turns to pull the chain, shouting, "You're a turd! I'm flushing you down the toilet!" Then they saw me grinning at them and got embarrassed and ran off.

The icy clean water felt superb on my skin. I ran my fingers through my tangled hair, sloshing all the salt away, then hurried back to Davinia. She let out an indignant squawk as I sprayed her with water droplets from my hair.

"That was *so good*," I breathed. "Aren't you going in? Come on, I'm starving now. Have a swim before lunch!"

"God, Chloe, will you stop being so revoltingly hearty! Have you got conditioner?"

"What?"

"Spray-on conditioner. Your hair will look like coconut matting if you don't condition it when you've been in the sea." Efficiently, she rummaged in her bag and came out with a small pink bottle. "Here. Spray it on, brush it through. Leave it in. And put some more *cream* on, Chloe! *God!*"

Laughing, I did as I was told, flattered by her attention. "You know," she said, considering me, "you have really, really good bone structure. You should wear your hair back off your face more." Obediently, I forked it back with my fingers. "That's better. You'd suit it layered a bit, you know. If there was a single hairdresser on this island that didn't only have the skills of a *sheep shearer*, we could get it done."

She stood up and tied her sarong round her waist, and flicked back her gorgeous hair. *God, I thought, she's stunning. I'm glad I'm with her. Some of her stunningness might reflect onto me.* I felt like—I dunno, the bargain version. Ordinary face, ordinary mousy brown hair, slimmer body than hers but more *ordinary* . . .

"OK," she said. "Let's get lunch."

"Aren't you going to swim?"

"Later. Put the umbrella down, leave the mats and towels here, no one'll take them."

"You sure about that?"

"No. But it doesn't exactly matter if they *do*. Daddy'll get us new ones."

Davinia insisted that we walk farther on along the beach, past the great outcrop of rocks where the local boys were diving. "I am not going anywhere near The Cabin," she said. "There'll be people we know along there. . . . They kind of *gather* here every year, like migrating rats."

"Do rats migrate?"

"Whatever. They all head for the same spot and meet up again and scream about how incredible it is that they've bumped into one another. They are so unspeakably thick. And they go on about how much you've grown. I mean—I *really* don't want to be told that!"

It was weird, walking on the sand, you had to go slow, kind of lope along. It made me feel all swaying and sexy, like one of those women with jugs on their heads. Plus it was like being a celebrity, walking along the shoreline with Davinia. I loved her confidence. People stared at us, and a few boys called out. She kept her eyes straight ahead as she glided on, but I knew she was collecting each and every glance and storing it, feeding off it.

We doubled back on ourselves round another outcrop of rocks, and Davinia pointed ahead to a white-painted shed at the end of a winding track coming down to the beach. "That place," she said, "is OK. Because it's a trek you don't get many ghastly little kids or dribbly old people in there." A huge fir tree with cones like hand grenades grew next to it, shading the ramshackle collection of benches and tables laid out on the sand. "The other reason I like it is it's kind of anonymous. I never bump into anyone I know here."

She strode up to the café and dumped her beach bag on one of the few spare tables left. It was at the edge of the group, and only part-shaded by the great spread of the tree, but that suited us. We sat down opposite each other on the worn wooden benches, and I wiggled my toes in the hot sand. "Is the food any good?" I asked.

"It's food." Davinia shrugged.

A smiling, mahogany-tanned man bounded up to us, wearing a well-washed white T-shirt, and handed us two worn-looking menu cards. "Two beers, please," said Davinia, glancing at the card. "And I'll have a tuna salad. Chloe?"

"Are the beers all for you?"

"Funny. One each."

"OK, I'll have the burger and salad. And some chips."

"Burger and chips?" Davinia repeated, all disapproving.

"I've been swimming," I said virtuously. "I've worked up an appetite."

"Hmm," said Davinia. "I'll have chips too."

A soft breeze was moving the branches above our heads, making a *shushshuuush* sound. Davinia was craning her neck, looking at something behind me, then she subsided back down and put the menu card up in front of her face. "Don't look round," she hissed. "I think it's those goons from the plane. One of them keeps smirking at me. Oh, God. Oh, *shit*. They're coming over."

"Mind if we join you, girls?"

I looked up. It was him, it was *him*, the wonderful arrogant loathsome boy from the plane. He had a pair of forest-green bathers on, and nothing else, and he was standing next to the boy with bleached hair and crooked teeth.

Standing beside us, asking to join us.

"Only there aren't any other tables," said the blond one cockily. "I mean—we could try and squeeze six of us onto that one, but . . ."

I felt like my throat had cemented up. I looked

at Davinia. Most of me wanted her to tell them to sod off but a terrible, treacherous bit of me wanted her to say yes, join us.

She looked back at me and sighed heavily, then she flopped her menu at the space beside her, as though bestowing a momentous favor. "Go ahead," she said.

And *he* levered himself into the place next to her, and the one with bleached hair plunked down next to me.

The terrible treacherous bit of me felt crushed, wanted to know why he'd sat next to Davinia, and not next to me. Although . . . now I could look at him. He had a wonderful chest and shoulders and neck, all brown, with white flecks of salt and sand glittering his skin . . . and he was smiling at me, knowing and sure of himself and hateful.

"Thanks, ladies," said the boy next to me. "You were on the plane with us coming over, weren't you?"

"Yeah," said Davinia. "You were sitting behind us, weren't you? Making a load of noise."

"Oh, come on, we kept it down once the complaints started coming in," *he* said, and grinned at me, and I felt my face respond, although I'm not sure what it did, I just hope it didn't glow too much.

Then he raised his hands all cocky like he was asking for a truce, and said, "I'm Alex—that's Frazer. What are you two called?"

Davinia sighed wearily again, and said, "I'm Davinia, that's Chloe."

I was glad she was doing all the talking for us because I was pretty sure I'd lost the power of speech.

*Alex. Alex. What a great name. Shut up, Chloe, you traitor.*

"Didn't see you on the ferry," Alex said.

My heart was thumping with the thought that maybe he was *looking* for us, looking for *me*, while Davinia drawled, "We drove on."

The waiter appeared with our food and drink, and took the boys' order, and I sheltered behind all the activity, and all the time his face was there across the table from me. "So, you girls been here before?" said Frazer breezily.

"Yes," said Davinia, mouth full. She was really tucking in. "I've been coming here since I was about three years old."

"Wow! D'your parents own a place, or something?"

"Part-own."

I thought I really should enter the conversation, so I squeaked, "It's my first time." Then I realized how sexual that sounded and went red.

"Yeah?" said Alex, grinning at me again.

I wanted to crawl under the table and hide, but instead I snapped, "It's a beautiful island, isn't it?"

"Gorgeous," he said, rolling the word round his mouth.

I glared down at my plate and after a pause, Frazer asked, "So where is your place, then?"

"Quite near here," said Davinia, and filled her mouth again. I made myself cut a chip in two, put half in my cement-mouth, and chewed.

"Not gonna give us the address, then?"

"Well spotted. Look—I'm trying to *eat*, OK?"

"All right, moody! Why'd you let us sit here if you're going to freeze us out?"

"I didn't think I had a choice. There weren't any other seats. That doesn't mean we have to become best friends, though, does it?"

"No chance," Frazer rapped back, "not with someone as up their own arse as you are, darling."

"Oh, fuck you. Clear off if you're going to get abusive."

"*Me* abusive? You're the one being snotty as hell. *And* swearing. Give us a chip." He reached across to her plate, and she batted at his hand, and her glass of beer tipped over. As the beer flowed off the table into her lap, she shot to her feet, snarling.

"Oh, you fucking *wanker*!" She sounded really vicious. Hateful.

"Hey, no need for that!" said Alex. "It was an accident!"

"*He's* a fucking accident! Oh, God—I'm *soaked*!"

"It may have escaped your notice, Duchess, but we're at the *beach*? Where getting soaked is part of it all?"

"*Don't you patronize me, you idiot,*" she hissed, right in his face.

Alex drew back, fast. He looked half disgusted, half . . . *afraid*. I didn't blame him. Jesus, she'd changed. Medusa, or whatever. I half-expected to see little venomous snakes writhing in her hair. I reached out and put a calming hand on her arm, but she shook me off.

"Come on, Chloe!" she spat. "We're going. I take it you idiots won't mind getting our bill, since you've *spilled our drinks* all over me?"

"You need to relax, babe," said Alex bravely. "You'll give yourself a coronary."

"Yeah," said Frazer. "And it was only one drink that got spilled."

"Oh, really?" said Davinia. "Well, I can soon sort that out."

Then she picked up my glass and tossed my

beer straight in Frazer's face.

"*You fucking bitch,*" said Frazer, dripping. Then he scrambled to his feet and his hand shot out and slapped her face.

And Davinia opened her mouth and screamed. I mean really *screamed.* On and on and on. Everyone in the café—on the *beach*—had stopped and turned round and was staring. I pushed past Alex, put my arm round her. "*Shhhhh!*" I said. "*Shhhhh!*"

She stopped screaming, and shook me off violently. "*Are you going to let him get away with that?*" she squawked.

It was weird, unreal, like I was watching myself from a distance. What was I supposed to do? Start a punch-up? "*What the hell were you thinking of?*" I shouted at Frazer, like I was following a script. "*What kind of a creep hits a girl?*"

"*Yeah?*" roared Alex, at me. "*What kind of a girl chucks a drink at someone just 'cos he's accidentally knocked a glass over?*"

"*You are so out of order!*" I railed. Our faces were inches apart. "He is so out of order, hitting her!"

"He's got a quick temper. Just like she has. And *she* started it!"

"She didn't *hit* him!"

"Chucking a drink at someone—that's just as bad!"

"No it's *not*!"

The waiter appeared at our side. "Please, you must go," he said. "You must fight away from here."

"Don't worry, we're going!" I said. "And *they're* paying our bill." I put my arm back round Davinia's shoulders and this time she left it there. Then I shepherded her out of the café.

Davinia was so quiet as we walked along the beach that I thought she had to be in shock. A couple of years ago, this psychette in the year below had slapped me, and I was so shocked by it I'd gone very silent and kind of distanced. I hadn't wanted to hit her back, I'd just locked myself in the bathroom and then I'd *sobbed*.

We walked on, me waiting for Davinia to start sobbing, but she didn't. So then I thought: *Maybe she feels I let her down, maybe she knows I was following a script instead of feeling really angry on her behalf.*

The whole thing had been surreal. Alex's face shouting at me filled my mind.

"Dav, are you OK?" I whispered at last. "That was awful, are you OK?"

"Don't call me Dav," she said.

"D'you want to sit down for a bit?"

"*No*. Let's get back to where we left the umbrella and stuff, OK?"

"Sure."

"As far away from those cretins as we can get!"

"Absolutely!"

We walked on in silence, and soon we were back to where our reed mats lay stretched on the sand, with our towels beside them. I opened up the umbrella again; the afternoon sun was scorching. Davinia took off her sarong and stretched out on her back, then she turned on her side and pulled a bottle of sun oil from her bag, and started massaging oil onto her legs.

I was waiting for it to hit her. I was waiting for her to start swearing or crying or talking. But she just carried on oiling her legs, and her face looked calm, impassive.

And I realized it wasn't going to happen, the reaction I was waiting for. It was over, it was gone, she felt fine again.

I couldn't decide if I admired her for that or felt chilled by it. I stretched out beside her on my mat, and I felt all kind of alienated and alone, and my mind was boiling with everything that had happened—Alex shouting, Davinia screaming—and I felt full of this kind of weepy longing and before I knew it, I was thinking about Mum.

Oh, weird. Oh, freaky. In the months since Mum had left, I'd developed a very efficient blocking system that destroyed any thoughts about her. How come it wasn't working now? I rolled over on my side, full of this awful longing, and I knew I wanted to talk to Mum. She'd always listened so well to me, she'd always helped me sort things out. I wanted to tell her about Alex and about Davinia, how I'd practically adored her and now this gap was opening up and I didn't know what to do about it, I didn't know how to cope with feeling critical, I wanted to go back to how it was, because it was easy there, it was easy just worshipping her. . . .

And then the doppelganger slid into my mind, the one I'd met in the shopping mall just before we came away. What was it she'd said? *I'm not who you think I am.* I rolled over on my side, and stared at Davinia. Her profile was perfect, like a carving, still and perfect. Eyelashes dark on honey-brown cheeks, just a few freckles, perfect, straight nose, and that envy-making full mouth, slicked with gloss. She was so still. Even her eyelids were still, no movement underneath them.

Why couldn't I be like her? Why was I so restless all the time?

"Coming for a swim?" I breathed. She didn't answer. I stood up and headed for the shoreline.

I stayed in the sea for ages. I swam out for a bit, then I treaded water, and sometimes I floated on my back with my hair like seaweed and my arms and legs like a starfish. Nobody bothered me—I was too far out. I gently surged up and down with the waves, and looked up at the unreal blue of the sky, and felt far more at peace than I'd felt staked out on the beach. My ears were full of water but I could hear the local boys shouting as they jumped off the rocks. I looked back at the beach a few times to check that Davinia wasn't worried about me, but she hadn't moved.

Shouting attracted my attention. I reared up and treaded water and saw that the shouting was from the rocks. Some other boys had climbed up there, and the diving boys were shouting at them. . . . The incomers had light skin compared to the deep tan of the locals, they had to be holiday makers. . . .

And then I realized it was Alex.

Alex and his mates. Alex in his forest-green bathers. Although I'd've known him whatever color he was wearing.

Suspended safe in the sea, rising up and down

with the waves, I ogled him. He didn't have a text-book-perfect body, his shoulders were too broad for his height, but he was all energy and power. I felt like his shape was imprinting into me like his face had done, becoming my perfect male shape.

Oh, lord.

The local boys were challenging the English boys to dive like they were doing. They jostled them and gestured to the sea and then one of them would spring off the rocks, diving as they'd done since they were little kids.

And then Alex stepped forward. He was on the edge and the two groups of boys were behind him, waiting, egging him on. . . .

I was gripped by panic. I was thinking, if he dives he could kill himself, smash his head on the rocks, but if he bottles it, what would happen to him, how would he carry the shame? . . . I brought myself up sharp. Why should I care about him *carrying shame*? I'd *like* him to carry shame.

Suddenly he made a kind of lunging run, and sprang out and up in the air, and even at that distance I could see the courage it had taken, the nerve, and then he was down, down, he'd jumped farther out than the locals and that meant he was closer to this great vicious fist of a rock jutting from the sea, too close to it, *oh*, *God*, much too *close*. . . .

I shut my eyes. I was in absolute terror.

Then there was a great roar of approval and triumph from the boys on the rocks and I opened my eyes and saw Alex's head break the surface of the water, safe, and he was waving, waving. . . .

I felt kind of woozy with relief. He'd done it, he was a hero, he was alive. . . .

He was swimming now, an over-arm crawl out to sea, out toward me. Something inside me told me to get my head down and start swimming again but I was like a rabbit in the headlights, I couldn't move.

He came toward me. Then his head came up, and he looked at me. We were only a few meters apart. He knew who I was, and he knew I knew him.

Then he turned and swam back to the rocks again.

## CHAPTER 17

**WE USED TO HAVE A** cat at home who'd sleep for eight hours at a stretch, just dossed down on her little cat beanbag, and Davinia completely reminded me of her. When I plunked myself down beside her after my second beach shower of the day, she barely stirred.

Alex was inside me, like a secret. There was no way I was going to tell Davinia what I'd seen. The sun was getting cooler—the shadows on the beach were lengthening.

The couple next to us had bought two bottles of lager from a nearby beach bar and were sitting drinking them, leaning up against each other and gazing out at the sea. I watched them, throat tight, longing for it to be me, me and . . . someone. They'd be going back to their hotel room or apartment soon, and maybe they'd make love, all salty and warm from the sun, before they got showered.

Then they'd get dressed up to go out to some lovely little seafood restaurant and drink cold wine with their faces inches apart and then they'd wander back and make love again. . . . I was kind of cramped up with envy, just thinking about the lovely pattern of it.

Then Davinia suddenly sat up, and said, "God, I'm starving."

"*You're* starving—what about *me*?" I scoffed, although I wasn't hungry, not a bit. "You managed to put most of your meal away—I hardly touched mine!"

Davinia shrugged elegantly. "You could've brought that burger with you."

"*What?* That might've undermined things a bit, don't you think? Shouting at those idiots furiously but still remembering to grab my grub?" Davinia started giggling, and I joined in. "Honestly, Dav, sorry, but what made you chuck that drink at him?"

"Oh, I don't know. They were just—in my face. I suddenly felt like I'd had *enough*. You know what?" She glared at me.

"What?" I prompted.

"I reckon I was just pissed off that the only guys to hit on us were those wankers from the plane. The only guys *likely* to hit on us here."

I was seized by regret when she said that. In agreement with her or because *he* could've been hitting on *me*?

"It's such a . . . *backwater*," Davinia groaned on. "I'm not coming here next year. Definitely not."

There was a pause, then I said, "I can't believe you weren't more upset. You know—when he slapped you."

"I screamed, didn't I?"

"Er—*yes*! They must have heard you all over Caminos! But then you just seemed to . . . I dunno, shrug it off. *Forget* about it."

"That's 'cos I *did* forget about it. I've had a lot worse than that little shit landing one on me, I can tell you. And I've worked out a way to be free of it, to *not be a victim*. What you have to do is scream very loud. Or smash something or fight back, but only if you're sure of winning. Basically—you do something *violent* and *extremely noisy* and then you walk away and as you walk away you tell yourself you're moving on, leaving it all behind. It's practically Buddhist, honestly."

"And it really works? I mean—I'm not sure I could get over being slapped that easy, no matter how loud I screamed."

"Practice," said Davinia. "Trust me. I've had a *lot* of practice. Now come on, let's get back. And eat. And then let's *go out* tonight."

"To Hilly's, like you said."

"Yes. Hilly's is cool. Maybe we'll even pick up a couple of gorgeous men. You never know, there might just about be two on the island." She scrambled to her feet and started rolling her mat up, and grinning, I followed her.

That was more like it, I thought. Maybe Davinia was OK after all. Maybe she'd just been— I dunno. Tired.

We trudged into the flat to find Paul and Cassie in the process of making something sizzling and fabulous-smelling in a great iron pan on the stove. "Hello, girls!" said Cassie brightly. "Have you had a good day?"

"It was all right," said Davinia grudgingly. "When are we eating?"

I was waiting for her mum to say something along the lines of "Well, we're eating in half an hour—you're eating when you fix yourself something," but she didn't, she just said, "Almost ready. Five minutes? You timed that really well. You can join us on the balcony, or you can take yours onto the roof . . . or eat in here. . . ."

Davinia made no response; I glanced out onto the balcony. Its little table was laid for two with a bottle of wine in a silver ice bucket, and it was so obvious that they were planning a romantic meal that I blurted out, "Oh, let's just eat in here, ay, Davinia? Then we can get ready to go out. . . ."

"Where are you off to?" asked Paul, beaming his broad smile. I'd clearly said the right thing.

"Hilly's," said Davinia.

"Where?"

"*You've* never been there," snapped Davinia. Whenever she talked to her parents, she always sounded kind of sour, like she'd never forgive them for the restraints they put on her life. "It was new last year—it's near the harbor."

"Is it good?"

"It's OK. The clientele isn't totally geriatric, like the rest of the bars here."

"Talking of geriatrics," said Paul, "we bumped into the Stuart-Coxes today."

Davinia groaned theatrically.

"They're having one of their parties. Next week. Tuesday. You can always say you're busy!"

"No—we'll go," said Davinia, like she was bestowing an incredible favor. "It's a chance to get dressed up." She turned to me. "You'll *looove* their place—they've got a pool. And a wonderful music system, so if I bring some of my CDs along we can sneak them on when they get sozzled."

"No, you *can't*, Davinia," said Paul. Then he turned to me and said, "Their parties are pretty good, Chloe. They order in all this delicious food from one of the local restaurants—wall-to-wall lobsters, that kind of thing."

"And all the champagne you can tip down," added Davinia.

"But remember what happened last year," said Cassie. "Remember you said you'd take it much, much slower the next time. . . ."

"Oh, *what*?" huffed Davinia. "You're never going to forget that, are you? Nobody minded."

"Everyone was *very concerned* about you."

"I just needed a sleep!"

"Under the *food* table? Poor Ilse Parks nearly passed out when she saw your feet sticking out. . . ."

"Let's face it, Davinia, you passed out," added Paul.

"*Oh, get off my back, will you?!*" Davinia suddenly shrieked, and her mum and dad both sucked in a big breath, both at the same time, and turned to focus on the cooking. "I won't *come* to your stupid party if you're ashamed of me!!"

"Darling, don't be silly," soothed Cassie. "Come on, the dinner's ready."

"That stupid old cow Ilse Parks would make a fuss about anything! I'd've been OK if she hadn't tried to wake me up!"

"Let's drop it, shall we?" said Paul, piling the spicy-smelling mixture from the iron pan onto four bright yellow plates. "Here. Help yourselves to salad."

Then the two of them escaped onto the balcony, pulling the sliding glass door shut behind them.

I let out a little mew of pleasure and started to eat. Davinia grabbed a bottle of white wine from the fridge, uncorked it, and filled two glasses brimfull. "This is *fabulous*." I sighed. It was some kind of rice thing, with bits of pepper and ham and mushroom in it. "I am *so hungry*."

"Oh, stop going on about all the exercise you've done," Davinia snapped.

"I wasn't!"

"Yes, you were." She took a huge swig of wine. "On and on and *on*."

"Sod *off*! I'm hungry 'cos I didn't get my lunch 'cos you picked a fight with Frazer!"

"Oh, fuck off—*Frazer*?" She sneered and took another huge swig. "Since when have we been on chummy-wummy first-name terms with those idiots, ay?"

"I just remember his name," I muttered. Then, anxious to divert her, I said, "Tell me what happened at that party. When that old girl woke you up."

"I puked."

"What—instantaneously?"

"Just about. The stupid old cow wouldn't stop tugging on my arm, and I came to and threw up. A load of it went on her shoes."

"Bloody hell, Davinia, weren't you *embarrassed*? I'd've died. Right under the food table—it must have put everyone off taking another *bite*!"

"It did. But that was OK, because I convinced them . . . *God*, I was good . . . that the reason I'd been ill was food poisoning. So no one would've wanted another bite even if the food *hadn't* had a pile of vomit right in front of it! Clever, ay?"

"Diabolical!"

"My stupid parents realized the truth later, of course, 'cos no one else got sick. Actually—I suppose *everyone* realized the truth later. But I was away by then so who cares? *God*, they're so unspeakably boring, going on about it!" And she took another swig and emptied her glass.

## CHAPTER 18

WE REALLY ENJOYED GETTING tarted up to go out that night. Davinia seemed to have forgotten her ruling that Caminos just wasn't worth the effort. We showered and then we slathered on loads of fake tan—brilliant stuff that was slightly glittery and very brown, so you could see exactly where you were smearing it. It looked excellent on top of the pink beginnings of a tan we'd got on the beach earlier. Then we got out our fancy flip-flops and floppy skirts and skimpy tops, all in lush, bright colors, and we threw them all together like the feathers of tropical birds. Our hair dried fast and natural in the warm air.

The wine I'd managed to down before Davinia finished the bottle was sizzling in my bloodstream. I loved my slicked, bare skin, I loved wearing clothes so light I could hardly feel them. The sun had set and the night was nearly here—I couldn't wait to get out in it.

"Finishing touches, Chloe," said Davinia. "Perfume. Bangles. Rings." Laughing, I let her load me up, loving her attention, the feeling she thought I was worth it, and then we each took a tiny bag with just cash and a brush and lipstick in it, and Davinia made sure she had her keys and we danced out of the flat.

Cassie and Paul were still ensconced on the balcony, talking with their faces very close; they didn't see us go.

It was a long walk to the harbor, but I really enjoyed it. The cicadas sang and there was a feeling of festival in the air. People promenaded about, boys in cars slowed down to catcall us. Davinia dispatched them all with style, at the same time preening under their admiration, and I felt such status walking alongside her that I forgot about the criticisms I'd had for her earlier. After all, she was a night owl, wasn't she? The few times we'd gone out at home, it had taken her practically until midnight to start to get going.

Walking onto the harbor was like walking into a party. People were milling about, heading for the restaurants with their tables out under the stars and their strings of twinkling lights. Groups lounged on the low seawalls, talking, laughing, looking at the boats going by. The night sea shone. Davinia was in her element, sneering at the other tourists and the local kids' idea of fashion. ("Oh . . . my . . . *God*. That girl actually has 'You think I'm bad? Sometimes I'm not this good!' on her T-shirt. I mean—does she actually think it means something?") Then she pointed and said, "There's Hilly's, over there."

It didn't look much from the outside. It was in a slightly derelict-looking stone building, only the small sign showed there was a bar here. The door was black and forbidding, with a large brass knocker. I felt quite nervous just standing in front of it. "It doesn't want to pull people in off the road, it's *exclusive*," said Davinia. "Well, actually, it's not that exclusive. They seem to let *anyone* in." And she rapped loudly on the door.

It was opened immediately by a very tanned boy dressed all in black with slicked-back hair. "Is Cora here?" demanded Davinia.

"Can I ask you for your name, please?" he demanded back in a strong Maltese accent.

"She might not remember my name," countered Davinia, "but she'll know me when she sees me. . . ."

"I bet," the boy said, leering. And then this

incredibly throaty, sexy voice said, "Who is it, Saul?" and a fantastic woman swam into sight.

I say "swam" because she looked like a mermaid. She had an extraordinary mass of blond hair, all different colors from white to dark, and the skimpiest of pale pink tops that at first made her look naked from the waist up. Her hair was all tricked out in dreadlocks and tiny plaits, and haphazardly decorated with clips and slides. . . . I half expected to see shells and sea horses caught up in its tangles. Her waist was bare; she was wearing low-slung sea-green harem pants. She was barefoot and she had about fifteen silver bangles riding up each thin arm.

"*Cora!*" Davinia said.

"Darling, it's *you*!" cried Cora. "*Wel*come, welcome back . . . Oh, it's been too long, I've missed you. . . . How long is it?"

"Last summer," said Davinia.

"No! Longer, longer . . . And who is this beauty?" I felt really flattered as she lasered her amazing sea-green eyes at me.

"This is my friend Chloe. She's staying with me for the summer."

"How fabulous," purred Cora. "I'm so happy you two are here. Come on, come in . . . come and get a drink. The party's just starting."

We followed her down a plain, brick corridor with closed doors leading off it (one with a LADIES sign that I clocked for later) and then suddenly we were out under the stars again.

"You like it?" breathed Cora, turning to smile at me.

"It's amazing!" I squawked.

We were in a fantasy courtyard, open to the sky; all along its high brick walls were brackets holding flaming torches. "It's an old convent," Cora explained. "This was their quadrangle, where they'd meditate, walking up and down. Now it sees a bit more life, hmm?"

Very cool, bluesy music was playing. The people crowding the wide, impressive bar and lounging at the black tables were glossy and self-assured. Some of them were dressed up, some superconfidently underdressed, still in shorts and T-shirts. A good half of them looked young—under thirty, anyway. I scanned the faces for Alex—I couldn't help myself—but he wasn't there.

Cora led us over to an empty table, picked up two shiny purple cards lying on it, and handed them to us with a flourish as soon as we'd sat down. "Choose your cocktails!" She grinned and wandered off.

I watched her as she passed among her guests,

calling out to them, touching them, laughing with them. "She's some act," I breathed.

"It's OK here, isn't it?" enthused Davinia. "At least it's got some *style*."

"It's brilliant," I said. I loved the drama of it. The high walls made everything seem so intense. Behind Davinia's head a torch flared, lighting up her hair. "And the people," Davinia went on, "just a bit of a cut above, yeah?"

I pulled a face at her snobbish remark, but I could see what she meant. I felt a bit intimidated by everyone, to be honest. They all seemed so confident—the place was only half full but it was really humming. It was like we were in some little elite club. "Now," said Davinia, "cocktails. What are you gonna have?"

We chose a Bahama Mama and a Rosy Rum Cosmo, and as if she could read our minds, Cora was back at our sides, agreeing we'd chosen the best cocktails on offer. She signaled to the good-looking Maltese boy behind the bar, calling, "Hey—where's Zara? We have two very important ladies here who need her best shot. Where is she?"

There was a pause, and we both posed as people turned to look at us, then Zara swaggered out behind the bar. Her deep tan was shown off by her white tank top, and she clearly worked out. She had a terrific shape. Plus a tattoo of a chameleon on her arm and jet-black hair cropped very close to her finely shaped head. A group of men at the bar called out to her, and she grinned, acknowledging them, then she darted to the end of the bar and punched a couple of buttons on the music system. The music changed to a pounding 1980s disco beat.

"Bahama Mama and a Rosy Rum Cosmo, my angel!" shouted Cora. "And be *fast*, OK?" Zara stuck her tongue out at her, then picked up two silver cocktail shakers and at top speed added ice, rum, cranberry juice, coffee liqueur, pineapple juice . . . everything. She screwed the shakers' lids back on and raised them above her head like a couple of small dumbbells. And then she was dancing, strutting up and down behind the bar, shaking the cocktails for all she was worth.

"*Lovvvely* muscle definition," purred Cora, starting to dance too, undulating like seaweed. "All from this. Not from boring *weights*."

Zara, posturing, posing, poured the cocktails into two very tall glasses, added extra ice and two swizzle sticks, and pushed them across the bar. Cora jived over to pick them up. As she reached the bar, Zara leaned right over it, and Cora arched her head back, and they kissed on the mouth.

"Oh, yeah, I forgot to tell you that," Davinia said. "They're lesbians. Cool, ay?"

## CHAPTER 19

**PEOPLE WERE COMING IN** the bar in droves now, the courtyard was nearly full. The music stayed on loud, old 1980s stuff, and Zara was shaking cocktails nonstop, dancing behind the bar. It had its effect. People were standing up and dancing too, in groups or on their own—mixing in with each other and flirting and laughing. "C'mon, Davinia," I said, "let's dance!"

"In a minute," Davinia said, stirring her cocktail with her swizzle stick. It was transparent lilac with a naked girl on the end of it. "Not in the mood for cheesy eighties music."

The barman had come out from behind the bar to collect empty glasses. Cora swayed from table to table, group to group, delivering cocktails and taking orders. I got the feeling no one said *no* to her, not if she asked if you wanted another drink. She worked the room like a pimp, a first-rate cocktail pimp.

Soon she swam back to our table. "Come on, *girls,*" she purred. "One more little drink and then I want to see you dancing. The two best-looking girls in the place and they sit down all night? I don't think so." And she called out to Zara to get us two Champanskas. "You'll love them, darlings, honestly. Champagne and vodka. *They'll* get you moving."

Somehow Zara kept up with the incredible demand for cocktails, using the bar like a stage, sashaying up and down to the beat. The barman started issuing bills and taking money, and Saul the doorman was more in evidence too, escorting people out as well as in. There was no chance you could get away without paying.

It was some production. It was theatre, and the tourists were the audience and we were getting worked. Worked to buy cocktails and dance and make a great party . . . and buy more cocktails. It was all coming up to the boil in front of our eyes. Part of me loved it, but it made me really uneasy too.

"It's kind of . . . *false*, don't you think?" I muttered to Davinia. "The way Cora's making out she's everyone's best friend and everything."

"No she's not!" said Davinia scathingly. "She's just being a good hostess."

"Yeah, but it's more than that. I mean—there's a difference between making someone feel welcome and making out they're her best friend, isn't there? Like she was making out to us that we were really special."

"Darling, we *are*!"

"I know, I know! But she tells everyone they're special, she says the same things to everyone. . . ."

"I don't think she does."

"Oh, come on—she butters everyone up! It's so kind of *phoney*. . . ."

Then Davinia slammed her glass down and snapped, "Oh, Chloe, will you just *relax* and stop frigging *analyzing* everything!"

I sat back, as hurt as if she'd slapped me, and it hit me that this gap that had opened up between us, these critical thoughts I'd been having about her . . . it was a two-way process.

She'd been having them about me too.

What had she called me on the beach? *Revoltingly hearty*. She'd been as pissed off with me for swimming as I had been with her for not swimming. I'd been fed up with her for being sour but maybe she was sour because she was disappointed with me. She was *disappointed* with me. . . . Oh, *God*. I suddenly felt full of panic. It was the first time we'd spent any length of time together and it

135

wasn't working. I had to make it work. I had to save the holiday—I had to get it back to how it was between us.

*Dancing.* We jelled dancing. "OK," I said. "I'll shut up. Come on—let's *dance*!"

I got to my feet and dragged her to hers, and we found a space on the floor, and started moving. The music had entered the twenty-first century—it was stuff we liked. The cocktails had gone to my head, I was buzzing. I danced close to her and mirrored her and buoyed her up. I can't explain how I did it, I just did it—I was the background, she was the star. I was working just like Cora to make things good, to create a party. Two men in their thirties sidled up to us, danced alongside us—Davinia dispatched them with a flick of her fingers. I laughed out loud against the music and danced on, and we ordered more cocktails. *From now on*, I thought, *I'm not going to be such a bore, I'm not going to analyze everything, I'm just going to have* fun.

And I managed it for five whole days. I laid low, I made no demands on Davinia, I flattered her, I made her laugh. In the long silences I thought about Alex. We went to the beach in the day and at night we'd wander down to the little bars along the harbor and be waspish about all the other holiday makers or we'd ransack Paul's wine rack and get tipsy up on the roof under the stars. . . . It was OK. Then, on Tuesday, we got out of bed with vibrating hangovers after stealing two of his bottles of wine and went through to the kitchen for orange juice to find a note saying:

*Be back from the beach by 4 p.m. at the latest if you want to come to the Stuart-Coxes' party!*

"Fantastic!" I gushed. "I am *so* looking forward to it!"

"Let's not bother with the beach," said Davinia. "Let's just roast up on the roof, then we can take our time getting ready."

"Sure!" I enthused, although I hated the thought of being stuck on the roof all day with no sea to swim in. "Good idea. Now . . . can you face eating a slice of toast . . . ?"

Davinia seemed a lot happier sunbathing on the roof than she had been on the beach. Near the bathroom and other modern facilities. With my resolution to be a fun companion at the forefront of my mind, I really tried to chat and joke, but our hangovers got in the way and we were silent most of the time, apart from a few forays back to the flat for carbohydrates and water.

In the late afternoon, I cracked. I told her I wanted to get out, stretch my legs, but she sneered. "Oh, for God's sake, Chloe, what is *wrong* with you? Just relax, can't you?" After that, I didn't even dare ask her for the apartment key in case I irritated her even more. Just for something to do, I wandered down to our bedroom, went out on the balcony, and leaned over, looking at the wasteland with its prickly pears and chaotic flowers. The pretty, skinny cat was there again, going about its business as the heat of the day started to fade. I felt trapped, awful—like I'd give anything to be down there with it. I found myself examining the balcony on the floor below. It was wider than ours, and it had a really sturdy-looking table wedged along one side of it. And just as my mind was screaming, *Chloe! Don't! You'll break your leg, you'll smash the table, you'll get arrested, YOU'LL DIE!* I'd thrown my flip-flops ahead of me and climbed over the balcony. Then I'd slid down the rails, hung by my hands from the bottom, let go, and dropped like a cat.

*BANG!!* Phew! Safe. Heart hammering, legs wobbly, but safe. Table unbroken. Windows of the flat empty. It was easy-peasy to chuck over my flip-flops again, climb over that railing, drop to the sun-baked ground—and *go*.

I hitched up my sarong so I looked pretty much respectable, and strode out. I was on an adrenaline rush from my daring escape and I felt fabulous, walking through the wild open space. A little track took me up alongside some walled-in patches of land where squashes were growing, but no one was about—it was still too hot to start watering anything. The clean, island air flowed past me and a crowd of chattering sparrows flew up from a bush as I passed. And suddenly without warning, I felt full of agony about Mum, about missing her. What was happening, why was I thinking about her again? It didn't make sense. I should be totally wrapped up in the moment, in the heat and the freedom and the exoticness of everything—why was I thinking about her? In a place she'd never been, that held no connections to her?

Maybe that was it. Maybe at home my blocking system worked so well because there were bits of her everywhere, and I had to be always on guard. But on Caminos, with the sun and the sea and the sound of the cicadas at night . . . some wall had come down and let her in.

I walked on, faster. I was breathing deeply. I knew I was understanding something. The track turned into a rough and stony road, with a low wall built of rocks running alongside it. There were goats on the other side of the wall, grazing among the wiry shrubs. *Maybe it's safe to think about Mum here*, I thought, *because there's no chance I can contact her. At home, I was so determined not to get in touch, to reject her, to punish her, that I censored any thought of her. She was dead as far as I was concerned—finished. But here, she's far away, and I can't see her, so it's safe now, it's safe to think about her. . . .*

I stopped dead then, I stopped and put out a hand to the low rock wall to steady myself. My head wheeled. I felt like I was standing on the edge of a high building, swaying, about to fall.

It wasn't safe to think about her, not safe at all.

I walked on for a while, then I thought I'd better head back in case Davinia got concerned about me. Although I was pretty sure she wouldn't even have noticed I'd gone. I was longing to talk about what had happened to me, about all these feelings that had come in, but I knew I couldn't even try to talk to Davinia. She'd be impatient, bored, a bit repulsed, maybe. She'd say: *Oh, God, Chloe, I don't know what your problem is with your mother—I can't wait to get away from mine*. Then she'd say, *Look— parents are unutterably* boring. *Come on, stop looking so down. Let's have a drink.*

I could phone Dad, but I knew if I even so much as *mentioned* I'd been thinking about Mum he'd be all over me, trying to get me to contact her. He was pretty generous, really, the way he kept trying to persuade me to get in touch with her, after the way she'd treated him, unless . . .

Unless he was doing it for me, not her. Yes, that was it, that had to be it. He knew I needed her.

That thought was so overwhelming and disturbing I kicked it out of my head right away.

I got back to the apartment block and screamed, *"Davinia!"* There was no way I could climb back up again, so I just had to hope she heard me, with her iPod in and everything.

*"DAVINIA!!!!"*

Silence. No sign of her head looking over the edge of the roof.

I called again.

Nothing.

Oh, *shit*. Maybe someone else would hear, maybe if I went round to the front, someone would let me in the main doors. . . . I filled my lungs again, and absolutely shrieked, *"DAVINIA!!!!!!"*

Two windows above me were pushed wide open, people peered out and then, at last, Davinia's head poked bemusedly over the roof edge railings. *"Shit!!"* she squawked, and disappeared. Two minutes later, she was opening the back door to the apartment block and letting me in.

"I thought you'd fallen off the frigging *roof!*" she yelped. "When I saw you down there that's all I could think—that you'd fallen *off!* Only as I came down the steps I realized that of course you couldn't have or you wouldn't exactly be standing up and shouting, would you?"

"Not exactly." I laughed.

"So what the hell happened?"

"I . . . I jumped. It was an impulse thing. I was on our balcony looking out and I really fancied a walk and I . . . *jumped.*"

"*God,* you make such a thing out of being athletic, don't you? *Jumping* out of a *window* with a *hangover!* *God!* Next time, ask me for the keys, OK?"

We went to the kitchen and collected more refreshments, and headed back to the roof "for the last of the rays," as Davinia put it. Honestly, the way she talked, the sun was just in existence to give her a tan. A *safe* tan—she slathered on about a bottle of expensive oil every day. But the excitement seemed to have bucked her up—she grinned at me and, as she smoothed yet more oil into her legs, she murmured, "Hedonism."

"Y'what?" I said.

"Hedonism. It's my religion. D'you know what

that word *means*, Chlo?"

"Um . . . you like the nice things in life?"

"*Pleasure.*" She purred the word. "God, I'm feeling better, thank *God*. Yes—my religion is pleasure."

"You could get very fat with a religion like that. I mean—if you just ate chocolate all the time. . . ."

"Ah, that's where you're wrong. It's all a question of balance. Hedonism means you also enjoy having a fabulous sexy slim body. So you'd have to balance the pleasure of that with the pleasure of chocolate. But the point is—you *really enjoy* both." And she carried on smoothing in sun oil, right down to her feet, concentrating on each red-tipped toe as though she loved it passionately.

Something nagged at me, snagged like a torn nail catching on nylon. "And how does it work with people?" I asked.

"People are no different. You stick with the ones that give you pleasure."

"But—OK. You're with someone you really like. They go through a bad patch. Do you dump them just 'cos you're no longer having a good time with them?"

Davinia switched to the toes on her other foot and started adoring them. "Oh, for goodness' sake. You're at it again—why d'you have to *analyze* everything so much?"

"I don't!" I said quickly. "I was just . . . thinking about it."

"Thinking, analyzing . . . it's all the same. It does my head in. Anyway. I guess my answer is . . . yes, ultimately, I'd dump them. If they showed no sign of snapping out of it."

"Snapping out of it—suppose it was cancer or something?"

"Oh, for Christ's sake, Chloe! Why are you on such a *downer* the whole time?"

I turned away, stung, and before I could stop myself I blurted out, "Why are *you* so fucking *superficial* the whole time?"

Shit, I'd said it. It was out in the air. Inside my head, the sound of a great ripping, a tearing, a rending. The sound of our friendship ending. Oh, *shit*.

Davinia didn't respond. There was a thrumming silence. At last I turned back to her and saw that she'd plugged her iPod in her ears and her expression told me she hadn't heard what I'd said at all.

Either that, or she wasn't bothered by it.

Half an hour later, Davinia decided we should start getting ready for the party.

## CHAPTER 20

### DAMAGE LIMITATION.

It was all I could think about as we got ready to go out. I was feeling all confused and churned up and . . . *scared*, almost, with everything that had been going on in my head. I told myself to concentrate on the here and now, put everything I had into being a Good Friend again. So I flattered Davinia; I made jokes, I gave out energy like a dynamo. I didn't blame Davinia for being pissed off with me. *I* was pissed off with me. It wasn't Davinia who'd changed—she'd always been like this—it was me. Getting all morbid about Mum, getting all serious and boring . . . some part of me had woken up to what Davinia was like and I didn't like it. I wanted to stay in my dream.

Well—I had nowhere else to go, did I?

I threw myself into getting ready for the party. This time there were no-holds-barred—we were going for the best we could look. And as we showered and got made up and chose our clothes, we laughed and fussed and preened ourselves, and I knew I was acting but the fear receded a bit and I started to feel better.

Davinia was good at this. And she was generous—she wanted me to look the best I could. She did my eye makeup for me, far more dramatically than I usually do, and it looked stunning. Then she picked out the exact right top to go with the skirt I was wearing, and made me wear heels when I'd been going to play it safe with flip-flops. When I stood in front of the thin full-length mirror inside the wardrobe door, I simultaneously thought, *That doesn't look like me* and *I've never ever looked as good as this before,* and I grinned at her reflection behind me in the glass.

"Well?" she demanded.

"It's fantastic," I said. "I feel great." I was acting again. I didn't feel great, but that was OK. I could act, and then maybe it would come true. "Thank you."

"Anytime, babe. You *look* great."

I was full of relief that she seemed to like me again. "Shall I do something with my hair?" I asked.

"No," she said firmly. "Just keep it down. It's

gorgeous when you've just washed it. Just try this on." And she handed me a perfect neck chain, all shiny and delicate.

"Can I really borrow this?" I asked. It looked pretty valuable.

"Sure." She shrugged. "It's just right with that top."

Davinia looked amazing, of course—far better than me. But I wasn't completely out of her league, and I felt grateful to her for the help she'd given me. "We look really hot," she announced. "There's Daddy shouting. Hey—put a bikini in your bag. We might want a drunken swim at the end of the night, when it doesn't matter about our makeup getting messed up. OK, let's go."

Paul had booked a taxi to take us to the party. He said he intended to really enjoy himself. The Stuart-Cox residence was some ways away, along a narrow, craggy winding road with fields on either side full of goats scrubbing for what little green had survived the intense heat. The car climbed up and up, then, following Paul's directions, stopped by a swanky ranch-style gate. "We'll walk from here," said Paul. "They don't like cars stirring up the dust near the house."

"I love this place," Davinia said as we got

out of the taxi. "It's like a time warp. The Stuart-Coxes were Fabulous People or something, in the 1970s. . . ."

"Beautiful People," corrected Cassie.

"Whatever," snapped Davinia. "They did drugs and modeled and stuff, and bought a bit of land here and . . ."

"She was a model, he was a photographer," interrupted Cassie. "A real cliché, really."

"Look, Mummy, d'you mind *butting out* and having your own conversation?"

"Don't be so rude, Davinia," said Paul automatically.

"I just thought you'd like to know the *facts*," said Cassie.

"No," said Davinia. "Facts are unspeakably boring." She linked her arm in mine, holding me back, until her parents had walked on for a couple of meters. "As I was saying," she went on, "they bought this bit of land for about five quid or something, and built a house, right back when people had only just started coming to Caminos for holidays, and it was really undiscovered and cool, and they had all these rock stars and famous people to stay with them. . . ."

"Wow, really?" I asked, impressed. I was wobbling on my heels but there was something really glam and sexy about walking in high heels along a hot, dusty track. Like you were in a fashion shoot or something.

"Well, OK, not *really* famous people," she admitted, "but it was kind of cool, for back then. . . . It was kind of a glamorous scene, you know. And now they're old and they still have parties and it's OK. Mr. Stuart-Cox adores me. Dirty old git keeps taking my photo."

"D'you mind?"

"Not at all. He takes fabulous shots, even though he's about ninety or something."

"So are we going to be the only young people here?" I demanded.

"No. That's what's good about it. If there's anyone interesting on the island, they'll be here. Last year, OK, I puked and blew it. But the year before, when I was fifteen, I got taken under the wing of these fantastic people, they took me out in their speedboat and everything. . . ."

"Wow. D'you still see them?"

"No. Why would I? God, I hope there's some attractive men here. Otherwise we're stuffed for the rest of the holiday."

Alex punched into my mind and I punched him out again. "Yeah, let's hope," I said.

We'd reached the house. It must have made

the whole island talk when it was first built—it was space-age and blocky, with acres of glass, some with loose white blinds fluttering. It dramatically set off the huge spiky desert plants growing all around it. Already, we could hear music, laughter, and loud talk coming from inside, and a few people were gathered in front, talking animatedly like you do when you want to signal that you're having a great time.

Then an extraordinary older woman tottered grandly from the wide doorway, holding one hand out to Paul and languidly waving a cigarette holder in the other. She was all drifting mauve silk and massive dangly earrings; her white hair was piled on her head and she was wearing snakeskin platform shoes. Paul seized her hand, bowed, and kissed it, then Cassie too ducked down and air-kissed her on both cheeks. "That's Deborah Stuart-Cox," hissed Davinia. "Don't *ever* call her Debby."

Paul beckoned to us and we hurried over to join them. Deborah turned an appraising eye on us, and said, "So. Your little girl's *really* grown up now, hasn't she?" There was no warmth in her voice, and I knew Davinia, who was neurotic about her curves, would interpret it as a comment that she'd put on too much weight. "And this is—"

"Chloe, her best friend," said Paul.

"Welcome, Chloe," said Deborah. "Welcome to my party." As I thanked her, she gave me the once over and, surreptitiously, I studied her back. Her eyes were almost hostile—like she was in competition with me or something. She must have been a proper beauty when she was young—behind all the well-applied makeup, you could still see it shine. Then I noticed her earlobes and I had to clamp my mouth shut to stop myself giggling. They were about three times as long as most people's—pulled out of shape by years of wearing heavy earrings like the ones she was wearing now.

"Come inside," Deborah drawled, "it's too hot out here. Come and get a drink."

We followed her into a huge room, split into three distinct levels, with a dramatic spiral staircase in the center and sparse, elegant furniture round the edges. The temperature was cool despite the great glass windows, all of them looking out onto stark, dramatic hilltops. The room was full of classy people, just like the ones who'd been at Hilly's, but what struck me more than the people were the photographs. They were hung everywhere there was wall space, they were mostly black and white and huge. And they were nearly all of Deborah when she'd been a lot, lot younger.

Davinia nudged me—an elderly man was

approaching us. "That's Anthony," she whispered. "Call him Tony and you're dead."

Anthony had a paunch and a short, cream-colored kaftany thing over cream-colored trousers. He ignored us and took Deborah's hand, all reverential, like she was the most important creature on the planet. "Are you all right, my darling?" he murmured.

"Yes, I'm fine," she murmured back.

"Shall I freshen up your drink?"

"In a while, perhaps."

Only then did he turn to us and welcome us, smiling, and ask Paul how his business was going. Davinia nudged me again. "Let's slide off," she whispered, "and get a drink."

We headed over to a long low table set up in front of one of the great windows. "They don't do waiters who come to us," said Davinia. "Not like at a normal posh party. Mummy told me it was considered stuffy and old-style when they were young. You have to forage for your own stuff." She ordered two glasses of champagne from the soulful-looking man behind the table, not exactly "foraging" as far as I could see, and then we headed over to look at a wall of photos. "She was one of the babes of her day," said Davinia. "Isn't she stunning?"

"Yes, but . . ." I trailed off. I wanted to talk about how weird it was to live surrounded by enormous images of yourself from forty or fifty years ago, how vain, how *sad*, but I couldn't risk Davinia getting pissed off with me again. I took a great swig of champagne and said, pointing, "I like that one. With the eyelashes."

"False ones. Ever tried them?"

"No."

"I did once. Practically glued my eyelids together. Anyway. Did you see how Anthony *adores* her? I want someone to feel that way about me, don't you?"

I nodded unhappily. It had looked like an act of nauseating phoniness to me, but who was I to judge?

"God, isn't there any food here?" Davinia snapped, glaring round at the crowded room. "You'd think they'd hand round a few canapés before the real food's served, wouldn't you? Come on, let's go and check out the talent."

I followed her through a space in one of the great glass walls. The heat hit me like some great gong reverberating deep inside me. I loved it, though I knew I wouldn't be able to stand it for long. We were on a wide terrace, with steps leading down to the swimming pool, which glittered in the sun. No one was in it—people in party clothes were grouped round the edge, under the sun umbrellas, drinking and talking. "Oh, *what*?" huffed Davinia. "Everyone here's at least forty. This is a dead loss. This is . . ." She broke off. At the far side of the pool a good-looking boy had reared up from a cane chair. "Hey—*Max*! *MAX!!*" he shouted. Davinia and I swung our eyes round in the direction he was shouting. Another good-looking boy was confidently loping across the terrace, a beer in each hand, heading for the first boy.

"Go and get some more champers," hissed Davinia.

"Oh—what?" I hissed back. "I've barely started mine."

"Fine. Give it to me and I'll down it."

I glared at her, lifted my glass, and took a huge mouthful. It was wonderful—fruity and alive.

"Damn," said Davinia. "They've got a girl with them. *Two* girls. No, hang on . . . *three*. And there's two more guys. Oh, that's all right—there's a big group of them. Get the champagne and we'll go and check them out. Grab a bottle if you can."

I made my way back through the party crowd. It was getting denser and noisier all the time as more and more people turned up. At the bar, I was given two fresh glasses of champagne—no question of just a refill. There was no way I was even going to *think* about trying to grab a bottle. I made my way back to Davinia.

"The bottles were out of reach," I said. "Here."

"Great." She took a huge mouthful. "Come on." And she high-heeled her way round the side of the pool, me wobbling a couple of steps behind, toward the group at the other side. "Hi!" she called out. "Don't I know you?"

Jesus, you had to admire her brazenness. You really did.

The two classy boys grinned right at her, but the rest of the party looked a bit hostile. Especially the girls.

"You know the Bartons, don't you?" Davinia powered on. "We met at one of their parties, last year."

"Maybe," said Max. "You look . . . familiar."

"Anyway"—she swung right over to the group, me cringing in her wake—"I'm Davinia. This is Chloe."

"Max," said Max, still grinning. "And Ollie. And—"

He was about to introduce the rest of the party, but Davinia burst in with, "When are we likely to get some frigging food round here, d'you know? I am about to *pass out*."

"You obviously haven't been to one of these parties before," said one of the girls tartly. "Food is always served after sunset."

"I have, actually," said Davinia, "but I guess I've just never noticed the *time* the food's served."

"Well, it's a bit more than *time*," said the girl. There was a real catfight brewing. "When the sun sets, all the big windows turn red—it's spectacular. Then the lights come on out here and they serve the food."

"Oh, yeah, I remember," said Davinia dismissively. "I guess last year I was . . . you know. Doing other things." The way she said it, she'd been having wild sex beyond the palm trees, not passed out under a table. Max laughed, kind of suggestively, and she laughed back at him, and said, "I don't always notice the *time*."

"Yeah, but it's not about *time*, is it?" said the girl, going all squeaky and indignant and pink. "It's the sunset, it's . . ." She trailed off. She was repeating herself and being boring and she knew it. I felt almost sorry for her.

"It's happening now," said Ollie. "Look."

The great globe of the sun was sinking behind the hills on the horizon; the low red light was striking the huge windows, flaring them into life.

"Come on," said Max. "Let's go and see it from the front." And then, kind of reluctantly, he put out a hand to the squeaky pink girl and said, "Coming, Pandora?"

CHAPTER 21

**AS WE FOLLOWED THE** group round to the front of the house, I whispered to Davinia that it looked like Max and Pandora were an item.

"I absolutely don't give a *shit*," Davinia hissed back, "whether they're an *item* or not. You saw the way he looked at me. She's *history*. Past tense, OK?"

I shrugged, kept walking.

"*Pandora*," she went on sneeringly. "What an absolutely *futile* and pretentious name."

I wanted to crack back that she wasn't exactly called *Jane*, but I kept my mouth shut. It hit me that my relationship with Davinia was increasingly carried on in silence. Not good.

A crowd of guests was standing at the front of the house, gazing like Druids at the sun. The great glass windows flamed with red light; for a few moments, the whole house seemed to be on fire.

Then the sun dropped, half disappeared behind the hills, everything black before it. I was feeling positively awed when, right at the front, Anthony raised his hands high in some kind of fake-religious salute and ruined everything. Deborah and a few others copied him. I was ready to throw up but everyone else burst out clapping and, like a coward, I joined in.

The flaming windows faded; the sun plunged completely out of sight. Right on cue, a mass of fairy lights sprang to twinkling life all over the garden, and the clapping increased, with a couple of cheers thrown in.

"Thank Christ," muttered Davinia. *"Food."*

"So not even intense lust can make you forget about your stomach?" I said.

"What? Oh. Don't be stupid. I can do both. Come on." And she sidewinded over to Max. "I could tear a lobster apart," she breathed, as she passed by him, "with my bare *teeth*."

Max laughed and Pandora glared, and then we all followed Davinia back round to the swimming pool. She catwalked along, swaying and sexy. Max, who was no longer holding Pandora's hand, ogled her arse fixedly. It did look pretty impressive, I had to admit.

We reached two large trestle tables that had

magically appeared in front of the pool. Three local women were running back and forth, carrying huge platters of the most amazing-looking goodies. The centerpiece was a kind of tower of ice, etched with ridges. Hanging off the ridges by their tails were row after row of gorgeous giant prawns. "Yumm*mmeee*!" drooled Davinia. She reached out and grabbed one and turned, ignoring the look of pure hatred shot at her by one of the women, to grin at us.

"Don't you think you should *wait*?" I hissed, but she ignored me, too. She was making a big play of peeling the prawn and eating it in ecstasy. Then she put her fingers in her mouth one by one, and sucked them clean. It was unbelievably crass and incredibly erotic and Max was lapping it up.

Then I noticed with dismay that Pandora had sidled up and was standing right next to me. "That is *so* out of order," she spat. "They hadn't finished laying it all out, she should wait until everyone's seen it. . . . *Look*, she's taking another!"

I hated agreeing with Pandora. I didn't want to be like her, all mealymouthed and indignant, I wanted to be reckless and arrogant like Davinia. I kind of humphed noncommittally. The local women were fussing round like angry bees as they finished arranging the table, getting as near to barging Davinia out of the way as they dared.

Then, just as Davinia was helping herself to a third prawn, Deborah heaved into view, purple silk flowing. "*Greeeeedy* girl," she cried, shooing Davinia away with a flap of her sleeve. If that'd been me, I'd've shriveled up with shame right there and then, but Davinia stumbled, giggling, over to Max, and the two of them laughed together, heads very close.

The three women bustled back to the house. Deborah finished inspecting the wonderful display of food, then raised her arms again (the Stuart-Coxes obviously had a real thing about raising their arms) and bleated out, "*Friends. Please. Enjoy. Share. The sun has gone down. Welcome to my party.*" There was another sycophantic round of clapping, and people began surging toward the tables, picking up plates to fill.

Then I spotted Max and Davinia heading, fast, toward the house. They weren't holding hands. They didn't need to. There was a kind of invisible, charged link between them.

I slid my eyes sideways to Pandora. She looked as though she'd been turned to stone. There was a long silence as we watched them disappear. I didn't know what to say.

And then a voice right behind me murmured, "Well, *they* seem to be getting it on, don't they?"

CHAPTER

22

**I SPUN ROUND. OLLIE WAS** up so close to me I could smell his breath. Beer, fags, and stale garlic. He wasn't such a dish close up. Close up, he looked a bit vacant.

"I expect they'll just be . . ." I stopped. All I could think of was them tearing each other's clothes off behind a door somewhere.

"Be *what*?" he insinuated, moving in on me even more closely and breathily. "Pandora's very upset," he added, as though that was a highly amusing thought.

There was a nasty pause. Before I'd got this close to him, I'd lined him up as someone who might wipe out the stupid obsession I seemed to be nurturing for Alex, even though Alex was vile and rude and arrogant and everything. But now—no way. Absolutely no way. Ollie just wasn't up to the job. An image of Alex jumping like a hero into the sea came into my head, and I stepped back. Ollie smirked like I was just being shy and came after me. And just then, thank *God*, Davinia and Max burst out from the house again, all kind of giggling and hunched over, carrying what looked like half a dozen champagne bottles between them. They scooted over for the farside of the pool, where we'd first seen Ollie rear his beautiful but vacant head.

"Come on!" Ollie cried, setting off after them.

I didn't want to be paired up with Ollie, but I did want to get to Davinia, so I hurried after him. Pandora was staggering along behind me like a stricken zombie and the rest of the group was behind us.

"Hey!" Max shouted. "Come and see what *we* got."

"Lots and lots of lovely champagne," gurgled Davinia. She'd popped the cork on one of the bottles and was pouring it straight down her throat. It spilled from her beautiful mouth and made glistening tracks into her wonderful cleavage. Max lunged forward as if he was about to lick it off, then he stopped and grinned at us.

"*All* her idea," he drawled. "She really is such a badly behaved *brat*!" He turned back to Davinia, saying, "Hey, gimme that! My turn!" and grabbed the bottle from her. Then he applied his mouth passionately to the bottle neck.

As though it was Davinia he was kissing.

"We thought we'd go in and clear out the champagne stocks while everyone was fighting over the food!" Davinia sniggered. "Here—you lot can have some!" And she *tossed*—literally tossed—a bottle at Pandora. Who clutched at it with a startled squeak, mouth gaping tragically. The boy next to her grabbed it and twisted off the cork, which shot like a bullet from the neck, followed by a great spurt of champagne.

Everyone cheered, and Davinia ran into the spray with her hands out and her mouth open, laughing and lapping with her tongue all pointy. Then she turned to Max, who was watching in goggle-eyed admiration, flicked the champagne from the ends of her fingers, cried, "Come on, let's go and grab some lobster before those pigs over there eat it all!" and danced off.

Everyone—and I mean *everyone*—was staring after her.

I was half in awe and half appalled.

"Yeah, come on!" Max jumped to his feet. "Let's go on another raiding party." Then—as if adding it made his elopement with Davinia absolutely A-OK—he added, "Coming, Pandora?"

He didn't wait for her answer, just set off. She death-walked after him. There was a pause, then, like Davinia was some sexy twenty-first-century Pied Piper, me and the rest of the group followed on.

When I got to the table, Max and Davinia were piling their plates, and she was giggling and stealing stuff from him and he was slapping her hand and calling her *naughty*, and Pandora was standing there with an empty plate, looking like she might suddenly smash it across Davinia's skull.

Or maybe her own skull, to put herself out of her misery.

Then Max and Davinia pranced off and I quickly filled my plate—fabulous stuff, salad and olive bread and wedges of lobster and crab and dangling prawns. I towered it high like I knew I was going to need the energy, then I left. Pandora—who'd put two slices of cucumber, a bit of ham, and a crust of bread on her plate—tagged along beside me. I glanced at her—she looked awful. She was like . . . *essence* of suffering. It kind of made me feel terrible.

Back at base camp, it took another ten minutes for Pandora to crack completely. The nine of us sat eating and laughing and drinking the champagne, and she watched Davinia glittering and swirling her hands and completely bewitching Max, then she suddenly dropped her plate, still with the two slices of cucumber, ham, and bread on it, and wailed, *"Max-I-need-to-speak-to-you-now-OK?"*

Then she scrambled up and scurried off, coming to a stop by a group of ornamental boulders. Max, sighing, got to his feet too, leaning in close to Davinia and muttering, "Shit, I'm in trouble."

Davinia didn't look at him. She just stared straight ahead and said loudly, "It's a mistake to let other people define what *trouble* is."

I don't think anyone—least of all her—knew what that meant exactly, but it came out as pretty profound and you could bet your life she meant it to suggest he should kick Pandora in the teeth.

A kind of hush had fallen on the group, everyone trying to keep on eating and drinking normally and not stare over at the couple by the ornamental boulders. Then it filtered through to me that everyone (apart from Ollie, who was still sitting uncomfortably close to me) had started to give Davinia sideways, hostile glances.

It felt like we shouldn't be sitting there with them anymore.

Maybe this had filtered through to Davinia too.

She dumped her plate, sprang to her feet, grabbed an unopened bottle of champagne, and said, "Come on, Chloe. Dessert time. Let's go, yeah?"

Keen to get away from the brewing hostility but most of all from Ollie, I scrambled up and followed her. We headed in the opposite direction to the way Max and Pandora had gone, but you could just about see them if you craned round. She'd got her head jammed up against his chest and she was clutching at his arm. He was staring out over her head like he was longing to escape.

Over by a shock of flowering bushes, Davinia and I found a tiny wrought-iron table with a little Moroccan-style lamp glimmering on it, and two tiny wrought-iron chairs, and sat down. "Brilliant," I said. "Are you gonna open that champagne?"

"You bet I am," Davinia said, twisting out the cork, opening it expertly with barely a pop. We'd brought our glasses with us too, and she filled them to the brim.

"It's a relief to be away from that lot," I went on, taking a swig. "I thought we were gonna get lynched or something."

Davinia didn't say anything. She was gazing into space as though she was working something out. "Are you very disappointed?" I asked.

"What, that he went off with Pandora? Well, he had to talk to her, didn't he?"

"Yeah. God, he *really* fancied you. I couldn't believe the risks he was taking in front of his girlfriend. No wonder she got so upset."

"She did, didn't she? Honestly, you'd've thought she'd have more pride."

I thought that was harsh, but I didn't say anything. "Ah, well," I went on. "You tried."

Davinia focused on me. "I *tried*? I tried *what*?"

"You know . . . what you said. To make her history."

"Chloe, you don't imagine for one minute that I've given up on him, do you?"

*"What?"*

"Why would I have given up on him, just 'cos she's dragged him off for a nauseating little guilt-inducing chat?"

"But . . . *Davinia*! Come on—you saw how desperate she was! I mean—fine, if they were pretty casual and everything, if they'd only just met, fair enough, but she's acting like they're *engaged*! And the way the others were reacting . . . like you'd broken up this dream couple! I mean—you saw them—they were looking at you in a really, really hostile way!"

"And your point is? Do you imagine I give a

tuppenny shit what way they were looking at me?"

"Well, why did you leave, then?"

"*What?* What planet are you from, Chloe? I left because Max had left, so there was no more reason to be there. I'd much sooner be swigging champagne alone with you."

I ignored the flush of pleasure I felt when she said that, and said, "What I *mean* is—*she* was devastated and *their* reaction shows just how serious Max and Pandora are."

"I still don't get your point. They could have been going out together since they were ten years old for all I care. He's after me, and he's going to have me. *God!* He's unutterably gorgeous. . . . He's got money. . . . He knows places on the island. . . . He can give us a really good time when we're here. Don't look at me like that, all moral high ground. It's his choice. I'm not going to drug him and make him dump Pandora, am I? Just make it . . . *easy* for him."

"Yeah? And how are you going to do that?"

"You've got to get my mobile number to him."

"*What?*"

"Well, I can't do it, can I? Not with that neurotic little bitch hanging off his arm." She flipped her bag onto the table and started rummaging for pen and paper. "Just walk over and slip it in his pocket or something. Leave the rest up to him."

I was silent. Actually I was *silenced*. It went through my mind to tell her how cruel she was being but then I thought—Max can just tear up her number if he wants to. He's the one who's supposed to care about Pandora, not Davinia. Or me.

"There!" she said, handing me a tightly folded wedge of green paper. "We'll go and get some dessert in a minute, maybe you'll get a chance then."

"Or maybe Pandora'll stab me with a cake knife."

"Oh, *Chloe*! Don't be so unspeakably feeble. What did you think of Ollie?"

"*What?*"

"I said—what did you think of Ollie?"

"I heard you. And not much. Why?"

"Because . . . *durgh*, you're being so *thick*! When Max calls me, I'm going to arrange for us to go out in a foursome, aren't I? *Obviously!*"

**CHAPTER 23**

**"NO WAY. NO WAY!"** I stared at Davinia, absolutely appalled.

"Don't be absurd, Chloe! As if I'd leave you on your own while I went out with Max! I could see the way Ollie was panting after you, he really likes you!"

"I don't give a shit if he likes me, I don't like him!"

"What's wrong with him?"

"Well, his voice for one thing. *Whaaaa, whaaa, whaaaa.* He sounds like a donkey."

"Oh, Chloe, honestly. Just 'cos he's had an education."

"*What?* I don't believe you said that." I was too drunk to remember not to say things that would piss Davinia off, so I plowed on. "Going to some posh privileged school is *not* the same as getting an education."

"Oh, *boring*. Not all your sociology shit again. He's not bad looking and he's got a great arse."

"Fuck that!"

"You're getting the idea!"

"Davinia, shut *up*! OK, he's good looking, but up close, he's so kind of soul-dead he gives me the creeps—"

"*Soul-dead*. What kind of a description is that? *Soul-dead*. You sound like some frigging elf out of *Lord of the Rings*." She went into a quavery falsetto. "Oh my lord, we are entering the dread region of the Wackadoos, the flesh-eating soul-dead. . . ."

"*Shut up!*" I was laughing, I couldn't help it. "I am not going to get off with some moronic creep just so you can shag off with his friend. OK?"

"OK. Your choice. If you really prefer to hang about on your own getting brain-numbingly bored rather than sit at a fabulous restaurant table across from Max and Ollie, that's your choice."

I was silent. I let it sink into me that her not going out with Max wasn't an option. If I refused to go out with Ollie, she'd happily abandon me. While I was thinking how to answer, she got complacently to her feet, and caroled, "Come on, let's get some pud. Then we can see if we can smuggle some decent sounds on and have a dance. And during all that, *somehow*, d'you think you'd be able to give that note to Max?"

Not even a great gooey pile of strawberries and meringue and cream and half a fat chocolate brownie and even more champagne could cheer me up. My finer side was telling me I should stand up to Davinia and tell her to get stuffed and do her own dirty work but my other, much bigger, cowardly side just wanted to keep in with her and not fall out.

The whole party was lifting off as people got drunker and more stupid. Someone put Dire Straits' *Sultans of Swing* on, and Davinia started boogying about in showy 1980s style, attracting masses of attention. In a kind of desperation I joined in, and as the music pounded I forgot about everything and started to enjoy myself just moving to the beat. Then I spotted Cassie weaving through to us, a slightly panicky look on her face. She shot me an indignant look (did she really think I was egging Davinia on? Davinia *never* needed egging on!), then she collared Davinia and towed her to the side of the floor. I guess she was worried about her daughter getting rat-assed and disgracing them. I stopped dancing and moved to the wall, and some old 1960s stuff came on, and Deborah and Anthony took the floor.

While I was watching our hosts twirl creakily about, Ollie slithered over to stand next to me. "Shame about Pandora being here, cramping Max's style," he murmured. "I was thinking what fun it would be for the four of us to get together, maybe fix up a date and all go out together."

"Has Davinia put you up to this?" I squawked.

"What?"

"Never mind."

He moved in closer. His mouth was all slack and repulsive. "Not that there are any rules about not going out as a twosome. . . ."

"I need the loo!" I squeaked. "Excuse me!"

Safely locked inside the Mediterranean-blue cloakroom, I pulled out the tightly folded wedge of green paper, and unfolded it.

*Don't fight it!!* Davinia had written. *I'm not!!* Then she'd scribbled down her mobile number, and two cartoon-style stars.

Stars *and* exclamation marks, I thought. Jesus, the confidence of the girl. It took your breath away.

I folded the note up again.

I came out of the cloakroom, the note hidden in my hand. Davinia was back on the dance floor, a one-woman show, and Max and Pandora had joined Ollie by the wall. It was now or never. I felt like an absolute two-face, an absolute Judas. In fact, thinking about it, Judas was quite nice compared to me.

I shuffled over.

Max and Pandora were standing underneath a huge blowup of Deborah in which she was wearing a bikini made of feathers. They looked up warily as I approached, and Pandora fixed herself onto Max's arm like a straitjacket. I smiled at her, all kind of wobbly and humble, and said, "Davinia's too embarrassed to come over herself, but she sent me over to say sorry."

"What for?" sniffed Pandora.

"Oh, you know. You've got a very attractive boyfriend and she got very carried away!" *And if you've got a brain,* I thought, *you'll admit to yourself how bloody carried away* he *got too.*

Pandora smiled at me, all watery, and I reached out, with the note clenched by my thumb into my palm, and patted her awkwardly on her arm, the one that was pressed up against Max. Then I made serious sympathetic eye contact with her, dropped my hand, found the lip of Max's linen-jacket pocket, pushed the note in, and jabbed my thumbnail into his leg, *hard,* hoping he wouldn't scream. I did this to alert him to the note and also because

I bloody *felt* like jabbing him.

Then I turned and walked slowly and traitorously away.

"Well?" hissed Davinia, zooming over to me. *"Well??!!"*

"Mission accomplished," I said as we turned to stare at them, "and poor old Pandora didn't suspect a thing. Although *look* at him! The idiot—he'll blow it. Oh, my God, *look* at him!"

Max was fumbling in his pocket, he'd drawn out the green note, any minute now Pandora would spot it and snatch it from him and read it and she'd know how it got there, she'd know it was me being a two-faced traitor, and she'd grab a bottle and smash it and race over and glass me in the face. . . .

"What a wanker," drawled Davinia, unmoved. "Luckily he's a sexy wanker."

Terrified, I watched as Pandora looked down, down toward Max's hand . . . and then Max kind of jumped at her, wrapped his arms round her head, and fixed his mouth on hers in the hugest soul kiss ever. Then his left hand came up like a cobra's head and flapped the green note. Ollie, smirking vacuously, caught on right away and took it from his fingers. Max carried on snogging Pandora as though she was his only source of oxygen and without her he'd die.

It was a very smooth operation.

When at last Max pulled away from Pandora, she was all pink and trembly with delight, you could see it even from a distance. "Jesus, what a heel," I muttered. "What a bastard. Don't you think he's a bastard?"

Davinia, smirking, said, "Maybe. But who wants a goody-goody?"

I was silent. We left the main room and wandered out to the terrace again. Davinia was silent too, absorbed no doubt in more lecherous plotting. Then she turned to me smiling like a starlet and said, "Fancy a swim? I want Max to see me in my bikini and *eat his heart out.*"

OK, I'D DRUNK FAR, *far* too much champagne. OK,
I was also kind of punch-drunk and reeling from
Davinia making me part of her all-out assault
attack on Max. But as she towed me inside again I
started to feel really spaced out and scared, like the
victim-heroine in one of those horror films where
she gets drugged and she's waiting for all kinds of
grotesque, obscene things to happen to her. . . . All
I could think was *I don't want to take my clothes off,
not here.* Davinia hauled me up the wide spiral
staircase, looking for a place to get changed, and as
I passed photo after photo of Deborah's huge,
blown-up face she looked more and more smirking
and *sinister* somehow and my head started to lurch
about. "I'm not sure I can swim, Dav," I groaned.
"I feel a bit sick."

"Well, cold water's exactly what you need,
then," she said briskly, as we reached the top of the

178

staircase. "Anyway, we're hardly going to *swim.* Just pose on the edge. . . . Maybe dive in . . ." She flung open a door. The room in front of us was practically filled by a huge circular bed, and on the bed a fully clothed woman was straddling a man who was stark naked and flat on his back and over by the *window* was . . .

"*Sorrr* ee!" cooed Davinia, giggling and slamming the door shut again.

"*Did you see that?*" I wailed.

"Hard to miss it, babe! She'll seriously mess her frock up if she's not careful."

"But there was someone standing there, by the window, a man, just *watching.* . . ."

"Oh, *Chloe*! Don't be so unspeakably depraved!"

"There *was*! Didn't you see him? It's not *me* who's depraved! I swear it, it was a *man*—"

"Maybe it was a coat stand," she said dismissively, storming on down the corridor. I lagged behind her, terrified of her opening another door, of what would be behind it.

"And actually, what the hell, who cares anyway? I told you the Stuart-Coxes were Fabulous People back in the day. They did orgies, free love, the whole bit. . . . They've got a name for it. Mummy and Daddy try and keep out of it . . . well, they *say* they do. . . ."

"But . . . that fuss over you puking last year . . . surely if they're having orgies . . ."

Davinia actually stopped walking to turn and glare at me. "Bit of a difference, wouldn't you say? Orgies are cool, puking on the carpet is *naff*! Why d'you have to remind me of it? Anyway they don't have orgies now. Not really." And she stormed on.

Ahead of us on the left, a door opened and two women came out, giggling. Davinia sprang forward. "Bathroom!" she said triumphantly, ushering me in and locking the door behind us. Then she stripped off like a speeded-up snake sloughing off its old skin. "Come *on*, Chlo!" she nagged. "We don't want to be the last ones at the pool, all the impact will go!"

"How d'you know anyone else *will* swim?" I wailed. "How d'you know we won't be the *only* ones?"

"Great for us, if we are. Now, we're gonna leave our clothes here—oh, come *on*, Chloe!" Naked, she lunged at my waist, seized my top, and yanked it over my head. Groaning, I pulled my skirt off too, and she started shimmying into her tiny bikini. She was reflected three times in the mirrors on the walls and she looked like a goddess transforming. Reluctantly, I got my bikini out of my bag.

"What we're going to do," she said, revolving slowly to see all three sides of her, "is leave our stuff over there, behind that urn thing, and we'll make an entrance, empty-handed . . . down the stairs, straight out to the pool, and dive in."

"Can you dive?" I muttered.

"OK, *wade* in. Smoothly. No giggling and stuff. All eyes will be on us. Max will *die.*"

"I don't *want* all eyes on us!"

"Oh, shut up, Chlo! Ready? Now come on."

She scooped up my clothes from the floor as I struggled with the tie of my bikini top and jammed them behind a huge decorative jar in the corner of the bathroom. Then she swept out of the door, and I followed her, and all along the corridor my brain was curdling, swaying. . . . I felt naked, exposed, awful. I wished I had something to clutch to me, a bag or a towel, for comfort. Ahead of me, Davinia was splaying her fingers like a model, elegant and free.

We wound our way down the staircase. But everyone had had the same idea of swimming at the same time—the place was suddenly full of bikinis and swimsuits and bathers. Two of the women were topless and they were older than my mum; it was *grotesque.* "Come on," hissed Davinia. *"Impact!* Straight out to the pool!"

As we stepped out onto the terrace the heat hit me like a flat iron. Out of the corner of my eye I saw Max, Pandora, and Ollie ogling us. Max looked like one of those cartoon dogs where their eyes are out on stalks and their tongues unfurl and hit the floor in lust.

At the edge of the pool, Anthony had set up a camera on a tripod. He saw us and his mouth splayed into a hideous leer, and he crouched over his camera, ready. He looked like one of those half-goat half-man things that are always carrying off wood nymphs. . . . *God*, everyone looked weird. Macabre. I started to feel I was tripping out or something. Could it really only be the champagne? Or were Deborah and Anthony such Beautiful People they'd baked hashish into the brownies?

"*Girls!*" called Anthony. "Oh, that's a lovely shot. Davinia, you are a peach, my duckling. Slide your strap down. *Yes.* Oh, look naughty for me. Oh, *yes.*"

I glanced at Davinia, hoping she'd yell, *Shut up, you disgusting old pedophile!* But she didn't. Her eyes flicked over to Max, still ogling her, then she turned deliberately back to Anthony and made a sexy pout at him, posing like a porn star. . . . Anthony's camera flashed manically like a speed camera on a motorway, and I knew the whole show was just to rev Max up some more: *I'm desirable, all these women here and it's me he's taking photos of.* . . . I wanted to throw up. An image of Alex jumping off the rocks flashed into my mind. I turned and almost ran toward the deep end of the pool, then I raised my arms, saw an empty space of water, and dived.

Underwater, my head cleared. Then my eyes. And I saw legs entwined, hands exploring bathers . . . Jesus, it was an underwater orgy. I came up for air a few feet from Davinia, who was lowering herself gingerly and posily into the water.

"All right, *show*-off," she said. "Just 'cos he wasn't taking pics of *you*."

"*What?* Oh, yeah, right. That's why I did it, right. Did he *get* a picture of me?"

"No. And you splashed Deborah."

"I'm *distraught*," I snapped, and I turned and swam to the shallow end of the pool, then back again, and back again. No one got in my way. Then I stood up and made for the steps. Anthony was waiting for me.

"Beautiful dive," he wheezed. "But I missed it. Will you do it again for me?"

"Sorry, I feel sick," I said, and waded up the steps. He ducked down and started flashing away and I had a strong urge to tip him and his tripod into the water.

There was a sudden burst of clapping from the deep end of the pool. Deborah had dropped her floaty mauve silk dress to the floor, revealed an extraordinary ivory-colored corset beneath, and *yet again* raised her hands to the sky. But this time less in pagan worship than to show off her figure. Whinnying like a horse, Anthony swiveled his camera and started clicking her like a madman. Amid cheers and more clapping, Deborah plonked her way over to the edge of the pool, kicked off her snakeskin platform shoes, and dropped into the water.

"Aren't they *terrific*?" said Paul, who'd silently appeared at my side. "Still so full of life. Hope you're having a good time, Chloe!"

## CHAPTER 25

**DAVINIA AND I DIDN'T** discuss the party when we got home. Although I was absolutely gagging to discuss it with someone. She'd gone into a kind of catatonic state over Max. What we did do was discuss him or not talk at all.

And over the next few days, what we did was:

1. wait for Max to call Davinia's mobile.
2. sunbathe.
3. eat.
4. sleep.

*Waiting for Max to call.* This was ongoing, even when we slept.

*Sunbathing.* I had to pressure Davinia to go to the beach. She said it was "all crowded up with children, idiots, and ugly people," so she was content just to sunbathe on the roof. When I did get her to the beach she still wouldn't swim. "It's the salt," she said, rubbing more oil into her nut-brown arms. "I can't bear it. All this sand's bad enough."

"But—don't you want to do *any* exercise?" I pleaded.

"No. Absolutely none. Although I s'pose I don't want to come back from here a huge blob. Hey—that little hotel, near the flat? That's got a pool we can use! God—why didn't I think of it before? All you have to do is buy a drink or something. I went there last year, they loved having me, I raised the standard from all the unspeakably sad old porkers, frankly."

"I bet you did," I said ungraciously. "And I've seen the pool from the road. It's the size of a small slice of toast."

"God, Chloe—why are you so *negative*?"

"I'm not the one who's negative!" I erupted. "The sea's much better than that tiny pool! The waves . . . the . . . *space* of it . . . swimming out to the horizon, no edges . . ."

"No *edges*?" she snapped. "Of course there aren't any frigging edges, it's the sea, isn't it? You make me tired." Then she rolled over on her side with her back to me.

I got to my feet and trekked down to the shoreline, waded in deep, and swam for all I was worth. Something that I didn't want to think about had moved into my head and wouldn't budge. It was like—I wasn't new anymore, she was done with me somehow. She was making absolutely no effort with me at all. She wanted to move on to the next person.

And me . . . I wanted to move on too.

*Why did I ever think you were exciting,* Davinia? I railed to myself, as I plowed through the waves. *You're boring as shit. You're dull. You're plastic.* Your *horizon stops with where* you *end, and you don't get excited by anything outside yourself. You make me* sick.

It was heresy, it was treachery, but it made me feel better. I slowed down, let the thoughts come. Davinia's ideas about pleasure, her sense of existence—it was true, they didn't move beyond the bounds of her own small self. That was why she had such surety, such confidence. She focused on what would be good for her, like a fox searching for its next meal. It was so unbelievably *limited.* This place with its heat and its smells and its beauty . . . it passed her by unless it was giving her some kind of concrete pleasure. Unless it was making her brown, or making her laugh, or serving her up with a long, cold drink, it was like she didn't actually see it.

And because I wasn't new anymore, she'd stopped seeing me.

*Eating.* We ate out all the time, lunch and evening, which was usually fun but I was growing scared my funds were running down. When I mentioned this to Davinia, she just shrugged in an irritated way as though that was entirely my own concern and nothing to do with her at all. Then she used it as an excuse to squash my suggestion about going back to Hilly's—"I thought you were short of money? Let's just have another drink here."

Paul and Cassie took us out to lunch a couple of times, which was great as they paid, but mostly they'd just leave us alone, relieved that their daughter was not causing trouble. They'd say things like "Call if you're going to be later than midnight, OK?" and "Make sure your bedroom's tidy, the cleaner's coming tomorrow." It would be me who had to remember these instructions of course; Davinia barely registered them.

*Sleeping.* She *slept.* God, did she sleep. Ten hours at night and on the roof and the beach, too.

\* \* \*

And in the list of things we did, there was a fifth, hidden category, applicable only to me. Any time we were out at the beach, in town, at a restaurant or bar or café—I'd be scanning the place for Alex. I'd stopped lecturing myself on what a gob-mouthed, vain, cocksure git he was, I'd given up reminding myself I hated him. I was just filled with wanting to see him again.

But there was absolutely no sign of him. *He's gone home*, I told myself. *He's had a week here, and flown home. Forget him.* But I couldn't. I fantasized about him all the time. I fantasized about lying on the sand with him, walking along the shoreline hand in hand. Coming face-to-face with him in the sea. The worse things got with Davinia, the more I moved into my head with Alex.

And things with Davinia were bad. We were hardly talking now, never mind having a laugh. She wouldn't explore the island with me, she wouldn't go clubbing, she wouldn't head out to another beach to get a change of scene. It got so if I heard the words "Oh, I can't be *bothered*, Chloe!" one more time, I'd punch her very hard in the middle of her beautiful, symmetrical face.

I tried to stop this slide into outright dislike of Davinia, of course. I'd tell myself all friends went through rough patches, I'd tell myself she'd gone into this vegetative-type state because she was angsting over Max calling, but I knew that wasn't true. She *was* waiting for him to call—she'd kind of put herself on hold till he called—but she wasn't that bothered.

This was just *her*. It was what she was, all she was.

On the fifth morning after Deborah and Anthony's party I cracked. I brought Davinia a cup of tea in bed, prodded her awake, and said, "You might be waiting for Max to call, but I'm not. And I'm getting really bored just sitting around eating and drinking in the evenings. I want to go out again, I want to go dancing!"

She opened one eye blearily and took the tea without comment. "Bloody hell," she groaned. "Have you been brooding about this all night or something?"

"*No.* I just want to do it, OK?"

"Anyway, I thought you were short of money?"

"Look—if we fix dinner here, we'll save loads of money!"

"*Cook?*"

"We don't have to cook, we can have salad!"

"You still have to get it ready! This is meant to be a *holiday*, Chloe!"

"*I'll* do it! The fridge is always jammed full of fabulous stuff, and your mum's always telling us to help ourselves!"

"*God!* OK, then. Now let me get some more sleep."

And she rolled over in bed and turned her back on me.

But I knew I'd won.

That night, after a lovely smoked salmon salad prepared by me with absolutely no help from Davinia, we set off for Hilly's. It was already heaving when we walked into the courtyard, but Cora still found time to swim over and greet us like long lost sisters. "Where have you *been*? Every night, I've been looking for you, and you didn't come! Have you found another bar, hmm? A bar you prefer?"

"Of course not!" gushed Davinia. "It's just . . . Chloe's a bit tight on cash. Aren't you, Chloe?"

I glared at her, as Cora reached out and stroked my arm. "Pooooor baby!" she soothed. "I'll give you a little job here, if you like!"

"Oh, yeah, and what'll *I* do if she works here?" Davinia laughed, all incredulous, like I was her maid and not allowed any time off. "*She's* all right! You can phone your dad and ask for more, can't you, Chloe?"

"Not everyone's daddy is as rich and . . . *indulgent* as yours, Davinia darling," murmured Cora, then she turned to me and smiled. "Two cocktails for the price of one, special price for you beautiful ladies. And Davinia will pay, yes?"

Somewhat sourly, Davinia gave our order, and Cora floated serenely off.

"*Are* you going to call him?" she demanded, as we found an empty table under a flaming torch and sat down.

"Call who?"

"Your dad."

"What, to ask for more money? No, I'm not! He's really stretched since the divorce, and with my school fees and everything . . ."

Davinia didn't have to tell me how unutterably boring she thought I was—it was screened all over her face. She drummed her fingers in an irritated way on the table, and moaned, "*God*, I wish Max would call me. I don't know what on earth's stopping him."

I wasn't in the mood to soft-pedal with her. "His girlfriend, maybe?" I said.

"Yes. I guess he does have to be careful."

"Or perhaps he just doesn't want to finish with her? Or *cheat* on her?"

"OK, OK. Have it your way, *sourpuss*. You

know you ought to be hoping he'll call soon too."

"*Me?* Why?"

"Because going out in a foursome'll help with your cash-flow problem, won't it? I mean—they'll pay!"

I couldn't think of anything to say to this that wasn't very, very rude, so I kept quiet. Then our cocktails arrived, all pink and festive looking. "Maybe this'll cheer you up," said Davinia.

*I doubt it,* I thought.

It hadn't worked, coming to Hilly's. I wanted to dance, I wanted to have fun, but not with Davinia. I'd got to the point where I was utterly, heartily sick of her.

Then I looked up and saw Alex standing by the bar.

**MY HEART STARTED THUDDING** away at twice its usual speed. There he was, my fantasy, at the bar. I felt thrown, weird, like I'd actually *done* all the things with him that I'd been fantasizing about . . . like I *knew* him, like I could just walk over to him and say hello. For a split second, panic filled me, as though I'd been on the verge of racing over and smacking a big kiss on his face.

He'd gotten even browner. He was wearing jeans and a white T-shirt and his hair looked wet still, and as I stared at him I wanted him so badly I'm amazed I kept standing and didn't just kind of flow across the floor toward him and wrap myself round his legs.

*Dignity, Chloe. Shape up and stop this right now. You might fancy him but you also hate him, remember?*

He was with Frazer and another of their group, a stocky boy with black hair. And he was chatting animatedly to two women. *Women*, not girls. They had to be getting on for thirty, at least. They were in these cheesy, sophisticated frocks with big, propped-up cleavages, and they looked all kind of stale and sure of themselves and I *loathed* them. I wanted to run over and shove them away from him and shout, *Go and get someone your own age, you raddled old cradle-snatchers!*

But I didn't, of course. I took in a deep breath and told myself to calm down. I told myself they were just chatting. I told myself they were probably friends of Frazer's parents or something.

But their body language was telling me something different. One of the women was moving in closer and closer to Alex all the time. She had bleached blond hair, cut short and glamorous, and green eye shadow and masses of flashy gold jewelry and she was very brown and so *confident*. She was leaning in closer and closer to Alex and she kept opening her mouth very wide to laugh, and he was staring at her like a rabbit caught in the headlights.

Like I'd stared at him, in the sea.

I felt sick.

"God, Chloe, what's up?" Davinia yawned. "You're being really boring tonight." Her tone said: *Even more boring than usual.*

I didn't answer her, just carried on staring at Alex as the woman talked and laughed right at him, touching him on the arm to emphasize what she was saying, and then the music switched to something with a fantastic beat, and she grabbed his arm all sure of herself and pulled him onto the floor.

And then they were dancing together. He wasn't moving much—he looked pretty inhibited to be honest—but he still looked wonderful. His eyes were on her face and her body as she pranced around him, all showy and sure of herself. And all the time they were drawing closer together and I couldn't take my eyes away, it was torture but I had to see, I had to be witness to it, whatever happened.

"Well, shall we *dance*, then?" snapped Davinia. "I mean, if we're not going to *talk* about anything. . . ." Then she broke off and crowed, "Oh . . . my . . . *God.*"

"What?" I yapped.

"D'you see what I see? That yob—the one who hit me! Over by the bar, chatting up that old slapper. Oh, my *God*. Look at his clothes. Oh, what a gonk. I can't believe Cora let him in. Talk about letting her standards slip. Look—there's the other one." She pointed with her chin at Alex. "God, look at him slavering all over that woman. How sad. What is he—a gigolo?"

"What's a gigolo?" I muttered.

"A kept man. A younger man who gets an older woman to pay for him. My great-great uncle was one, apparently. You should see the *photos* of him. . . . They're seriously glam, he was such a smoothy!" Then she picked up her cocktail, sipped it, and announced, "I'm going to get Cora to chuck them out."

"*What!?* You can't do that!"

"No? Watch me. I'll tell her they attacked me."

"But they didn't! I mean—it was ages ago—and you threw a drink over Frazer, he retaliated!"

"*God*, Chloe, will you stop calling them by their *names*? They don't have names, they're scum. And when did you become so frigging *fair* about everything? Whose side are you on?"

"Yours, of course. But . . ."

"I just want a little more *revenge,* that's all. It'll liven up the evening. Oh, God—look! *Yuck!*"

Frazer was in the process of towing the other woman onto the dance floor, leaving his dark-haired mate to prop the bar up glumly on his own. They joined Alex and his dance partner, forming a kind of foot-shuffling, arm-waving square.

"Oh, how *revolting,*" gloated Davinia. "God—look at those two sad cows. Think of actually *paying* those two thugs to—"

"Davinia, you have absolutely no proof that they're *paying* anything."

"Whatever. OK, I won't tell Cora to chuck them out. I've thought of something better. Let's go and screw up their gigolo earnings for the night, ay? Let's go and dance *right* near them and really mess things up!"

"*No!* Davinia, no—I don't want to—I *don't want*—"

But she was on her feet and away across the floor. She positioned herself right near Frazer and started dancing and then she started *beckoning* to me with both hands, all dramatic and eager and openmouthed, like she was in a dance video or something.

The only way to stop her *beckoning* and drawing all that attention to herself and to me (as the object of the beckoning) was to join her on the floor.

So I did.

In sheer horror at where I was, I shut out everything but the tiny space right ahead of me and the sound of the music. I danced like someone coming round from a full anesthetic. I didn't look at Davinia and I certainly didn't look at Alex. And then the music changed.

It was music I loved; music Davinia and I were good at moving to. We started to dance together, and soon people were looking at us. I sensed Alex was looking too, and I danced really well, really tight to the music, feeling my body was looking good. Davinia kept moving back, taking more and more space, until finally, inevitably, she barged into Frazer.

"Sorr-*eee*!" she squawked, all phonily apologetic as she spun round. Then she gasped, "Oh, my God—it's *you*! You're not gonna punch me in the *face* again, are you?"

"*What?*" gasped the woman he was dancing with.

"Don't be fucking *stupid*," growled Frazer.

"He punched me," Davinia called to the woman, over the music. "I spilled a drink on him, and he *punched* me!"

"You fucking *threw* it at me!"

"And you *punched* her?" demanded the woman, aghast.

"No! No—I . . ."

"OK, he slapped me," shrilled Davinia. "But *even so*!"

"What the *hell* are you up to, ay?" Alex pushed past Frazer, thrust his face right up to Davinia. "What sort of shitty little game are you up to now?"

"What's going on?" demanded Alex's cradle-snatcher, her green-rimmed eyes snapping.

Alex, keeping his eyes on us, answered with, "These two are fucking psychotic. They're to be avoided, trust me. I don't know what they're up to, coming over here, following us about—"

I couldn't bear it. "We're not following you about!" I wailed.

"No? You dance right up close to us, you knock into Frazer—"

Everything in me wanted to scream, *It wasn't me—it was her!* But I thought that would make me look even worse than I already did, so I didn't.

"Oh, *Alex*!" cried the cradle-snatcher. "They *fancy* you, that's all." She leaned across to us, all-powerful woman of the world. "I suggest you clear off," she gurgled, as though we were a huge joke. "Find your own fellas."

"Oh, my God," gasped Davinia, going for an Oscar, "you're so *wrong*! I wouldn't touch him with the longest barge pole in the *world*! He's violent—they're *both* violent—"

"Who's violent?" Cora had silently swum up behind us. "What's going on, Davinia? You're all causing a disturbance—everyone's looking!"

There was a pause. Frazer and his woman were face-to-face; we could hear her hissing "and I don't like the way you *swear* so much either!"

"I don't want to have to turn the music off," said Cora, sweet and steely. "Have you resolved your differences?"

"If they clear off," barked Alex, pointing at us, "and keep out of our way—"

"Or *what*?" wailed Davinia, really working the wounded victim act. "Or you'll *hit* us again?"

"Did he *hit* you?" demanded Cora.

"Oh, look, this is getting really ridiculous," said the cradle-snatcher bossily. "They seem to have had some kind of row before, but it's over and in the past and my boy here doesn't want to have anything to do with them. . . ."

"Your boy?" repeated Cora. "Is he your son?"

I wanted to punch the air and shout, *YEAH!* but I managed not to. The cradle-snatcher looked as though someone had got her with a poisoned dart. She sagged down and went kind of pinched and pale and twitchy, then she turned on her heel and tottered off in the direction of the Ladies'. Her friend, sensing a tragedy, let go of Frazer and hurried off after her.

"Oh, fucking terrific," snarled Alex, right in Cora's face. "What did you have to say that for?"

"An innocent mistake! Some women have their children very young!"

"Not that fucking young!"

"Oh—easily!" cooed Cora. "She's thirty-five at least, and *you* . . . you should be with girls your own age. Like these two here."

"I'd sooner roast my goolies on a barbecue. Come on, Frazer. We won't get any joy now, not now she's said that. They'll be in the bog for hours. Round up Sam and let's go. Let's leave the bitches from hell to it."

## CHAPTER 27

**"CELEBRATION COCKTAILS NOW,** don't you think?" cooed Davinia.

*I won't even be able to fantasize about him now. That was grotesque. Truly grotesque.*

"That, I tell you, followed a script!" she went on. "Oh, that was such *fun!*"

*He hates me. He hates me.*

"Are you going to tell me what that was all about?" asked Cora, smiling.

"Just a bit of revenge. Don't worry, Cora, they really are bastards. You wouldn't want them here."

"Well, I didn't want those *women* here. I can't exactly ban them, but I'm glad of a chance to get them to leave."

"You know them?" Davinia asked.

"They've been here before. They're *predatory*," said Cora.

"*Predatory?* They're *desperate*, they're *sick*—

going after those two yobs!"

Cora smiled, and I wondered why she cared about the cradle-snatchers, but I was too depressed to open my mouth, and she told us to take care, and left us.

Davinia was fizzing with triumph. She sashayed over to the bar, hailed Zara, and ordered us fresh cocktails. Zara went into her full workout mixing them, grinning at Davinia like she really fancied her. Which—thinking about it—she probably did. Then we found an empty table, and Davinia started reliving her triumph, not noticing or caring that I wasn't saying a single solitary word. "That *showed* him," she crowed. "No one whacks *me* and gets away with it. Oh, God, that was *sweeeeet*!"

And then her mobile went.

Usually at this time, it would be Cassie, checking up where we were, that we were safe. But Davinia didn't snarl into her phone like she did when her mum called. She said, *"Heeeeey!"* and then "No . . . not at all! Of course I do, of course I understand!" and then *"Yeaaaaah! Lovely!"* and it dawned on me that it was Max calling her. At long last.

She mewed and cooed at him for quite a bit longer; then she said, "Absolutely. Oh, fabulous!

See you then, then!" slipped her phone back in her bag, and grinned at me like she'd just pulled off the most amazing coup in the history of the world.

"That," she said, "was Max."

"You don't say," I said tiredly.

"Chloe, aren't you *happy* for me?"

"Of course I am," I croaked, forcing myself to sound glad. "What was his excuse for leaving it so long?"

"Oh, Chloe, don't be an idiot! He had to ditch Pandora, didn't he? She was devastated, he said. He had to go slow, he had to be a gentleman about it. He's such a sweet guy—I'd've just told her to piss off. Oh, my God, I'm on cloud TEN here! *Bliss, bliss, blissy-blissy bliss!* We're meeting them tomorrow, seven thirty, at The Trident restaurant . . . it's wonderful, Chloe, so swish, I've been there before but only with Mummy and Da—"

"Er . . . excuse me? *We're* meeting *them*?"

"Oh, don't be daft! What sort of friend would I be if I left you behind?"

"But—you agreed to meet them—without even asking me?"

"Oh, Chloe, come on. It wasn't that sort of conversation. He was pouring his *heart* out to me . . . telling me how awful it had been, ditching

Pandora. . . . She's been stalking him, apparently, texting him nonstop. . . . I could hardly break off while he was opening his soul to me to check date details with you, could I? It would have been so . . . *naff*."

"Oh, right. Naff, right. Well, maybe you can leave it till tomorrow till his soul's closed up again and phone him back and say it'll just be you meeting him."

Davinia shot me a look of pure loathing. "You know, I really don't know what's wrong with you. You've changed. If I thought you'd be like *this* on holiday . . ."

She didn't need to say the rest. Again, I felt that sense of fear restricting me, telling me to play it safe. I was here on my own with her, in her parents' flat—I was dependent on her. I was beyond saving the friendship, but I had to keep things from falling apart completely.

I was desperate. I said the one thing I knew would turn her on to me again.

"Oh, Davinia, I'm sorry I'm being a cow. It's just . . . you and Max'll make such a great couple and I don't fancy Ollie, not a bit, and I'm just *jealous* of you, OK? I'm *jealous*."

After that, Davinia was kindness itself. We talked it all through and she persuaded me that it was OK just to go along for the meal. . . . It would be a night out, it would save money. And it would help *her* because she'd built him up so much in her mind she felt really nervous about seeing him again. She told me I'd love the restaurant and I might "warm" to Ollie once I'd spent some time with him but even if I didn't, it didn't matter, no strings, I didn't have to snog him or anything, I'd just say *no* to the next date, that was all.

We didn't discuss what would happen if I did say *no* to a next date, and she started a full-on relationship with Max. That wasn't even touched on.

The next evening, Davinia was in meltdown. She locked herself in the bathroom and did the makeover to end makeovers on herself waxing, conditioning, exfoliating, the lot. It was like she'd got me to say yes to the evening, so she could ignore me now. She did give me a fabulous, pinky-purple low-cut top that was too tight on her—but then she could afford to be generous, couldn't she?

I stood in front of the long mirror on our bedroom wall, waiting to get in the bathroom, admiring the top. I needed a bit of polishing up, sure, but I was tanned and my mousy hair had gone all blond in the sun and the swimming had shaped me up and given me this glow and I looked really good, the best I'd ever looked. But instead of feeling great about it, I was flooded with something like grief, that here I was, looking like this, going out to a really fabulous restaurant on this amazing island in the heat and I was meeting . . . *Ollie*.

Not Alex, it would never be Alex, he hated me . . . *Ollie*.

The one thing I'm good at, though—the one thing I've had to be good at, ever since Mum walked out and Dad collapsed and everything—is picking myself up and pulling myself together and making the best of a bad job. "OK, it's Ollie and not Alex," I told myself, "and that is a seriously sad substitution, but everything else is in place. You *do* look great and Caminos is great and you're going out in the sultry night air with the cicadas singing to this utterly cool restaurant. And just like Deborah back in the old days, you are going to be one of the Beautiful People tonight and *nothing* can take that away from you, *nothing*."

That night was the first night it was me and not Davinia who suggested nicking a bottle of white wine from Paul's vast stock and substituting it for one in the fridge, which we opened and downed. That night was the first night I actually managed to down more of the bottle than Davinia, too. I was pretty half-cut by the time we wobbled out of the escalator and out into the night air.

Davinia had booked a cab to take us to the restaurant. We could've walked, but her heels were too high for comfort. The cab driver put a real premium on speed, shooting through the narrow streets and swerving across little squares, each with its own church looming over it. At the corner of one he had a standoff with a truck coming the other way, both of them refusing to back down. As the drivers shouted, I stared out at the bar we'd drawn up alongside. There were the usual tourists drinking quite separately from the group of local men. . . . I sat back in my seat in shock. Alex and Frazer were there among a group of local boys, all of them dressed in torn, dirty shorts and T-shirts and workmen's boots, laughing, having a great time.

"Oh, my *GOD*," Davinia gurgled. "Look at *that*."

"Don't stare," I hissed, unable to wrench my eyes away from Alex. He looked gorgeous—all tanned and dusty, face in profile, hair messed up.

"What've they *done*—gone native? Look at them—they're *filthy*. Oh, *gross*."

Alex's arm was sunburned; it made his muscles stand out. He shifted on his chair to talk to the boy next to him and something in the movement kind of stabbed me with longing, with loss, with God knows what. . . . "That's the trouble with this island," Davinia was saying. "You keep bumping into the same unspeakably awful people the whole time."

Then the taxi driver lost the standoff with the truck, reversed so hard I thought we were going to crash into the wall behind, and spun off down a different road.

Alex hadn't even looked up.

**THE RESTAURANT WAS EVERY** bit as wonderful as Davinia had said it would be, but the minute I walked through its wide, stained-wood doors, I hated it. It was like a beautiful, very self-conscious woman. Not self-conscious in the awkward, embarrassed sense, self-conscious in the "look at me, worship me, aren't I amazing" sense.

Which made it the perfect venue for Davinia, of course.

It had statues and fountains and hangings, but they were all over the top and pretentious and you felt they weren't there because someone genuinely liked them, they were there as stage props, they were there to impress.

But naturally I didn't show what I felt. I acted awed and cooed and oooed as we tottered toward the smarmy waiter who approached us. Davinia gave Max's name and the waiter checked his book.

"Aaaah," he said. "I'm afraid the . . . *gentlemen* are not here yet. But do come through."

His stress on the word *gentlemen* suggested he thought they were nothing of the sort, to keep us waiting like this. I tended to agree with him. We were ten minutes late ourselves so where *were* those bastards?

"They'd better not've stood us up," I hissed, as we negotiated our way past huge overflowing terra-cotta pots and down three wide marble steps into the dining room. All the other diners turned and sneered at us, then carried on eating.

"Of course they haven't," Davinia hissed back.

We were shown to our table, an intimate rectangle in the corner. "You sit there, diagonally across from me," she ordered. "Then Max can sit opposite me. Lovers *always* sit opposite. And stop looking so frigging *anxious*! Nobody stands *me* up."

She was right. No sooner had we taken our seats when Max and Ollie came steaming in, braying out apologies at the tops of their voices. "We went diving!" Max said. "We totally lost track of the time!"

"Flattering," I muttered.

"It's OK," purred Davinia. "Just get us some champagne and we'll forget all about it."

You had to admire her. You really did. The

champagne arrived, and menus the size of barn doors, and Max and Ollie raved on about their diving trip, and their friend's really, really amazing speedboat, and how he let them drive it even though they hadn't got a license. . . . I sipped my champagne and looked at the menu and tried to remember what I'd resolved about being one of the Beautiful People, but it was no good. I kept seeing Alex's dusty face, wishing I was sitting outside that scruffy bar with him. The menu was a joke, full of words like *jus* and *parfait*. We ordered and I had no idea what I'd asked for except it was bound to be like the restaurant itself, tarted up and pretentious.

And then, to put the icing on the cake, Ollie started getting fruity.

It was OK at first. The two boys were just boring on about diving, and giving us patronizing advice about which food to order, and making a big, big deal about which wine to get. But then Max leaned in closer across the table to Davinia and started to tell her in a low, meaningful voice what he'd been through with Pandora. I could tell it was all cobblers—I reckon he hadn't even finished with Pandora, just sneaked out for the night. But Davinia was lapping it up. In fact Davinia was looking more impressed than I'd ever seen her look before.

In fact, Davinia was looking *smitten*. Oh, my God. Her eyes were round and trusting and her nose was practically touching his as he talked. They'd both forgotten to eat.

It was then that I sensed Ollie creaking his chair closer to the table and leaning in toward me. "They seem pretty thick, don't they?" he wheezed.

I ignored him and carried on trying to pierce a tiny, frilly lettuce leaf with my fork.

"I feel positively in the way, don't you?" he said.

*You are in the way, mate,* I thought, *right in my way.* But I couldn't just keep on ignoring him, could I? So I gave a little measly smile and a kind of agreeing cough.

Ollie took this as the big green light, of course. His leg pressed against mine under the table as he murmured, "He's very keen on your friend, you know. Very keen."

"Has he really dumped Pandora?" I demanded.

"Heeeey! Suspicious!" he oiled, and brought his hand down to cover mine.

I resisted a very strong desire to stab it with my fork, pulled my hand from underneath his sweaty mitt, and repeated, "Has he?"

"Of *course* he has. *Loooook* . . . the relationship was on its way out anyway. You saw that at the party. It's just . . . Pandora was so hysterical afterward, he had to take it slow, you know what I mean? He had to . . ."

I heard a sucking noise to my left and glanced up. Oh, my *God!* Max and Davinia were snogging, right across the table. All kind of frenzied and passionate, like they didn't care who was looking because they were just *overcome* by intense desire and had to go with it. Max was actually standing up to get at her, his arse was a good six inches off his seat. Ollie let out a *phewwww* of breath and brought his hammy head closer to mine. *Don't get any ideas,* I thought savagely, drawing back. *I'd never kiss you, never. I'd sooner let an oozing slug push its way into my mouth than your tongue.*

The rampant lovers broke apart, all breathless and *wow!* and giggly, just as an indignant-looking waiter bore down on our table to ask if "everything was all right."

"All right?" breezed Max. "I'll say it's all right. Now—let's have some more wine, shall we?"

And so it went on. We had main courses, we had dessert, and Davinia and Max didn't go in for any more snogging but all the time they were getting hotter and hotter as they bantered and flirted across the table. Which kept kind of shifting and . . . *bucking*, practically, as though they were bloody nearly having sex underneath it. All I can say is—their legs were very entwined. And all these plans were flying about, too—plans that involved us going out in a foursome—on the boat, to this great club they knew tomorrow night, to a "very secluded beach I know . . . and I mean you could get up to *anything* there and no one would see you, *hergh-hergh-hergh.*"

It was enough to make you start screaming, it really was. I wanted to jump up on the table and shout, *Reality check, everyone! This is not going to* happen! *Am I* invisible*? Has no one noticed I find Ollie* utterly repulsive *and there's no way I want to be part of your sleazy plans?*

I didn't, of course. It would have been swimming too hard against the tide. I just sat there silently, leaning as far to my *left* as possible to keep away from Max lustfully threshing about and as far *back* in my seat as possible to keep out of Ollie's breath range. I chewed and swallowed and tried to work out why Ollie had looked pretty good at first but now he made me want to gag. I decided it was his voice, it was what he did with his eyes and his mouth, but most of all it was just what he said and *who he was* that completely turned me off.

I looked across the table at Davinia. She was

rolling her eyes as Max spooned raspberry pavlova into her mouth. She looked like an idiot. How could I ever have idolized her so much? How could I ever think I might be a lesbian because of the way I felt about her? I was just besotted and envious and fascinated by the way she looked, that was all. The way she moved and smiled and sneered at people and laughed. It was like a picture of a girl in a magazine who's so beautiful and perfect and so much better than you that it hurts. And you think—if I was like *her*, if I looked like *her*, then I'd be happy. And then you realize it's just a stupid picture, and the model probably feels like shit because she's cold and she hasn't eaten for a week and it's all just an illusion. . . .

Just a stupid illusion.

Davinia was just a stupid illusion.

She was just very, very good at the act, that's all.

And when I realized that, she stopped looking so beautiful and started to look fake and false and even repulsive.

Silently, I grabbed the wine bottle and emptied it into my glass. Max glanced at me disapprovingly. "Another bottle, guys?" he said. "Or shall we just get the bill and get outta here? Anyone want coffee?"

"Not for me," said Ollie. He was still smirking at me across the table. It hadn't filtered through into his rock-hard cranium that I loathed him. Or maybe he didn't care that I loathed him, maybe he thought he'd still get a snog.

Max was reviewing the bill, an old hand at this. "OK, ladies, the champagne's on me, but we're going to have to split the rest, I'm afraid. Bit more than I thought it'd be."

I was waiting for Davinia to hit the roof, but she didn't. She picked up her bag all docile, and said, "So what's the damage then, Maxy-boo?"

"Well—let's see. Pricey place, this. OK—with a tip, split by four, it's—"

He named a figure that froze the marrow in my bones, and went on, "You don't mind, do you? Feminism and all that. And then the next time . . . it'll definitely be on us, OK?"

*What NEXT TIME?* I raged silently. *I've got to pay out a sum of money that normally lasts me a YEAR on one of the crappiest nights of my LIFE and you seriously imagine there'll EVER be a NEXT TIME?*

I felt sick, awful. I didn't know what to do. I had the money in my bank account but it would just about clear it out. And then what would I do for the rest of the holiday?

But I just wasn't brave enough to make a fuss.

Like a coward, with shaking fingers I got my bank card—the one we'd specially arranged for this holiday—out of my bag, and pushed it across the table to Max.

CHAPTER
29

**THAT CRAVEN ACT OF** submission seemed to galvanize me. I stomped through to the hotel vestibule and asked the snooty headwaiter to get us a cab. No discussion. If Davinia wanted to hang about groping Max, I'd wrestle the apartment keys off her and go back on my own.

We all spilled out onto the cobbled pavement, into the warm night air. My throat felt like it had barbed wire round it with the effort not to cry or swear or both, but I managed to announce in the voice of a strangled mouse that the waiter had said the cab would be about five minutes.

By now it had finally, finally filtered through to everyone that I was in a Mood. Ollie leaned up against the wall in a resigned way and lit up his twentieth fag of the evening. Max and Davinia were half snogging and half whispering together and I heard "she'll come round" and "God, I wish it was just the two of us here" and other phrases not exactly likely to cheer me up.

At last, the cab came rattling round the corner and I wrenched its door open and shot into it at top speed. I knew I was acting like a neurotic cow, not even saying good-bye to Max and Ollie, but I didn't care. Every cell in my body was screaming to get out of there.

After what felt like an hour—after Max and Davinia had had another long bout of frenzied kissing and exchanged pledges about meeting up again—Davinia got into the cab and we roared away. Then she leaned over to me and said, "Listen—it's OK. Don't worry about it."

"Don't worry about what?" I grated out. There were so many things to worry about—being suddenly totally broke was probably the main one—that I couldn't wait to hear what she'd choose.

"Dragging me off like that," she said, soothingly. "It's OK. It kind of spoiled the end of the evening but—it's OK. I could see you were upset, and Max is just great like that, he understood, he told me I had to look after you, that's what friends are for. Isn't he *great*?"

I *knew* what she was like—and I knew she was drunk—but even so, this total, blind *complacency*— it was too much. I couldn't speak.

"I'm gonna see him tomorrow anyway," she went on. "He's phoning, we're going to go to that beach he was on about, God, he's so hot, he's—"

"Davinia, I'm sodding well *broke* after that meal," I hissed.

"It was a bit steep, wasn't it?" She giggled. "Don't worry. I'll get the cab. Oh, come on, Chloe—don't look so miserable! You know—it was the wine that bumped the bill up. Max chose the best—he's like that." She giggled again. "After all, he chose *me*, didn't he?"

"I'm sorry," I croaked, "but it's really upset me. They had no *right* to ask us out like they were gonna pay and choose the most expensive place on the island and order all that wine and—"

"Oh, Chloe! *Boring!* Look—I am in *love* here, I mean seriously deeply in love, and all you can do is whinge on about the restaurant bill! It wasn't even that bad. How much d'you think that meal at The Cabin cost, the first night we got here?"

"Not half as much as that one."

"Actually, it did. The Cabin makes out it's all beach-style and everything but for the classy stuff on the menu it charges a *lot*, trust me. And the lunch Mummy and Daddy paid for the other day— that was loads—and the food at the Stuart-Coxes' party would've cost more than the whole lot put together!"

Her point was clear. I was on a freebie holiday with lots of extras thrown in so I'd better not moan about anything.

"Come on," she said, "cheer up. Look, Chloe—I know what your *real* problem is." The cab drew to a stop outside the apartment gates and we got out, and Davinia—with a saintly air—paid the fare. Then she linked her arm into mine and went on, "It's Ollie, isn't it? Look—OK, you don't fancy him. But that doesn't mean you can't just come along and have *fun*! Max would feel as bad about leaving Ollie out as I would about you. We both value our friends."

I had a choice. I could project a violent stream of vomit into the shrubbery, or I could keep quiet. Guess what? I kept quiet.

"You'll feel better in the morning," she breezed on. "More *positive*. You're just a bit drunk."

We went into the main doors of the apartment, and up in the lift. I knew Davinia was dying to go into a big gurgling review about how irresistible Max was, and I suppose it showed she had some sensitivity that she kept quiet. *Almost* quiet. What she actually did was *hum*.

Her *hum* was essence of gloating self-satisfaction with a lot of lechery thrown in, and I had to *really steel* myself not to put my hands over my ears.

I played up feeling drunk and ill and got into bed as quickly as I could. As sleep obliterated me, I told myself that I'd work it all out in the morning, but deep down I knew I wouldn't, I'd be stuck in this same mess. I had a choice. I'd kowtow to Davinia yet again, I'd phone Dad and screw some more money out of him, I'd go along with her and Max and Ollie and pretend to be happy—hey, why not go the whole hog, I could pretend I fancied Ollie, couldn't I, let him snog me, so we could make up a real foursome. . . .

Or I could . . . I could *what*?

I guess sleep was my one refuge. I slept. And slept. Even when I was aware of Davinia getting out of bed before me, an unheard-of event, and leaving the bedroom, I went back to sleep.

It was the light in the bedroom that finally woke me up properly, late-morning, white-hot light. As I stumbled through to the bathroom I could hear voices, Davinia and her parents talking. I locked myself in and peed, washed my hands, brushed my hair, tried to make myself look a little less grim. I'd have to go and join them, wouldn't I, at least to say hello, or I'd look like a real weirdo.

All three of them turned to smile at me as I walked into the main room, kind of bright, assessing smiles. "Sleepyhead!" caroled Davinia. "You were out like a dead *log*." I resisted the strong impulse to snap back that it was the first time *she'd* been out of bed first since the holiday began—and sniggered weakly. "Listen," she went on, "Max has phoned. He's sorted it out for us to go out in the speedboat with them—they'll be here in an hour to pick us up. We can do a tour round the island. It'll be *amazing*!"

There was a silence, which I was clearly expected to fill with an explosion of joy.

"Don't worry," said Paul firmly and genially. "The lad can manage a boat. Turns out we know his parents."

It killed me the way knowing someone's parents was, for other parents, a guarantee of good behavior, a talisman against anything going wrong.

"I'm not sure about going out in a boat today," I muttered. "I feel pretty rough, I—"

"You'll feel better when you're out in the air," interrupted Cassie, just as firm as Paul, and it suddenly hit me what Davinia had done. She'd got up early to get her parents on her side, to tell them

about the wonderful couple of boys we'd met—
*hey!* they knew Max's parents!—and how we were
all going to have a great time together. And if I
wanted to back out, well, that was me being a sad
pain, me being difficult, awkward, *ungrateful.*

I hated playing the feeble sick card, I really
hated it, but it was the only card I had. "Look—I
really do feel rough," I croaked. "I'm gonna go
back to bed. I'd hate to spoil the trip for you,
Davinia, by getting sick . . . *you* go."

Then I put my hand up to my mouth, miming
being about to throw up, turned on my heel, scurried back to the bathroom, and locked myself in.

I sat on the closed lid of the toilet and put my
head in my hands. Oh, shit, this had to be about as
bad as it could get, didn't it? The three of them
were out there discussing what a pathetic failure I
was as a holiday guest (I kind of agreed with them,
choosing solitary bed over a speedboat trip *was*
pretty pathetic), and what's more I hadn't solved a
thing by it, because Davinia would want to go on
seeing Max, wouldn't she, so what was I going to
do, stay in bed for the rest of the bloody holiday?
Mum surfaced in my head again, choking up my
throat, and I slammed her down.

I had to get out of the bathroom, or they'd
come checking to see if I was OK. I pulled the

chain and scuttled out, praying that the corridor would be empty. It was. So was our bedroom. I jumped into my bed and pulled the sheet over my head.

Not long afterward, Davinia came back in the room. She put a tinkling glass down by the side of my bed and in the voice of a ministering saint whispered, "Got you some water." I pretended to be passed out. I heard her moving about, imagined her collecting beach bag, bikini, sun oil . . . I was ready to scream with frustration, being cooped up under the covers like that, envying her, thinking of the day she was going to have with someone she fancied like crazy. . . . Alex slid into my mind and I forced him out again.

And on top of all that, I was beginning to feel really, really thirsty. And hungry. If I've been drinking the night before, I crave water, lots of it, and carbs. But I had to keep on acting dead.

At last, Davinia tiptoed out of the room, shutting the door behind her. I shoved back the sheet and downed the water she'd brought me. I craned my ears, but it was hard to hear what was going on in the flat, so I slipped out of bed and opened the door just a crack, then shot back into bed again. Before long, I heard the apartment bell go, and heard Davinia calling, *"Byeeee!"* and Paul and

Cassie telling her to have a good time and be safe and put sun cream on.

One gone, two to go. I waited, listening, under my sheet, for what seemed like hours. My stomach felt like it was eating itself, I was so desperate for some food. I didn't care about the dire situation I was in anymore, only getting some food down my throat. I could hear Paul and Cassie moving about, clearing up in the kitchen, talking in quiet, contented voices. *Piss off!* I screamed silently. *Stop fussing about—GO!!*

At last, they went. And with the sound of the flat door closing I bolted out of bed, raced into the kitchen, and rammed my head in the fridge. It would be pretty bloody embarrassing if they got to the car, realized they'd forgotten something, and came back, but too bad, I'd have to pretend I was getting a raw egg hangover cure or something. . . .

*Bliss.* Lovely, fresh ham, tomatoes, creamy white butter . . . I ate it with crusty bread and a big mug of tea, then I had a banana and some nuts.

Physically, I felt a lot, lot better, but unfortunately that meant I once again started to think about the mess I was in. I was staying in the flat of someone I'd started to loathe, my bank balance was down to about half a pound, I had no friends here . . . oh, but it was good to be in the flat alone, without Davinia. It started to feel as if parts of me that had been all clenched up and wary, policing what I said and did, were able to flow free at last.

I went back to our room, opened the window, and hopped out onto the narrow balcony, turned my face up to the heat of the sun. Raising my arms above my head, I stretched out the muscles in my shoulders and back. They were sore from all the swimming I'd done and it felt deeply pleasurable. I rested my hands on the rail and scanned the wasteland for cats, but there was no movement. I examined my hands. They were lovely and brown, and my nails were long and white-tipped—the sun and the sea had strengthened them. They were ragged, though; they desperately needed filing.

I thought of Davinia last night racing about the bathroom, getting herself tarted up for Max, chucking wax-strips around, screaming at me to lend her my mascara, and decided there and then to have a grooming session. For starters I'd give my hair some serious conditioning with that expensive stuff of Cassie's she'd got tucked away in her sponge bag. She'd never notice a bit missing.

It was great just to take all the time I wanted in the bathroom. Cassie and Davinia moaned on so much about the awfulness of there only being one bathroom in the flat, of having to share and not have your own en suite, that usually I raced through showering as fast as I could. But now I could wallow.

First, I waxed my legs, using Davinia's wax strips. I'm not particularly hairy so it didn't take long. Then I stepped in the shower and luxuriated in the pounding water. When I'd washed my hair, I hopped out and scooped up a dollop of Cassie's miracle conditioner. I smoothed it in, got back in the shower, and exfoliated with some gorgeous-smelling papaya stuff. I was a bit nervous of scraping my tan off, but I knew the dry skin was on its way out anyway.

Then I got out, still with the miracle conditioner doing its work feeding and restoring my salt-spoiled hair, and sat, dripping, on the edge of the bath. I cut my toenails; I filed away all the dry skin on my feet. I massaged vitamin E oil (courtesy of Cassie again) into my cuticles and they softened and pushed back perfectly; my nails shone. Then I got back into the shower and rinsed out the miracle conditioner.

It really was a miracle—my hair felt all soft and springy as I dried it off and combed it through. Some payback impulse must've been working away in me; I nicked Davinia's expensive body cream and lathered it on, all over. My skin just kept drinking it up and I kept rubbing it in.

I felt fabulous when I'd finished. I gathered up my stuff and walked, naked, down the corridor to our room, enjoying the slightly risky thrill of it, the air on my super-moisturized skin. I stood in front of the mirror and loved what I saw. I wanted to make up my eyes, gloss my lips, load silver bangles on my brown arms, put my best bra on, and my silky turquoise top . . . adorn myself, like an Arabian princess, and then go out and . . .

My fantasy stopped sharp. I couldn't go out. I realized with a rush of anger and almost-panic that I hadn't got a key to the flat. It was just assumed that I'd be with Davinia all the time, that she'd take me along with her, and if she didn't I'd be left behind like a bag she wasn't using.

Shit! Shit, shit, *shit*!!

If I went out how would I get back in again? They'd all gone out and left me alone without a key. Selfish *bastards*. Maybe if I left the door on the latch, and didn't go out for long, it would be OK, no one would break in, would they?

I went back and tried the front door. It was locked. They'd gone out and Chubb-locked the door, like they always did, for security, and locked me in. Selfish *bastards*! This wave of horrible claustrophobic panic washed over me. I couldn't get *out*,

I couldn't even get up onto the *roof*, could I? *I was locked in.*

And then I remembered our bedroom balcony, and my daring jump to freedom.

**IT WAS EVERY BIT AS** easy this time round. I even left a note on my bed saying: DON'T WORRY ABOUT ME—I FEEL BETTER—I'M GOING OUT FOR A BIT. I pulled on shorts and a T-shirt, stepped out on the balcony, slid the window shut after me, and dropped safely onto the table on the balcony below. Blank windows stared reassuringly back at me; no one yelled at me. It wasn't until I'd climbed over the second lot of railings and landed on the parched ground beneath that it hit me I had no way of getting back in again. Davinia wasn't up on the roof to shout to this time.

I stood still for a minute, gripped by panic. Then I told myself it was too late to worry about it, and maybe my subconscious had *made* me jump before I'd realized because I so desperately had to get out.

Then I started to walk.

233

It felt good, loping along in the heat. I didn't cross the wasteland like I had done the last time I jumped; instead I wandered along the dirt track behind the apartments and came out on the road. There, I stopped for a minute. If I went left, I'd get to the harbor; right, I'd get to the beach we always went to. I was pondering this when a little red-and-cream bus trundled by. I'd suggested getting a bus once, at the start of the holiday, to explore the island, but Davinia had reacted as though I'd suggested smearing goat shit on her face. Public transport was too utterly beneath her.

The bus was going in the direction of Victoria, one of the main towns—we'd driven there last week when Cassie and Paul had taken us out to lunch. Victoria was pretty and its main square looked inviting, but the others hadn't wanted to spend time there and we'd just driven straight back again.

On an impulse, I headed after the bus. I decided I'd find its stop and I wouldn't just go to the harbor or the beach, I'd go to Victoria.

The bus stop took me about fifteen minutes to reach, walking along the edge of the dusty road. I was worried there'd turn out to be only two buses a day, or something, but I took it to be a hopeful sign that two middle-aged local women were standing by the stop, talking furiously. I sidled up behind them; they glanced at me and went on talking. The sun beat down on my head and I prayed that the bus would come soon. For a start, I was worried that Davinia's parents might drive by and spot me, stop, and haul me back with them because I was supposed to be ill. My arms started to prick with sunburn—I pulled a bottle of sun cream out of my bag and was just unscrewing the lid when another little bus drew into sight. Dust fanned round its wheels and it had VICTORIA on a battered sign in front of it.

I got on behind the woman, and as I paid I asked the driver if he'd shout me when we reached Victoria.

"You can't miss it," he assured me. "It's where I turn around and come back again."

I loved the bus ride. It was pure retro, with minimal suspension, leather straps, and battered formica seat backs, and a little faded shrine by the driver. Up higher than in the car, driving along at a more leisurely pace, I could see into the fields, look at the little houses as we drove by with their geraniums and statues of Holy Mary.

It took us twenty minutes and three more stops to get to Victoria. At the last-but-one stop, a group of three girls and two boys got on, laughing and noisy, hair wet from swimming. They were German and I couldn't understand what they were saying but their pleasure with themselves and with one another didn't need to be explained. One of the boys had got sunburned, and they were mocking him and tending him. . . . It made me feel really lonely. I gazed steadfastly out of the window, trying to look aloof and mysterious.

We arrived in Victoria. I checked which bus stop I'd need for my return journey, then I set off to explore. The main square was shady with large trees overhanging, a market in the center, and little shops and cafés all round. I admired the woven shawls and baskets, the silver filigree jewelry. There was a little butterfly brooch that I really coveted, but I knew I had to save all my money just to survive.

I bought five postcards, because to buy fewer seemed too pathetic, and decided I'd sit at a café under the trees, treat myself to a cappuccino, and write them. I'd always felt inhibited about buying postcards in front of Davinia because I knew she'd sneer at such sad, touristy behavior, but I also knew Dad would be disappointed if he didn't get at least one from the holiday. I wrote one to him, one

to my gran, and then—God knows why—one to
Abby that said:

> Hi Abby,
>     Bet I'm the last person you expected to get a card
> from. The island is HOT and beautiful and brilliant,
> but you were 80% right about Davinia. No—90%
> right. She's totally self-centered and she's trying to
> force me to date this CREEP just because she's got the
> hots for his friend! I'd sooner slit my wrists because
> I'm in love with someone else. He's gorgeous but he
> hates me. Aren't holidays supposed to be relaxing?!
>     Abby, I wish we hadn't fallen out. Maybe see
> you when I get back?
>     Lots of love (honest!),
>     Chloe xxx

I didn't stick a stamp on it. I wasn't sure I was
going to send it. It was pathetic, making out I had
something going on with Alex, even hatred, when
I'd hardly spoken to him. And I didn't really want
to see Abby when I got back—the postcard was just
a kind of bleak insurance policy against being completely friendless. And I was completely friendless—I had absolutely no idea who to send the
other two cards to.

I sat there, sipping the cappuccino as slowly as I could, all weird and adrift, out of kilter with myself, like everything inside me was shifting about and I wasn't sure who I was anymore, what I wanted, what I liked, when I heard a voice behind me say, "And what are *you* doing out all on your own, darling, hmm?"

CHAPTER 31

T WAS CORA. SHE LOOKED very different in the real ight of day, away from the bar. Older, less glamrous . . . more human somehow. I liked her more. She had a huge wicker basket full of shiny red peppers over her arm and she was wearing a plain T-shirt and shorts and very little makeup. Her extraordinary hair was simply tied back, no clips or spangles or shells in its coils.

"Oh, I just fancied a break," I said.

Cora plonked her basket down on the ground. "You want to be alone? Or can I get you another coffee? I'm desperate for a coffee."

Free coffee—it was too tempting. I said thank you, and pulled out a chair for her, and she beckoned to the waiter.

"What's wrong?" she asked.

"Nothing," I muttered.

"Come on," she said. "You can't fool me. You

didn't just fancy a break, did you? You're upset
Has Davinia gone and found herself a boyfriend o
something?"

It was so amazing and—I don't know—*sedu*
*tive*, to have someone actually see me, take notic
of *me*, that I gulped out, "Yes. How did you know?

Cora shrugged. "She does it every yea
Sometimes the friend finds a boyfriend too, some
times not."

"Well, she wanted me to have a boyfriend too
that's part of the trouble," I said . . . and then
found myself telling Cora everything, all abou
Deborah and Anthony's party and Max and Ollie
And then the coffee arrived and I went on to te
her about the awful posh meal where I spent a
my money and how I was absolutely broke nov
and I didn't want to ask my dad for more mone
because he'd been through so much with my mun
walking out and . . . and Cora listened, she *listened*
Her attention was like food to me, nourishmen
that up till then I hadn't known I'd needed. Sh
put in the odd prompting question and she kep
picking up my hand and squeezing it and strokin
my arm and it was so comforting and nice, I jus
went on talking.

"Oh, God—*sorry*!" I mumbled at last. "I've beer
going on and *on*—sorry!"

"Don't be absurd," she said. "You needed to talk. Now. It seems your most pressing problem is lack of money, and the need to have something to do while Davinia is running around being in love. Why don't you come and work for me? That would solve both problems in one go."

I stared at her dumbly.

"Don't look so shocked! I don't mean full-time, I couldn't afford that. But Hilly's is *expanding*."

"Expanding?" I echoed. "How?"

"Into lunchtimes! It's so exciting! We decided it was a waste of an expensive facility to leave it shut up all through the day, so we've started doing lunches. That's what these are for." She nodded toward her basket. "These are the best peppers on the island. We're specializing in simple, fresh, local food—this marvelous local lady is helping us."

"How fantastic! Is it going well?"

"It's only been going two weeks so far, so early, early days . . . but yes . . . it's taking off. We're getting busier."

"But won't you be completely knackered? I mean—the bar opens every night, doesn't it?"

Cora crinkled up her wonderful sea-green eyes and laughed. "We'll be *totally* knackered. But then we'll have enough money to see us through the winter. And we're only doing lunches Wednesday to Sunday. We need a wonderful waitress to help us! What do you say?"

"I . . . I don't know what to say! I mean—thank you, it's—"

"Have you ever done this sort of work before?"

"Yes. I used to do Saturdays, at Greedies. It was this . . . kind of upmarket greasy spoon caf near me."

"So there you are! An experienced waitress! And maybe you can help in the evenings too. I mean—we can be flexible, we can fit round Davinia and her . . . *schedule*. You can't serve drinks because you're not eighteen, but you could clear glasses, wash up. . . ."

It was too good an offer.

As if she was picking up on my thoughts, Cora sat back. "Sorry, I'm rushing you," she purred. "You want to think about it, of course you do. . . ."

"It's a fantastic offer," I muttered. "It's just . . . I don't know how they'd all take it, me just clearing off and working. And shouldn't you . . . I mean, shouldn't you check with Zara?"

"She leaves the front of house to me. And anyway, she'll be thrilled!"

"She won't be . . . she won't be . . . ?"

I was staring hot-faced at the table. And Cora suddenly threw back her head and laughed. "You mean *jealous*, don't you, darling? You mean she might think I fancy you? Oh, my God—you haven't realized. Well, why should you? You think we're lesbians, don't you?"

"Davinia *told* me you were! And you do kind of . . . *act* it."

"And that's what it is, an *act*. I adore Zara, I love to kiss her, but I'm not a lesbian. Since we're being so frank—I'm celibate. I have been for the last three years, since my divorce. I find it a very refreshing state to live in."

"But *why* . . . everyone *thinks* . . ."

"Two women on their own, on this traditional little island, running a bar? We put out that we were lesbians to protect ourselves—so we could still dress up and flaunt and do all the things you have to do to give your bar a buzz and make it commercial without constantly having *men* trying it on with you. Or only the very arrogant ones who think we're only lesbians because we've never had a real man. *Ha!*"

"Blimey," I muttered. I was still taking it in. "It's some act. Don't you ever get real lesbians coming after you?"

Cora preened. "Occasionally. But they recognize our devotion to each other and back off. Why are you looking like that? You think we're wrong to do it, you think we're insulting real lesbians? We do it to survive. And we don't hurt anyone."

"I wasn't thinking that at all. I was just thinking how . . . *different* people can turn out to be. You know—when you get below the surface."

"*Aah*," she said meaningfully, as if she knew I wasn't just talking about her.

"And I was thinking how much I'd like to work for you! But I'll have to . . . feel my way first, OK?"

Cora waved an imperious hand for the bill. "Of course you must, my darling. You know where we are."

## CHAPTER 32

I WAS REVVING ON THE bus on the way home, head full of plans. The more I thought about it, the more perfect working at Hilly's was. Why should Davinia and her parents object? It would sort out my money problems and give me something to do while Davinia saw Max, *and* it would give Davinia and me a much-needed break from each other. Who knows—we might even start liking each other again.

I was so deep in thought I stayed on the bus as it sailed right past our apartment block, but the next stop was only a ten-minute walk back. I told myself I was absolutely banned from worrying about there not being anyone in the flat to let me in until I'd pressed the bell and got no response.

Happily, I *did* get a response. Through the crackly entrance speaker, Cassie said, "Oh, it's you!" then she pressed the buzzer, and I was in. I raced up the marble-clad stairs two at a time, nearly giving a small green lizard on the first-floor landing wall a heart attack.

The flat door was already open when I arrived, and I dashed in.

To face what felt like a tribunal.

Cassie and Paul were sitting in the main room, and they looked up at me but didn't smile. "Did you see my note?" I faltered.

"Yes," said Cassie. "We came back from the beach early so we could check that you were OK."

"Oh look—I'm *sorry*," I said. "I felt so much better—"

"In your note, you said you were going out for a *bit*," said Paul. "*We've* been back nearly an hour. Hardly a *bit*."

"Even if you left right before we got here," added Cassie.

"I'm *sorry*," I repeated. "I ended up getting the bus to Victoria, I dunno, it was just an impulse . . ."

I trailed off and they looked at me stonily. I could understand why they were pissed off with me but . . . why were they *so* pissed off? For one mad minute I thought Cassie had found out about me nicking her conditioner and posh stuff. They hadn't said they were glad I was better, they hadn't asked how I'd got out of the flat. They were just really, really put out that they'd had to cut their beach session short.

Paul cleared his throat. "Well, as you're not really ill, I think it's a real shame you didn't stick with Davinia today. Safety in numbers and all that. I mean—she's gone out alone with two boys."

"She'll be all right!" I cried.

"I hope so," said Cassie meaningfully. "I mean—OK, if you were ill you couldn't go out on the speedboat. But you obviously weren't *that* ill."

I felt myself go red. She was accusing me of lying. Well, OK—I *had* lied. But for very good reasons! It was time they knew the truth.

"Look," I said, looking hard at the floor, "OK, I wasn't at death's door. But the thing is—Davinia thinks Max is great, but I *really* don't. And Ollie's worse. That meal we all had out together—I *hated* it. It was awful. There's no way I want to make up a foursome with Ollie again. He makes my skin crawl, to be honest."

"Poor boy," said Cassie coldly. "What a horrible thing to have said about you."

I looked up, stung by her response, to see the two of them still glaring at me. I'd thought I could win them round to my point of view but I'd failed massively.

There was a nasty, drawn-out pause. Then Paul

said, kind of forced-heartily, "Chloe, aren't you taking all this a bit seriously? We're not asking you to marry Ollie. Just . . . get *along* with him."

"Davinia likes the boys," put in Cassie. "She was telling me how great they are. So they can't be *that* bad."

"The thing is, you came on holiday with Davinia," said Paul, "so we hoped you'd stick by her. *You* know."

*Yes, I do know*, I thought miserably. *This holiday has terms attached to it, and those terms are that I "stick by" Davinia like her bloody* servant *no matter what.*

I wished I'd had the courage to say it out loud, but I didn't.

"Anyway," Cassie went on, "there's a big festa tomorrow night—festas on Caminos are wonderful. Processions, fireworks—we thought we'd all go. And if Davinia wants the boys to come too—well, I hope at least you'll be civil to them, OK?"

At least I was brave enough not to smile and agree. I just kind of nodded, turned on my heel, and went back to our bedroom.

I felt like bursting into tears when I got there. I'd thought Cassie and Paul were so *nice* but really they were just kind of . . . *suave*, and worldly.

They'd been "nice" to me because I was useful to them, and because it fitted the image they had of themselves, as "nice" people, but now I'd come up against them the niceness had stopped sharp.

They were terrified of their own daughter, scared of her going off like a car alarm if you rattled her, and I'd helped prevent that. I was here to keep Davinia on the straight and narrow, keep her occupied—I didn't count in my own right. I thought back to the times they'd used me to hurry her up—"Go and give her another shout, will you, Chloe, darling?"—or watch that she didn't drink too much—"Don't let her overdo it, Chloe!"—and it made me feel more and more that I'd been employed as a maid.

God, what a shitty situation. What's that phrase, "An apple doesn't fall too far from its tree"? I could see now why Davinia was so self-obsessed and selfish. I could really see it.

So much for thinking they'd be OK about Cora's offer of a job. I could just imagine how that would go down. So here I was, no money, no key to the flat—no *food* unless I play-acted everything was fine and joined them at their meals. Or managed to raid the fridge.

I was getting very hungry again. *Shit!*

\* \* \*

Another hour went by, while I brooded all hunched up on my bed. I could hear the sounds of the two of them drifting in and out of the bathroom and their bedroom, getting ready (I hoped) to go out. I was dreading one of them knocking on the door, wanting to come in for another little talk, but they didn't.

There was no sign of Davinia either. With any luck she'd come back from her boat trip even more keen on Max and wouldn't give a toss about what I did for the rest of the holiday. I decided I'd appeal to her finer side (ha!), tell her I desperately didn't want to spend time with Ollie, and enlist her support in me working for Cora.

At last, Cassie and Paul went out again, not even calling out good-bye, which was a relief and hurtful both at the same time. I raced out on another reccy to the fridge, piled up my plate, and shot back to the bedroom. I'd taken some fruit too, and half a packet of oatmeal-and-raisin cookies, and I hid them at the back of the drawer of my bedside table as survival rations.

What did you do on your holiday, Chloe? Hid in my room and ate stolen food. Counted the days—twenty-seven more days—a sodding *lifetime*—until I'd be on the plane home again. God, was I sad or *what*?

Davinia didn't get back that night until very, very late. I'd drifted off to sleep and she woke me by landing on the end of my bed, squawking, "God, have you been tucked up all *day*?" in a very scathing voice.

Then—before I could answer—she went on, "I have had *the* most *amazing* time. Oh, my *God*, it was the *best*! You should've seen the speedboat, Chloe! So classy! We went off to this little island, there's only a hotel on it, it's *so* exclusive, and tied the boat up and then just drifted up to the hotel and all these people were looking at us, wondering who we were . . . most of them were unspeakably hideous and fat but some of them had style, and Max knew this really fantastic crowd, and we all had lunch together, this amazing buffet thing, it was fabulous!"

"Great," I croaked. "I'm glad you had a good day. I—"

"*God*, you should've come, though. It was dire having Ollie tagging along. No *privacy*. After lunch we went for a wander in among these sand dunes, near where we'd moored the boat, and Max was getting really hot, whispering in my ear about how he wanted to *lay me down* behind one. . . ." She shrieked with laughter. "We have to do it soon,

Chloe, I swear. I'm gonna *burn up* if we don't! He's so hot, just the touch of his hand practically gives me a multiple orgasm. . . ."

I had this strong desire to clap my hands over my ears. "Too much information, Davinia," I croaked.

"He's just so unutterably fabulous," she blithered on, "you should see him without his clothes on. . . . Don't look like that—in his bathers, I mean!" She shrieked again. "I can't keep my hands off him . . . and he's the same. I mean . . . he *adores* me, he's always whispering dirty things in my ear about what he wants to do to me. . . ."

I knew I could wait for the apocalypse before Davinia asked me how I was, how I'd spent the day. "Did your parents tell you about their plans for tomorrow?" I asked.

"The festa? Yeah—fabulous. I'm gonna really dress up. Something utterly revealing but glamorous. I thought my terra-cotta-and-mint dress with the swishy skirt—"

"And will Max and Ollie be coming along?"

"Well, I think poor Ollie has taken the hint that you're not that keen on him, Chloe! He was talking about going along with some other friends. But Max'll be there. Later."

"Why later?"

"He's still getting trouble from Pandora, can you believe it? She's actually threatened she's gonna top herself. How selfish is that? And he's too *sweet* to just let her go ahead and do it."

"Oh, that *is* sweet."

"Yeah. He's probably going to see her again tomorrow evening, to try and sort her out, but he'll be along to the festa later. . . . I just hope we can connect up. I mean, I hope our mobiles work with all the fireworks and everything. . . . Max thought they might not."

By this time I didn't so much *smell* a rat as have it force my nostril open with its little paws and run straight up my nose. I mean—how thick was she? How absolutely sure of her own gorgeousness that it didn't cross her mind that Max might not put *her* before everything else in his life? He obviously hadn't broken up with Pandora at all. He was indulging in the time-honored pursuit of two-timing. He'd see Pandora, then race on and see Davinia, and he'd tell her his mobile was off because of the *fireworks* . . . ?

Davinia got off my bed and stripped off all her clothes, dropping them on the floor. Then she stood naked in the moonlight in front of the full-length mirror. "Lucky Max," she purred, raising her arms above her head. "How can he *bear* to *wait*?"

CHAPTER 33

DESPITE EVERYTHING, THE NEXT evening the excitement of the festa fizzled through to me. Davinia and I had spent the day quietly on the beach and I'd done a huge amount of swimming and I felt good and relaxed. As we were getting ready, sounds of the festa preparations drifted in through the open windows—children shouting, scraps of band music, a drum beating. . . . Davinia was oblivious, of course. She wouldn't have heard a nuclear strike. She was absolutely focused on making herself look gorgeous for the night ahead.

Which, in her terra-cotta-and-mint dress with the swishy skirt, and her hair all piled on top, and wonderful, festive earrings—she did. I didn't have the heart to tart myself up much, but I felt good in a plain white vest and short dusty pink skirt.

The festa was being held on the opposite side of the island, so we got in the car and drove there.

Cassie had agreed not to drink and take us all back. Except that Davinia, of course, planned to take off with Max.

When she told her parents this, there was a distinct shift in the car. "How *definite* is that arrangement, darling?" asked Cassie tentatively.

"*Absolutely* definite."

"But you did say he might not be able to get in touch with you, there might not be network coverage. . . ."

"Let's do what we did last year," said Paul firmly. "Just in case we can't get in touch by mobile. Mummy and I will be in the Good Friends bar at eleven o'clock. You remember where that is?"

"Yes," said Davinia grudgingly, "it's that one by the church in the main square."

"That's it. You be there too at eleven o'clock, no later, if you want a lift home."

"OK," said Davinia sulkily, "but I won't need one. Max has got a car."

"So he's not going to drink?" said Paul.

"Oh, for GOD'S SAKE," erupted Davinia, "why can't you just TRUST me for once? If he drinks, I won't get in a car with him, will I?"

"Of course not, darling," soothed Cassie. "Look—I'm going to give you the cab fare home too, just in case." And she handed a significant roll of notes over her shoulder to Davinia, who took it like it was her absolute due and shoved it in her little glitzy bag.

I cleared my throat. "It might just be me coming back with you," I said. "If Davinia's going off with Max, I mean. . . ."

"Well, won't your young man be there?" demanded Paul, sounding irritated.

"He's not *my young man*," I snapped.

"Look, Chloe, we've been through this," said Cassie wearily. "You know we think you girls should stick together. These festas can get a bit wild."

Seething, I didn't answer, and soon we were parked on a side street and heading toward the noise of the festa.

I hadn't realized it was a religious festival. We turned the corner to see an extraordinary statue being carried on a platform—a weeping Madonna with makeup like a 1930s film starlet, all red-bow mouth and sooty eyelashes. A band followed her, with children carrying flowers, and people surging happily along behind. There was a real party atmosphere. "Where are they taking her?" I asked, but just then huge silver fireworks lit up the sky in front of us, and no one answered. "OK, we're off!"

said Davinia, air-kissing first Paul and then Cassie.

"Be careful," said Cassie. "Phone me when you've hooked up with the boys. . . ."

"Will do," said Davinia, and we were off.

"It's all a bit naff in a way," said Davinia as we headed down to the main square ahead of the procession, "but it's fun. The bars are *packed*, and they do these little barbecue thingies out on the street—are you hungry?"

"Not yet," I said.

"Come on—let's get a drink. There's Good Friends, by the way."

I marked it, by the spindly towered church. I thought I might need it later. Then I watched Davinia sashaying ahead of me, attracting all eyes, and wished I'd dressed up a bit more. A little girl with a basket of yellow chrysanthemums ran over and gave her one of them and, laughing, she tucked it behind her ear. Men were calling out to her, asking her to join them for a drink—she floated by like a queen. Soon we were sitting side by side on a bench outside a bar, watching the crowds pass by, sipping white wine.

And I reckoned it was time to set the record straight.

"OK, Davinia," I said, "you've gotta pick up the

tab for this. I told you I'm broke."

"No problem. We'll use the taxi money. Max won't let me down."

"And that's the other thing. You'll want to be on your own with him. What'll I do? Apart from go all green and prickly?"

"*What?* Oh—gooseberry. Ha bloody ha. Well, either he'll give you a lift back or you can catch Mummy and Daddy at Good Friends."

Neither of us commented on the fact that I was supposed to keep her company until her lover turned up, and then bugger off. Neither of us commented on the extreme irony of the name of the bar. I swallowed down a big gulp of wine to cool my burning resentment.

When we'd emptied our glasses, we moved on through the noisy crowds to the next bar, where a little barbecue was sending out roast-chicken scents into the warm night. Davinia bought two pieces, wrapped in napkins, and as we ate it she obsessed about not getting grease down her front. We moved off again, then stopped at another bar for another glass of cold wine. It should have been fun, but it wasn't. Everyone we passed seemed to be having a better time than us—not that that was hard. Davinia was tight-lipped and silent, and she kept patting her bag. Probably willing her phone to ring.

The crowds were getting noisier now, more boisterous, as the children and old people went home and alcohol took its effect. Fireworks filled the sky as the evening reached its climax. And it began to dawn on me that Max wasn't going to come. I decided to wait till 10:30, then gently steer Davinia to Good Friends to get a lift back with her parents.

I couldn't bear to think about what would happen after that. Davinia *rejected*? It *really* didn't bear thinking about.

Then, suddenly—at 10:20—her phone went off. Frenziedly, she scooped it out of her bag. Her face split in a grin as she answered it, like someone had injected her with a happy drug. She was suddenly all energy and animation, squealing "*Yes*," she'd be at the Tribune bar, "*yes*," she'd get the drinks in . . . then she cooed, "*good-byeeee*," and straightaway phoned Cassie. "We've hooked up with Max, OK?" she squawked. "Just wanted to let you know!" Then she turned to me, face positively glowing. "Come on! He'll be here in a minute— let's get a bottle in!" And set off across to the Tribune.

I followed in her incandescent wake, muttering, "I bet he'll be really fed up when he sees I'm here."

"Oh, *Chloe*! Don't be *stupid*! I told you—he's not like that! Anyway—the festa's practically over. We can drop you off at the flat and you can cover for me with Mummy and Daddy."

*Great.* Party *on.*

We'd barely sat down at a tiny table on the pavement when Max strolled up, twirling his car keys, grinning supersexily at Davinia and ignoring me. "Yo, gorgeous!" he called, and she kind of *sprang* at him, nearly knocking the bloody table over—I only just saved the wine. They snogged heatedly for about ten minutes, then they sat down next to me. In between kisses, Max had got stuck into his tale of woe about stopping Pandora from topping herself—Davinia was lapping it up, saying, "Poor Maxy baby!" and "You're too *nice*!" and stroking his face.

While I made serious inroads into the bottle of wine. When Max discovered it was empty, he stood up, pulling Davinia with him, saying, "Come on, sexy. . . . Let's go to that *beach* I was telling you about. That *deserted beach*."

"You're on." Davinia giggled.

"OK to drop me off first?" I asked stiffly.

"No, *sorry*!" said Max, smiling happily. "The car's a two-seater—only room for me and the ol' girl!"

My stomach seized with panic, while Davinia squawked, "Don't you *dare* call me an old girl!" and batted at his chest, all turned on by his rudeness.

"Sorry, my angel. My *queen*," he said. Davinia gurgled lecherously and took his arm.

For a moment I really thought they were just going to walk away and leave me there.

"Hang *on*!" I wailed. "What do I do? What—"

"Oh, *Chloe*," snapped Davinia, "Mummy'll give you a lift! You remember where Good Friends is, don't you?"

"What? *No!*"

"Yes, you do! It's that way—then left onto the main square. You'll be there by eleven, if you run."

"But, *Davinia*—"

"Don't stand there dithering! *RUN!*"

*Why* did I run? Why didn't I *insist* Max gave me a lift, even if it meant leaving precious Davinia on her own for a bit? Why didn't I grab taxi money off them?

I don't know, but I didn't. I *ran*.

I took two wrong turnings, I scooted through the middle of a crowd of drunk lads who tried to grab me, then I nearly bashed into a priest as, still running, I checked my watch. Only five to eleven—*Calm down, Chloe!* It was going to be OK—

I could see the spindly towered church ahead of me. And anyway, Paul and Cassie wouldn't leave on the dot, would they?

I shot across the main square, weaving my way through all the people, and ran into the Good Friends. Three drunk men lounging at a table by the door cheered when I ran in, called to me to join them. I skirted by a tired-looking woman sweeping up broken glass and went into the dark recess at the back of the bar. I could hardly bear what my eyes told me. A young couple all meshed up together across a table; an old man asleep with his head tipped back against the wall. And no one else.

I scurried back to the sweeping woman. "Is there an upstairs here?" I squeaked. "A down-stairs?"

She shook her head. "Closing soon," she said. "Closing soon."

CHAPTER

34

I COULDN'T ADMIT IT TO myself, I couldn't admit the evidence of my own eyes—that Cassie and Paul weren't there. I kept looking at my watch as if the fact that it was only just on eleven would suddenly magic them both right there in front of me. Then, spotting the little WC sign, I raced over and wrenched open the door on a tiny, smelly cubicle. Did I really think they'd both be crammed in there together?

It was hopeless. They'd gone. Probably as soon as they got Davinia's phone call.

"Closing now," said the sweeping woman, not meeting my eyes. She didn't care what had happened to me, who I was looking for, she just wanted me out of her bar. The three drunk men were lurching to their feet—one of them took hold of my arm and as I wrenched myself away he slurred, "Heeyy . . . easy! We know another bar—you come with us. . . ."

I ran out into the street. It hit me that the crowd in the square was ninety percent male, ninety percent drunk, and they were all milling about like they didn't want the party to end, like they hadn't had enough action yet. I suddenly felt really scared. I was miles away from the apartment. . . . The buses would have stopped running. . . . I didn't have the money for a taxi. . . . A group of local boys were shouting at me to come over and join them. They probably thought all tourists were absolute sluts. I was out on my own late at night, I had to be an absolute slut. They started to walk toward me and I fled. Not too far, though. I had it in my mind that I should stay in the square, stay near people, to keep safe. . . . I scurried over to a shuttered ice-cream stall, pulled my mobile from my pocket, and called Davinia. Part of my brain knew this was hopeless—she'd be writhing about on the deserted beach with Max by now— but I had to try.

She didn't answer, of course. I left a semi-hysterical message about calling as soon as she possibly could because I was *stranded* and rang off. *OK, think,* Chloe, *think!* I needed to find a proper taxi rank, not just pick up a cab on a road that could be driven by a rapist. And then when I got back to the flat I'd tell him to wait and I'd bloody well wake Cassie and Paul up, I'd *lean* on the bell till they woke up. . . .

Suppose they hadn't gone straight home, though. Suppose they'd gone on somewhere else. . . . I didn't have their mobile numbers, of course. It was just *assumed* I'd always be with Davinia and wouldn't need it. Like it was *assumed* I'd be with her tonight. Even though I'd said I might need a lift back with them. . . .

A great wave of self-pity washed over me, and my throat filled up with tears. I'd slipped through the net, hadn't I—I was just so *small* and unimportant that I'd dropped right through Cassie and Paul's net. They hadn't given me a thought. They'd have waited in Good Friends till the sun came up for their daughter, but *me*? I was off their radar screen. And Davinia—it wouldn't occur to her to call to check if I was safe. Even after she finished screwing Max and was lounging on the sand all ecstatic, it wouldn't occur to her. Maybe they'd all remember me in the morning when they saw my bed hadn't been slept in, just minutes before the local police turned up to ask if they could come and identify my body. . . .

I started to shake. I could feel my legs tremble and my right hand kept kind of *jumping*; it was horrible. *Stop it, Chloe, pull yourself together!* I spotted a middle-aged couple walking along with two young teenage boys, and made a beeline for them. I dived in front of the woman and blurted out, "Is there a taxi rank near here, please?" The woman glared at me as though I'd offered to shag both her sons for a tenner, barked out, *"Taxis finished!"* and walked on. Three boys were calling out to me from across the square, heading toward me. *Jesus*, this was getting worse every minute. Heart hammering, I scurried away from them. I had to leave the square, I'd *run*, that's what I'd do, I'd run down the side streets and find a policeman or a bar with a light on still, they'd have to take me in, they'd have to help me, wouldn't they?

I set off running, and a man shouted at me and I ran faster, it was crazy, what did I think I was going to do, run till I dropped? And then I heard motorbikes behind me—oh, *great*, now some mad biker gang was after me—I speeded up and a bike growled to a halt just ahead of me and this dark, helmeted head turned to me and said, "You all right? What you running from?"

CHAPTER
35

THE BIKER PULLED HIS helmet off. It was Frazer. Relief flooded into me. Why, though? Why was I relieved when he hated me? 'What's up, is someone after you?" he said.

I was taking in great gulps of air, trying to answer. The second bike wheeled forward and stopped, and the biker pulled his helmet off.

*Alex!* While my blood was chanting *Alex! Alex! ALEX!!!* my brain was thinking. *They'll never help me, they hate me, they'll laugh at the state I'm in. . . .*

"Where's your bitchy friend?" Alex said.

"She's . . . she's on a beach," I muttered.

"And you came here on your own?" asked Frazer.

"I missed my lift back. I was meant to meet her parents in a bar, but they'd gone when I got there."

"What d'you mean they'd *gone* when you *got* there?" repeated Alex. God, but his face was fantastic. I loved the way his mouth moved, when he spoke. "They just up and left you?"

"Well, I'm not sure they knew I was coming...," I said, and then—*Christ!*—I started crying. I really didn't mean to. It was the relief of being with them, even if they were going to laugh and ride off, and it was the awfulness of the last half hour, finding the bar empty, and not knowing what the hell I was going to do. . . .

"Bloody hell, don't start that," said Frazer. "Hey—you're OK. I'll give you a lift back."

"Why should you?" I hiccupped. "After Davinia threw a drink at you and messed things up with those women you were after and—"

"Don't remind me or I might change my mind. Where you staying?"

"It's a block of flats called Belvedere Mansions," I said. "It's kind of up above the harbor. Are you really gonna give me a lift back? I'd be so grateful, I don't even have cab money. . . ."

"Well, we're not going to leave you here on your own, are we?"

"I'll take her," said Alex grudgingly. "My bike's bigger."

"*What?* No, it isn't, mate. It's . . . OK, you take her."

What had passed between them? I didn't see

anything—I just knew that, fast as a snake strike, Alex had changed Frazer's mind.

I just knew that I was going on Alex's bike.

For some reason, he wanted to take me.

Two minutes later I had my arms round his waist and my face pressed up against his back, and I was feeling every muscle move as he maneuvered the bike out onto the coast road. *Careful, careful, careful,* I chanted to myself. Remember how arrogant he was on the plane, remember he hates you, remember what he's like, pulling that cradlesnatcher, pulling anyone he can get his hands on, probably. Don't get blown away by his face. Or his body. *Careful.*

Ten minutes later, we were roaring through the gates of the Belvedere Mansions. As soon as I'd got off the bike, he did too. "So let's see you in safe," he said gruffly, walking ahead of me to the large entrance doors.

"I'll have to ring the buzzer. God, I hope they're in."

"How come you don't have a key?"

"Well—Davinia's got one."

"Not much use if she doesn't stick with you, is it?"

"No."

"So she went off with some guy, did she?"

"Yes. He's called Max and he's a sleazy, lying . . . *shit*."

"They're a good match, then."

I laughed, and he said, "So which is your bell?"

"God, I don't think I can do this. Wake them up, I mean."

"*What?!* They abandon you on your own in town at midnight, and you feel bad about waking them up?"

I smiled and pushed the buzzer. Alex put his thumb on top of my finger, and pressed it down hard, keeping it pressed down. I stared at the side of his face as he glared at the intercom. "They're not answering, are they?" he said.

"They're out," I muttered. "Or asleep."

He pressed the buzzer again, so hard it made me jump. "They're really not there," I said.

"OK, so what are you gonna do now? Sleep in the doorway?"

"I climbed out the bedroom window once, to get out. . . . It's a bit high up, but maybe . . ."

"To get *out*? Why didn't you just walk out the door?"

"They Chubb-locked it. For safety."

"Bloody hell. This gets better. Suppose there'd been a fire?"

I hadn't thought of that. It didn't seem to

matter anymore, though. Nothing mattered but the fact that I was standing right up close to him, and he seemed very energized by Davinia's parents' treatment of me.

"OK, show me," he said. "Show me the window, yeah?"

We set off round the side of the building. It was pitch-black except where splashes of light came through windows where people were still awake.

Could he feel the energy coming off me? Could he feel every bit of me kind of . . . *craning* toward him? It was so powerful in me, how could he miss it? And yet he seemed cut off and focused on the ground ahead of him. He still hated me, that was it. What was it he'd said at Hilly's? That he'd sooner roast his goolies on a barbecue than have anything to do with either me or Davinia. You couldn't accuse him of not putting things plain, could you? He was just the type of guy who'd help someone who was in trouble, even if he hated you.

We reached the back of the apartment block. "There," I said, pointing. "I jumped onto that table. . . . It's really strong."

"And you don't think the window's locked?"

"We never lock it. We're s'posed to, but we forget."

"Right," he said, then—just like when he'd

dived off the rocks—he made a kind of lunging run at the bottom balcony, sprang up, and got a grip on the top of the railings. Then he heaved himself over. "Come on," he called, beckoning.

There was no way I could reach the bar at the top, like he'd done. I stretched up as far as I could and he reached down and took hold of my hands, then before I could worry about being too heavy for him to lift, he'd hauled and I'd scrambled, up, up, and over.

"Athletic!" he said admiringly. "All that swimming you do."

There was a kind of thump between us. *He knew I swam a lot?* "OK," he said hurriedly, "we just repeat that performance, from the table." He hopped up on it, and I followed him, and then he was over the rails of our balcony, hauling me up after him again, and I pulled back the sliding door and we clambered over the sill.

And then we were standing face-to-face in the dark bedroom.

"So," he said, "are you just gonna let them get away with this?"

"What d'you mean?"

"They've treated you like shit. Like you don't count. Are you just going to let them get away with it?"

Suddenly the front door banged, and I heard Cassie's voice, calling out something about "checking their room," and I gasped. "It's them! Maybe you should go! I don't want them to—"

I was going to say I didn't want them to give him a hard time, but he was off before I finished my sentence. He just grinned at me, all kind of knowing and sneering, then he jumped out of the window, and I heard the bang on the table just as Cassie came though the door.

"What are you doing standing here in the dark?" she said.

"I just climbed in. Through the window."

"Where's Davinia?"

"With Max."

"Her phone's off. I keep calling her."

"I know it's off. I tried to call her when I missed you at Good Friends."

"What? Weren't you *with* her?"

"I would've been in the way."

"Honestly, you *girls*—so she went off with Max?"

"Yes. In his little two-seater. There wasn't *room* for me."

Cassie glared at me like it was my fault her daughter was such a cow, then she turned on her heel and left, calling out, "Let me know if she calls you, OK?"

I didn't answer. I stood there letting it sink in that Cassie clearly didn't give a tuppenny shit about me—not even enough to ask how I'd got back—and realized I didn't care. Not anymore.

I went over to the window, climbed out onto the narrow balcony again, and rested my arms on the railing. It was pitch-black below, but I could hear the wild creepers stirring in the warm breeze, and the sound of the cicadas.

And then I heard the sound of a motorbike starting up and roaring away.

## CHAPTER 36

I SUPPOSE IT WAS about dawn when Davinia landed on the end of my bed, because there was a pale, bleak light all around her. "Did you cover for me?" she hissed.

"What d'you mean?"

"I dunno . . . tell them I was in the bathroom, put a bolster in my bed . . ."

"A *bolster*? For Christ's sake, *bolsters* only exist in school stories—"

"Chloe, *shut up*! Do they think I'm *here*?"

*"I've no sodding idea!"*

"I *thought* I heard the door go!" Paul strode into our room, barefoot in a dark paisley silk dressing gown. "Davinia, do you have any *idea* how worried your mother has been?"

Davinia shrugged sulkily. "Yeah? How come she's not standing next to you then?"

"Because two hours ago, I forced two of her

275

sleeping tablets down her throat! Why did you have your phone off?"

*Because she didn't want to be interrupted shagging,* I thought. Davinia shrugged again, even more sulkily, and said, "The battery went flat."

"That's no excuse," Paul said furiously. "You behaved with complete *selfishness*, Davinia. You *contact us* if you want to stay out beyond the agreed time. Your mother's too bloody soft on you. She gives you too much rope, and you *hang* yourself. I would have insisted you came to the Good Friends, to get a lift back with us."

"I phoned to say I'd met Max, didn't I?" Davinia pouted.

"At ten thirty! It's now four fifty! That's more than six hours unaccounted for!" I got the feeling Paul was loving this, throwing restraint to the winds at last and having a real go at his daughter. "If you want to go back to having curfews and being grounded, you're going exactly the right way about it—"

"*Paul!* Paul—why didn't you *wake* me!" Cassie flew across the room and threw her arms round Davinia. "Are you OK, baby?"

"Yes. I'm *sorry*, Mummy. . . . My battery went flat. . . ."

"So long as you're safe," she slurred, voice still

fogged up by the sleeping pills. "God, I've been so *worried*!"

Davinia didn't exactly stick two fingers up at her dad behind her mum's head, but by her triumphant look she might just as well have done. "Oh, you shouldn't have worried," she soothed. "Max is great. He didn't drink and he drove me all the way home and saw me in. . . ."

"Davinia, that is not the point!" snapped Paul.

"She's home now," said Cassie.

"Cassie, have you *quite forgotten* the state you were in last night?"

"Mummy, I'm *sorry*," said Davinia. Cassie hugged her again and Davinia smirked. She was playing her parents like the experienced little brain-manipulator she was.

"Look, the whole thing was a cock-up best forgotten," said Cassie. "The way you two girls split up and everything. I know Chloe didn't want to team up with Ollie, but"—(Oh, *what*!? This was suddenly all going to be *my* fault?!)—"I'd feel so much safer if you were all in a foursome. . . ."

"Well, I'm *really sorry*," I hissed, "but I'm not going out with someone who makes me want to *throw up* just so you can feel Davinia's got a keeper!"

Three pairs of eyes turned on me in disgust,

like I'd suddenly let rip with a gigantic fart. Well, I'd started now. Something in me wasn't going to let me stop.

"*Davinia* just drove off with Max in his little two-seater leaving me on the street," I raved, "and you two cleared off from Good Friends well before eleven! I was stranded! No money—Davinia had it all! How d'you think I got home?!"

"Excuse *me*!" said Paul, enormously offended. "We didn't need to wait, Davinia phoned us. . . ."

"About *her*! Not about me, about *her*!"

"Well, really, Chloe," said Cassie icily, "you're seventeen—we didn't bring you on holiday to have to look *after* you—"

I was exhausted. My dreams had been full of Alex, riding away from me. And I'd just been yanked out of a deep sleep by Davinia.

I shrieked, "*FUCK YOU!*" and burrowed under the sheet.

There was a booming silence. Then I heard three pairs of feet troop from the bedroom, and close the door behind them.

SEVEN THIRTY THE NEXT morning saw me climbing over our balcony and dropping onto the table below again. It was getting to be a real habit.

After screaming *Fuck you!* at my hosts, I'd escaped back to a nasty, anxious sleep. Then woken an hour or so later, heart thudding with panic. The hump in the other bed told me Davinia had come back in and was sleeping. So they obviously all thought I wasn't quite certifiable, liable to throttle her while she slept or anything.

I sat up in bed. "You're going to have to face them," I told myself. "Be calm and reasonable. Tell them you need your own set of keys to the flat, so you don't have to keep hurling yourself out of the window. Tell them you're going to start working at Hilly's. Tell them you want as little as possible to do with Davinia until you fly home."

Oh, right. There was no way I was going to

even begin to tell them that. I couldn't bear the thought of looking at any one of them again.

I crept out of bed and started grabbing some of my more useful, general clothes, and my makeup and stuff, and shoving it in a backpack. I went for speed over quietness, relying on Davinia being too literally shagged out to wake and challenge me. I was shaking with the need to get away; I felt like my head might explode and shatter in rage if any of them tried to speak to me ever again. It crossed my mind that maybe I was having a kind of break-down.

I had a plan in my mind, a sort of plan. I was going to go and throw myself on Cora's mercy, beg for a place to stay—under a counter, in a closet, anywhere—and tell her I'd work for my keep. Then I'd somehow get my flight brought forward, no matter how much it cost.

Just so long as I wouldn't have to see any of them ever again.

I felt better once I was hurrying along the road toward the harbor. A fig tree was leaning over the dry stone wall, laden with fat purple figs. I stood there and pulled off four, one after the other, peeled back the dusty skins, and ate the centers that looked like a mass of worms but tasted sweet and nourishing. The air was fresh, the sun bright and starting to get hot. The ferry had just left, I could see it churning its way toward the horizon; crates of fresh produce were piled on the quayside ready for the restaurants to pick up. It wasn't until I got within sight of Hilly's forbidding, black door with its big brass knocker that the doubt crashed in.

It *was* Thursday today, wasn't it? And Cora *had* said they'd started opening for lunch on Wednesdays—hadn't she? Oh, God, I couldn't remember. Maybe it was Wednesday and Thursday they were *shut*. . . .

I checked my watch, saw it was 7:50. I looked up; Hilly's black door stared blankly back at me. I decided I'd knock at 8:00. I knew I'd only made that decision to put off the awful moment when I'd discover that no one was in, but it comforted me to have a plan.

Eight o'clock arrived. The Caminos bells tolled out the hour ominously with their cracked, gothic notes. I walked over to Hilly's and knocked. No answer. I knocked again, more loudly. Still no answer.

I had about three pounds in my purse and very little more in my bank account. Suppose I had to rent a room for tonight? Suppose I starved?

I wandered back to the harbor edge, and stood

looking down at the water. A dead fish kept butting up against the concrete wall, and slopping away again, in a kind of hopeless repetition. I kept looking from the fish back to Hilly's door, but it stayed shut. I had absolutely no idea what to do. All I could think of was phoning Dad, wailing, *Help!* and getting him to transfer money to my account, but it felt like such a failure, running to him like that. I shot another desperate look at Hilly's door.

This time, it was ajar, and a tiny black car with its boot open was parked right up near it.

Hope pulsed into me. The door suddenly burst wide open and Zara hurried out. She picked up a box of tomatoes and squashes from the boot and slammed it shut.

I hesitated—then I *ran*. I got to the door just as she'd closed it and hammered the big brass knocker down.

The door sprang bad-temperedly open again. "Yes?" she barked.

"Zara—hi! It's me, it's . . . Chloe," I stuttered. "Did Cora mention that I might . . . that . . . that she'd offered me a job?"

Zara screwed her face up, shook her head. Then said, "Hang on, yes—waitressing?"

"Yes."

"We won't need any waitresses if we don't get the food cooked!"

"Sorry," I mumbled, "you're busy. . . ."

"I'll say I'm bloody busy! Can you iron?"

"What?"

"IRON! Can you bloody IRON? You know, hot thing, gets creases out . . ."

"Yes! Yes, of course I can!"

"Now?"

"Iron now? Yes! Yes, of course!"

"Brilliant. You're the first thing that's gone right since last night. Come in. Slam the door shut behind you."

So I stepped over the threshold, slammed the door, and followed Zara's military little form down the long, plain, brick corridor to the central courtyard. It looked so different in the day, with the sun coming in at an angle and striking one side of the high walls.

"Sorry I was so short with you," she said, dumping down her box on one of the black tables nearest to us. "Our wonderful cook's let us down. She's great, but she has these *crises* all the time. So Cora and I are doing the food. And Cora isn't bloody here yet. I'll kill her, I swear I will."

"I could help," I said. "I mean . . . chopping and stuff . . ."

"First things first. Let's shift these tables. Saul said he'd come in early, but I'm not holding my breath. Then you can put the cloths straight on."

Together, we shifted all twelve black tables from around the edges and arranged them evenly in the center. They were heavy—I was sweating by the time I'd finished—but I kept my end up with Zara, who grinned at me approvingly. "There!" she said as we put the last one down. "Now. Follow me."

We went back along the brick corridor and she threw open a door next to the Ladies'. Inside was a nice little square cell with a high, barred window. Stripes of sun lit up wide shelves on the far wall, all of them weighed down with piles of plates and boxes of glasses. An ironing board was set up in the center on the washed stone floor; two great baskets of heaped white linen stood beside it, steaming slightly.

"Tablecloths and napkins," said Zara. "Cora insists we have proper linen and she also insists we wash and line-dry them ourselves. Except they're not exactly dry yet."

I picked up a corner of cloth. "They'll be fine to iron," I said.

"That's what *she* said. She said iron them and put them over the tables to dry. Dunno what you'll do with the napkins, though. . . ."

"I can put them over the chair backs, one to each," I said. "Then fold them when they're dry."

Zara beamed. "Initiative," she said. "Like it. Coffee?"

"I'd *love* some," I said fervently.

Zara narrowed her eyes at me. "And some breakfast," she said. "I'll do you a roll. You look bushwhacked, sweetheart."

"I am, a bit. Zara, if—if Davinia or her parents turn up, could you not tell them I'm here? I mean, they almost certainly won't, but—"

"If they almost certainly won't, let's not worry about 'em. I'll shout you when the coffee's ready." And she marched off.

Maybe it was because I was strung out with emotional exhaustion, but as I picked the first tablecloth from the basket and started ironing I felt kind of at peace, floated away from the chaos of the world. A bit like a nun, in fact. Did nuns iron? They'd have to, wouldn't they, or they'd have wrinkly wimples? The creases fell satisfyingly away under the steaming iron, and the white cloth shone in the sunlight, and I imagined living the life of a nun, safe and contained and never troubled by rows with ex-friends and their parents or desire about boys like Alex. . . .

When I'd finished the tablecloth, I picked it up by its corners and headed back to the courtyard. There, I shook it out and let it fall evenly across one of the black tables. "Chlo-*eeee*! Coff-*eeeee*!" *Perfect timing*, I thought, heading in the direction of Zara's shout, round behind the bar and through a door into a big kitchen that can't have changed much since the place was a convent—white-washed walls, a big scrubbed table, and huge old cooking range in the corner.

"There," said Zara, nodding toward a tall mug and a plate with a wonderful, large ham-filled roll on it. "Get that down you."

The coffee was milky, not too hot. I drank it greedily, and munched the roll, and Zara said, "Listen, Chloe—not my business, but if you've run out on Davinia and her folks you need to at least tell them you're safe."

"Yes, but—"

"Look—something's obviously happened. Talk to Cora about it, she's the touchy-feely one. She'll be here soon. She'd bloody better be."

I was glad to get back to my cell, back to rhythmic working and not-thinking. I ironed steadily, taking the cloths in one by one to the courtyard, and one by one the black tables turned white, and then chair after chair, four at a time, had a napkin airing on its back.

I was laying out the last-but-eight napkins when Cora swam into the courtyard. "Chloe!" she sang. "My angel! Oh—this looks wonderful! Oh—perfect—I told Zara they'd dry beautifully in place, but she . . . *Zara!* Sweetness!"

The two women hugged each other, and kissed on the mouth, and Zara said, "If you'd been five minutes later you'd be a corpse by now, babes! Anyway—your little protégé has saved our bacon. She's been on the official payroll since eight thirty this morning. Everything's been delivered—I've washed the salad, I've made the coleslaw and the guacamole. Have you got the savory flans?"

"Fabulous, perfect flans."

"Then lunch is *on.*"

"Fan-tastic!" crowed Cora, and suddenly it *was* fantastic, and I was all infected by their enthusiasm, wanting to help. "What can I do?" I said. "After I've finished these."

"You can lay the tables, my darling," Cora said. "But—why are you here so early? Has something happened? Has—"

"Cora—later," said Zara firmly. "After the last customer has gone. When you've laid the tables, Chloe, we find you a waitress costume. Now— back to work!"

## CHAPTER 38

**SEVEN HOURS LATER,** I was slumped across the great kitchen table wearing a swishy white apron and my rust-colored shift dress that I'd pulled from my rucksack, spooning coleslaw into my mouth, feeling a) absolutely knackered, and b) really proud of myself. It was a great combination.

Hilly's was closed now until the evening. Zara had gone back home with the tablecloths to wash—she was going to *collapse*, she said, before the evening shift started. Saul was in the court-yard, moving the tables back all on his own. "He loves to be macho," Cora had purred, when I offered to help. "Leave him be."

The two huge dishwashers were rumbling away; the kitchen was tidy. It was 3:30 and I'd worked flat-out since 8:30. As soon as I'd laid the tables, I'd made an enormous fantastic fresh fruit salad in a great glass bowl. Then I'd got ready (Cora had French-plaited my hair for me, and told me I looked gorgeous) just in time for the first customers to arrive (with Saul) around midday. They'd been totally seduced by Cora's tale of woe about the missing cook and her promise of simple, fresh food; they filled three of the tables. Saul had taken charge of the drinks; Zara manned the kitchen; Cora and I did everything else between us.

It was like a dance; it worked. As the sun climbed higher in the sky and the courtyard grew too hot, Saul turned a large iron handle on the side wall and a great, tentlike blind cranked across the top, creating lovely shade. More and more customers came; soon, all the tables had been filled and we were on to a second sitting. The courtyard looked like a mad checkerboard as used tablecloths were whisked off and I laid fresh places on the black wood. The food kept coming. Saul helped clear. The last (rather drunk and very cheerful) guests left.

And now Cora was sitting down opposite me, pouring me a large glass of white wine. "Some of our *best*," she said. "Somebody left a whole half a bottle—can you *imagine*?"

I took a sip. It tasted like heaven. "And now, my darling," she murmured, "tell me *all* about it."

* * *

Cora was so unbelievably generous with her time. She must have been dying to get her head down too, like Zara, but she listened as I wailed on about what had happened to me the night of the festa, and why I'd escaped at first light this morning. She was particularly interested in the fact that the same boy she'd rescued from the cradle-snatcher in her bar was the boy who'd given me a lift home. "*Verrry* good looking," she said. "But more than that . . . he had integrity."

"*Integrity!?*"

"He saw you home, didn't he? Although that was also because he likes you. I could tell, the particular way he shouted at you. I'm glad I offended that dreadful woman. Next year, she could be going after my son."

I gawped at her. "Your *son*?"

"Yes. He's fourteen. At the moment he's with his *father*." She said "father" the way you might say "Satan"—kind of awed by the darkness of the word. "Zara has a fourteen-year-old son too. It's how we met." Then she laughed her gorgeous, mellow, heard-it-all laugh. "Hey—don't look so amazed, Chloe! The world really isn't all simple and neat, you know! More wine?"

I pushed my glass toward her again. "This is going to knock me out," I mumbled. "I'm soooo tired. God, what am I going to do? I *can't* go back to the flat. . . ."

"No, you can't. And you mustn't. But you must tell them where you are, and that you're safe." She looked at me warmly. "You can sleep here. I can't ask you back with me and Zara, we share a house with two other ladies and they would object. But I'll make you up a good bed in one of the storerooms. You can make yourself a little nest, a *lair*. You can be like a nun on a retreat. You won't be bothered. I'll ban Davinia and her parents from the bar."

My eyes whanged open like a doll's. "You can't do that!"

"It's my bar. I can do what I want. Your peace of mind comes first. Follow me."

So I did.

It was the "second" storeroom, and it was basically full of junk, so no one needed to come into it but me, apart from when the rubbish was carried through to be dumped in the yard. "*Clean* rubbish, though, darling," said Cora, flinging open the wide wooden door to the yard and letting the sun stream in. "Just bottles for recycling and boxes and stuff. Saul takes the waste food for his uncle's pigs."

Then with a flourish, she pulled a dust sheet

off a huge old brown leather sofa. "Here's your bed," she said. "I'll bring you sheets and a pillow from my house."

"Cora, this is perfect," I said. "Thank you so much."

"Oh, it's nothing, darling. But you can improve it. Hang up some drapes. Make it *yours*." Together we cleared a space round the sofa, and she found me a little table I could use and a lamp that worked. She even sorted me out a shower.

It was outside, but then as she said, the richest people in California showered outside. Basically it was a hose attached to a tap in the yard, but she promised me I wouldn't be spied on. Laughing, she dragged two straggly-looking little trees in big blue pots (throw outs, like the sofa, from the bar lobby) over to the hose and arranged them like a screen. "They'll hide your naughty bits," she said. "And now—I must go. You must rest. I'll leave your wages for today on your new bed."

I kind of threw myself at her and we hugged, then she left. I stood for a moment, looking round the tiny yard. The high whitewashed walls glared in the hot sun, reflecting white light on the terra-cotta brick floor, baked hard. The two great white gates were bolted on the inside. Cora was right; it wasn't exposed, not at all. I was longing for a shower, I hadn't washed since before the festa and that felt like . . . God, *years* ago. So much had happened since.

I went back into the storeroom. Several bank notes lay on the sofa, weighed down by an enormous black key. I picked it up. It was the key to the main entrance of Hilly's, it had to be. And Cora had just . . . *left* it for me.

So I could come and go.

So I'd be free.

I PULLED OUT MY mobile phone. I couldn't phone Davinia's parents; I didn't have their number. But I could phone her.

Two texts were waiting for me, both from Davinia.

WHERE THE FUCK ARE YOU????

and

CALL URGENTLY!!! PLEASE!!!

I took in a deep breath and dialed. It went straight to voice mail.

"Davinia, it's me," I said, my voice all flat and expressionless. "I'm sorry I didn't call earlier. I'm OK—I'm staying with Cora, she's given me a job." I took in another breath, wondering what to say— I knew I couldn't say I was sorry. "Tell your parents I'm OK," I barked, and rang off.

I felt brilliant once I'd done that, like a weight had lifted. I counted my pay—it was a fair rate, no more, no less, and it meant I was solvent again. I stowed it and the key in my bag, got clean shorts, underwear, and a T-shirt out of my backpack, then I stripped off all my clothes, picked up my wash bag, and walked naked out to the heat of the yard.

It was wonderful, showering under the hose. The water was warm for at least three minutes from lying in the water pipe in the sun, and I got my hair washed—then I finished off with icy cold. Hot sun, cold water, just like the beach. I sprayed water at the two thirsty potted trees, rinsing the dust from their leaves, and their earth drank it up.

I had no towel to dry with so I just stood there, dripping, as the sun dried me, then I went inside again.

I knew I should sleep, so I'd be OK for the evening shift, but I was too excited, too restless. I'd been at my lowest and most scared, and now life was turning toward me again. So I got dressed, picked up my bag, and walked back through the courtyard down the long brick corridor to the big black door.

I tried it—it was locked, just like the door at the apartment had been locked. But this time I had the key to it.

* * *

I walked and walked, well into the late afternoon, all along the coast road. I reached a kind of rocky outcrop and climbed, higher and higher, until I found myself on a stark, flat, circular rock platform. The huge glowing sun hung right in front of me. It was extraordinary, it was like something out of a sci-fi film—just these two disks, the rock, stuck out into space, and the sun, hanging there, and a great dome of blue sky, and me. It was like theatre, it was like being on a stage, but there was no one there to see me.

My eyes were half shut against the sun, and it glowed on my face. Slowly I sank down onto the rock and sat cross legged. The rock was hot, but not too hot. All I had to do was be. It felt like there was no room in this dramatic place for anything else.

Then I felt this welling inside me, and I knew I was letting go. All the tension and the trying-to-be-liked and hope and fear about Davinia—I was letting go of all of it. And then I was filled with feeling about Mum. It wasn't anger or misery or anguish, not anymore. The only word I could give it was grief, pure grief. It welled up inside me like water, and I felt like I had to slow my breathing, like when you see videos of women giving birth, so

I breathed slow and intentional, and then the tears came, streaming out of my eyes, but I was hardly making a sound.

I sat there cross-legged like some kind of mystic on this holy rock, just letting the grief pour out of me.

## CHAPTER 40

YOU'D THINK I'D BE wasted after an experience like that, wouldn't you? You'd think I'd be drained and exhausted, no use to anyone. But it wasn't like that at all. I reported for work in the bar at seven o'clock sharp, in a short, flared skirt and low-cut top and a fantastic necklace Cora loaned me, and I felt kind of empty and *free* and wonderful.

I didn't have to work too hard either. Cora told me to *circulate* and that's what I did. Filling little dishes on the bar with mixed nuts, clearing empty glasses, taking orders for drinks, and checking on the Ladies' every hour or so to give the basins a wipe and put in more loo paper. It was a doddle, it was fun. For the first few hours I was a bit on edge in case Davinia and her parents burst in, demanding to know what I was playing at, but as it got later I relaxed. I chatted and flirted and enjoyed the buzz and the music.

"Don't exhaust yourself, angel," said Cora, floating languidly by me, like seaweed. "We need you on laundry duty tomorrow."

"I won't," I said. "And Cora—thank you so much for letting me have a key."

"Well, of course you must have a key!" she said. "We have about a *hundred* of them! I suppose all the nuns handed them in, when the convent closed."

I got to bed about one in the morning. Cora had already put a pillow and sheets on the sofa. It felt a bit scary, knowing Cora and Zara were locking up, leaving me here alone. I bolted the door to the yard; air came in still, through a glassless, barred window high above the door, but it felt a bit stuffy in the room.

There was no bolt on the inside door. It made me feel scared to do it, but I shoved a pile of crates in front of the door. At least I'd wake up if someone pushed their way in. And there was no way I was schlepping all the way along to the Ladies' in the dark either. I'd already found a large, ceramic bowl in amongst the junk that I was going to use as a potty in the middle of the night if I needed to. I'd tip it out in the yard drain in the morning.

Now I just had to get to sleep.

I lay there on the wide sofa in the pitch black,

listening to all the night noises, mentally running through all the doors and windows to the place, telling myself Cora would have securely locked every one.

Then I thought about ghosts. Ghosts of nuns. The shapes at the corners of the storeroom looked really creepy.

Then I fell sound asleep.

I was up and in the kitchen with the kettle on by the time Zara arrived with her baskets of almost-dry tablecloths. We had breakfast together, then I got straight to work.

I knew I was kind of on hold, suspended, as I ironed away, but for now, it was what I wanted. I had no plans to phone Dad to tell him what had happened—I didn't see the need to, not yet.

I hadn't heard back from Davinia. I needed to get the rest of my stuff from the flat sometime—and I needed to change my flight if I didn't want to sit next to her on the plane. But that was all for later.

I still had the grief inside me about Mum. And the longing about Alex. But it was on hold too, and it was OK.

After the lunchtime session was over, Zara asked me if I wanted to go to the sea for a swim, and we got into her tiny black car and headed for a thin, rocky beach I'd never been to before. We didn't talk a lot, just headed into the waves and swam, then got back in the hot car all salty and wet. Back at Hilly's, I slooshed off in the hot yard, then lay drying, drifting off to sleep, on the crisp white sheet.

After an hour or so, I woke. I was making a clearing for myself in the storeroom, gradually shifting and tidying the junk. I had somewhere to hang clothes now too, all along the rail of an old bookcase, on hangers Cora gave me. It was starting to feel like home.

It went on like this for two more days. Sleeping, ironing, waitressing, swimming, showering in the yard, circulating in the bar. Without really discussing it, Cora promoted me to full-time work, as though she knew I needed it. For more reasons than the money, I mean. I wasn't looking forward to Monday, when there'd be no more lunches to do. The space of it alarmed me.

Then, on Sunday night, once again . . . Alex and Frazer turned up.

It was so completely what I'd been hoping for, it froze me. I came back from checking the Ladies' to see them standing at the bar. Alex was saying something heatedly to Frazer and his face was in profile; just the sight of his nose, his chin, had this calamitous effect on me. I prowled about the tables in a hopeless kind of way for a while, collecting glasses, then told myself I had to go over and speak to him and thank him for rescuing me after the festa. It wouldn't look like I fancied him if I did—it would look so weird if I *didn't* that *that* would look like I fancied him, because why would I avoid him unless I fancied him?

Oh, shut *up*, Chloe. Just fucking do it.

With three glasses in each hand, I made my way up, sidled in next to Alex, and pushed the glasses across the bar.

"Hello," Alex said, "what you doing that for, you got a job here or something?"

"Yes," I said, and I made myself turn to face him and it was like facing this blowtorch, it was too much, I had to look away again, and to make up for doing that, I started gabbling like an idiot. "I've completely run out of cash, I had to get a job, and I just met Cora in Victoria one day, and she offered me a job, I do clearing up and . . . and ironing . . ." Shit, Chloe. *Scintillating.* In desperation I gabbled on: "Listen, thanks so much for giving me a lift back the other night, God, I don't know what I'd've done if you hadn't. . . ."

His mouth lifted in a kind of sneer. "They didn't suspect anything, then? I got out of the way quick enough?"

"Yes. Well—Cassie came in and all she cared about was where Davinia was. . . ."

"And where was she? Shagging that posh jerk on a beach somewhere?"

"Yes. But I couldn't tell Cassie that. I went to sleep, and then Davinia woke me up. . . ." I made myself slide my eyes to his face again, but he wasn't looking at me. He was looking out over my head. He was looking for the cradle-snatcher, wasn't he? He was hoping she'd be here and he could pick up where he'd left off. . . .

"Anyway, I'd better go," I mumbled, and I shuffled off to put out more mixed nuts.

Frazer and Alex stayed by the bar, on and on. As I circulated and collected glasses, I kept looking over to them, wondering when they'd give up on the cradle-snatchers and go. They seemed to be arguing about something—once, Frazer shoved Alex backward, and Alex looked like he was going to take a swing at him.

When I came out of the Ladies' after my third check of the night, Alex was standing in the corridor outside. It was a total, terrifying, wonderful shock. But he was glaring at me like he loathed me. "Look—can you stop fucking about, please?" he snarled.

All I could think was that he was accusing me of stalking him again. "I only wanted to thank you," I said with as much dignity as I could manage.

"*What?*"

"And look—I work here—I've got to be here. Don't come here in future if you want to avoid me, OK?"

"Oh, come off it. Don't tell me you don't know what I'm talking about," he said. Then he came right up to me, and I didn't move, just stared back at him. Then he shot both hands out and got hold of my head and smacked his mouth on mine.

## CHAPTER 41

**IT WAS SO EXTREME** that my only options were to faint like a storybook heroine or shove him back, hard.

I shoved him back, hard, and snarled, "What the *fuck* d'you think you're doing?"

"Stop pissing around. God, I can't stand girls like you, *game* players—"

"Game players? *Game* players?"

"Yeah, fucking game players! You fancied me on the plane, I tried to chat you up, and you ignored me—"

"Tried to *chat me up*? You didn't chat me up—you invited me to say how gorgeous I thought you were!"

"Oh, bollocks." He snorted, and it might have been a laugh.

"You were all *'fancy some of this, do you, luv?'*"

"OK, OK. Look—we haven't had the best start—"

"The best *start*? Start to *what*? Your mate hits my mate—then we practically have a punch-up on the dance floor here and you think we're stalking you and you call us the bitches from hell or something, and—" I broke off. A couple of girls were heading toward us, goggling. We both glared at them and they disappeared into the Ladies', giggling.

"When do you knock off?" Alex asked.

"What?"

"I thought I could get you a drink. I thought we could talk about it. I thought . . ."

*Careful,* I told myself—but most of me didn't hear it. Most of me was focused on the pagan dance of triumph stampeding up my spine, taking over my head. "What's there to talk about?" I asked.

"Jesus. Look, Chloe, I admit I thought you were a posh stuck-up cow like your friend at first. But . . . look . . . Chloe, I think you're really hot, OK?"

I didn't know what to say. He had to be able to see it, he had to see how slayed I was by everything about him, he had to see how much I fancied him. He had to have the advantage. Maybe he was playing me, maybe this was some kind of twisted revenge. Or maybe . . .

Maybe he was telling the truth.

"OK," I said. "You get us a drink and find us a table, and I'll ask Cora if I can knock off for the night, OK?"

I turned and headed back to the courtyard and over to the bar where I could see Cora charming a couple of sturdy thirty-something men in nasty summer shirts. It had been so utterly exhilarating, laying into Alex like that. It had been such a turn-on. *Keep your head,* I nagged myself. *Don't go soft.* But everything in me was fizzing and potent with excitement.

Cora turned and put her arm round me. "Thank you, angel," she said. "How did you know I needed rescuing? Those two . . . uuuurgh! Still . . . nearly closing time."

"Cora," I said urgently, "if I do all the clearing up after you've shut up, can I knock off now? Only that boy's turned up—the one that rescued me . . ."

"Say no more, darling." She smirked.

"I mean—he may be a con artist. He may be a bastard. But I've got to see, haven't I? I've got to—"

"Chloe—go. *Go!*"

I went. Alex waved to me from a table in the corner. He had two cocktails in front of him and he failed to smile as I sat down. There was no sign of Frazer.

I couldn't keep my eyes off his mouth. I was full of how it had felt when it had hit mine, full of wanting to repeat the experience.

"So," he said, "are you gonna tell me what happened? I mean—you've run out on your posh friend, have you?"

"Yes," I said, picking up my drink, taking a sip. "It all got a bit dramatic right after you left. . . ." And I went on to tell him everything, from screaming *Fuck you* at my hosts at dawn, to dropping down from the balcony again and making my way to Hilly's to beg for a job. At first, I kept my eyes on the table as I spoke, but then more and more, I looked at him, and his eyes kept sliding to a point behind my head at first, but then more and more he looked straight at me, and our eyes were sparking off each other. Him saying I was really hot was in my blood like the cocktail, only more intoxicating. I knew I was telling my story well, and he was absorbed, listening, putting in the odd comment or question. . . .

"You want to find yourself a new friend," he said. "Davinia's an absolute sodding little cow. It didn't surprise me in the slightest when she just pissed off and left you on your own that festa night."

"Nor me," I said. "It was gonna happen, us having a bust-up. I needed to get out."

"What on earth made you go away with her in the first place?"

"I thought I was a lesbian."

*"Whaaaaat?"*

I laughed at his expression, and it came into my mind to start telling him everything, all about Mum leaving and *everything*, but luckily I stopped myself. "That's enough about me," I said. "What about you? How come you've been on the island so long? You're a rich bitch too, are you?"

"Far from it. Frazer's uncle's got a garage here. He needs extra help in the summer, doing up the motorbikes he rents out. And he's got a couple of derelict old cottages he's doing up to rent next summer. We came out on this deal that we get free food and lodging if we put in a few hours' work a day."

"Fantastic!"

"Yeah, it's OK. There were five of us at first, we shifted a load of rubble and shit from the cottages. Then the other three got bored and pissed off. Actually it's better now, just Frazer and me. We're staying at one of the cottages and doing up the other one, and Frazer's working at the garage— he's a bit of an engineer on the sly."

"Isn't his uncle paying you anything?"

"He slips us the odd twenty euros. And we're not working that hard. We don't need much, not here."

"And are you getting bored?"

"No. I love this place. I'd live here if I could."

The way he said it—so simple, so straight—I felt this rush of wanting to grab him.

I no longer doubted that he fancied me every bit as much as I fancied him. There was enough energy between us to turbocharge a tank. But I still didn't trust him. I didn't trust that this wasn't some kind of a trick, some bet he had on with Frazer, something to do with point scoring or revenge . . . or else he was just desperate. He'd been on the island all summer, he'd met no one, he was going to go mad for any girl, even me.

But all this began to matter less as an overpowering lust to kiss him grew.

A deal began to form itself in my head. *Let yourself kiss him. Let yourself enjoy that,* have *that. But no more.* You *be in charge. Then you'll be safe.*

"So—where are you sleeping?" he said. "In the kitchen?"

"No," I said. "In the storeroom." And I told him about my leather couch bed and my outdoor shower with its screen of trees in tubs.

"I'd love to see it," he said. "Especially the shower."

"It is pretty good. Saul's bringing me some of his uncle's pig-shit, to feed the trees with so they grow bigger."

"God, what about the stink?"

"It'll wear off. And I use a really gorgeous shower gel."

"I bet you do." He grinned. That was something else that was happening. From not smiling at all, he was suddenly showing me a lot of his excellent white teeth. Then he suddenly looked past my head again, his eyes widened, and he announced, "Hey—everyone's gone home!"

I spun round in my seat. It was true, the courtyard was empty.

This was ridiculous. I mean—I knew it was closing time, I'd been aware of the flow of people leaving the bar, I'd registered when Saul came over and pointedly collected our empty glasses, but . . . *when* had everyone gone?

"I'd better go," I said. "I told Cora I'd clear up. . . ."

"It's all been done," Alex said.

*When* did it happen? We weren't talking for that long. Were we? "Cora and Zara'll be in the kitchen, I'd better go," I repeated, and I stood up and hurried over to the kitchen, Alex right behind me.

As I'd kind of known it would be, the kitchen was empty. Cora and Zara had gone. They must have seen me talking to Alex and gone. Their thoughtfulness—their *approval*—it was too much, it was wonderful.

"Does this mean I'm locked in for the night?" said Alex, right behind my ear.

"No. I've got a key. Come on."

He followed me through into the storeroom, my bedroom. "This is where you sleep?" he said. "Oh, it's good. Show me the shower?"

I unlocked the back doors. "I have to sleep with them locked," I said. "I don't like it, it's stuffy, but I'm scared of someone climbing over those walls and . . ."

"You need a big dog," he said. "Sleeping at the foot of your bed, to protect you." He wandered out, turned the hose on, and sprayed water at the two little trees, grinning. Then he turned it off again and headed back to me, and I grabbed him.

That's exactly what I did, just like he'd grabbed me outside the Ladies'. Only he didn't push me off. We kissed, and it was the sort of kiss that you couldn't stop, that you had to go on with to see where it took you, an amazing kiss, me leading, him leading, me leading again. I didn't know I could kiss like that, I didn't know I was that good. We came up for air, and he said, "Blimey," and it was so touching and sweet the way he said it that I kissed him again, and his hand went over my breast and up onto my neck and stroked my shoulder and back to my breast again and then I realized he was walking backward, kind of shuffling backward, still kissing, towing me with him, and then he turned and the leather sofa hit the back of my knees and I sat down hard.

And he kind of fell on top of me, and I said, "OK, we're not doing this. We're not doing any more of this."

"You started it!"

"I know I did. Now I'm stopping it. But I'll see you tomorrow, if you want."

I don't know where I got the confidence, the courage, to say that, but I knew it was a kind of test. I waited for his reaction, to see if he'd passed.

"OK," he said. "When do you start work?"

"Not till nighttime. No lunches tomorrow."

"OK, I'll knock off early. Pick you up at twelve?"

"Great," I said. "I'll let you out." And I got the huge convent key from my bag.

CHAPTER
42

I NEVER DOUBTED THAT he'd be there. Which is incredible for me, Chloe the Mega-Self-Doubter with my not so much low as nonexistent self-esteem. I slept late and I showered slowly as the sun was heating up, then I dressed in my favorite skirt and top and wandered through to the kitchen to scavenge for breakfast. Cora was in there, making a big, big deal of checking the cutlery, laying it all out, and picking up the forks and squinting at them to make sure they were perfectly clean. "Hi, you," she said busily, not looking up. "I brought in some croissants. Help yourself."

"Cora," I said with a laugh, "are you here to check up on me?" She turned to me, eyes huge and innocent. "Make sure I haven't got anyone . . . staying over?"

"Oh, darling," she said, "you have who you want staying over, I just . . . I needed to make sure

315

you were OK. Not upset or confused. Or battered to death."

I spread out my hands. "Well, as you can see, I'm fine."

"You look more than fine, darling."

"Oh, *Cora*. Alex is wonderful. He's picking me up in an hour."

"He is? That's . . . *oooohhh*!" She danced over to me and hugged me tight.

"He's so gorgeous," I gasped. "It's all weird, it's all mad, I'm meant to be on holiday with Davinia, not working for you and staying here and about to get picked up by Alex. . . ."

"Go with it," she said. "Go with it, it's not mad. And I won't check up on you again."

At 11:55 I unlocked the convent door, walked out, and locked it behind me. Yes, I was that confident. And there was Alex, swerving in on his moped round by the harbor wall. He drew up beside me, smiling, and said, "Hi!"

"Hi!" I said back. It was kind of awkward, and I knew we weren't going to kiss, but it didn't matter, it was all for later, all of it.

"Here," he said. "I got you a helmet. Where d'you want to go?"

I shrugged. "Anywhere. Anywhere is brilliant.

Davinia and I just did the same thing over and over, trooped from the flat to the beach. . . . I'd love to see some of the coastline."

"Well, look—the cottages we're doing up? They're near the coast. I thought maybe you'd like to see them and—"

"I'd love to," I said fervently.

He grinned at me. "Hop on then. I promised Frazer I'd stop and pick up some lunch first."

We drove off. A bit of me was relieved that Frazer was going to be there, because the two of us on our own would be just too intense. That was for later.

At the little shop Alex bought ham and fresh bread and water, and I bought tomatoes and red peppers and grapes, and he laughed at me for being a health fiend, and we set off again. It was electric, just having my arms round him. After a bit I rested my cheek on his shirt and I heard or rather *felt* this kind of growl that could have been a laugh or it could have been a purr of pleasure. . . . It was frustrating, hugging his back. I wanted him to twist round, land his mouth on mine. . . . We'd crash and die if he did that, of course, but we'd die happy.

We headed along a narrow road that climbed the rocky hillside, and then we were bumping along a rough track with prickly pears on either side, and then Alex stopped the bike. "There's the cottages," he said. Two little semi-derelict buildings stood side by side, built from the same sandstone as the hill. The sound of hammering came from one of them. "And there's the view."

I looked out. All I could see was the stunning sweep of rocky coast, and the deep blue of the sea meeting the huge blue sky. It felt like we were alone in the universe.

"Ain't it fantastic?" he said. Then he shouted, *"Frazer!"*

Frazer emerged from the far cottage in a cloud of sandy dust. "'Bout time, mate!" he called. "I'm *starving*!" He grinned at me. "You sure you're on your own? You haven't got that poisonous cow with you?"

"I *told* you," said Alex, "they've fallen out."

"Oh, yeah—the dramatic dawn escape. That was pretty impressive, that was. Crack the food out, mate, I'm dying here."

We picked our way over the piles of rubble and I followed Alex into the first cottage. "This is where we're staying," he said. Inside were two mattresses, and two huge backpacks with piles of clothes beside them. "See? Not as fancy as your place, is it?" We walked through a doorway at the back into a tiny lobby with three rooms off it. "Here's the kitchen," said Alex, going through. He put the food down on a draining board next to an old sink half-hanging off the wall. "Running water, the works. There's a bathroom and a bedroom through there."

"It'll be fabulous when you've fixed it up," I said.

"Yeah, a right little love nest," he said, and grinned. I left him to wash the tomatoes and peppers, and looked into the other two rooms.

"Your bathroom's fancier than mine," I called. "It's actually got a bath."

"Yeah, but I wouldn't sit down in it. You'd get rust burns on your arse."

I laughed and wandered through to the bedroom. It was empty apart from a pile of rubble on the floor, but it had a wonderful feel to it, and a low window, its view divided between the rocky hill and the skyline. At night, I thought, you'd be able to hear cicadas, and the sea. . . .

"OK, let's go!" called Alex. We went outside to where Frazer was waiting in the shade of a huge old fig tree. As we ate they asked me questions about Davinia and my escape and I asked about their work at the cottages and they described how they were digging down into the foundations to lay new floors and how it was taking far longer than Frazer's uncle Harry liked. It was relaxed and good fun, and the three of us got on great, but all the time there was this tension, this waiting, between Alex and me. Whenever I looked up at him he was looking at me.

"OK," said Frazer, when we'd finished the food, "it's too hot to work now. Let's go for a swim, I need to wash off. *He's* OK of course—he had a sluice down before he picked you up."

I smiled at this evidence of Alex sprucing himself up for me, and Alex, sounding gorgeously embarrassed, muttered, "I forgot to tell you to bring your swimming stuff."

I shrugged. I had a set of pretty bra and pants on, and that would do fine. "That's OK, my underwear'll dry off."

"Great, let's go."

I hid my bag in the cottage, and we set off down a narrow, steep route that led straight down to the sea. We clambered down from rock to rock and Alex kept putting out his hand to help me and I kept taking it, even when I really didn't need to, and soon we arrived at a gorgeous little bay with three huge flat rocks washed smooth by the sea. "There's where you get in the sea," said Frazer, pointing. "Uncle Harry wants to put in a ladder there, like in a swimming pool. And hack out steps in the path we came down."

"So this might be the last year you'll see it all unspoiled like this," said Alex. "OK, let's go, yeah?"

The boys were obviously just going to jump in as they were, in their shorts. For a second I felt seized by embarrassment; then I thought—what the hell? My tan was good, I'd waxed my legs, it was the only body I had and it was OK. I kicked off my sandals and pulled off my T-shirt, and as one, they both turned away. Frazer was jumping off the edge into the sea as I took my shorts off.

"You gonna jump?" said Alex.

"Er . . . I don't think so. Can't I just climb down?" There was this heat between us because of me being in my underwear.

"Well, I'll give you a hand. I'll lower you so you don't hit the rocks, then you can just float off, OK?"

He braced himself to balance my weight and keep me safe as I kind of rappelled down the rock. It was a bit like hanging off the balcony at the flat, but this time I was dropping into cool water, not space, and I wasn't hanging on to a metal rail, I was hanging on to Alex. When the water was up to my waist he said, "OK?" and I said, "Yes!" and he let go. As I floated free he called out, "Don't kick yet! You'll hit your feet on the rocks!"

"It's beautiful!" I cried.

"Isn't it great?" he said, then he took a run and sprang out, just like he had done before when we'd been enemies, and landed in the sea and came up, safe and spluttering. Then he swam toward me. I took hold of his cold arm and our faces touched and we kissed, treading water. Then I let go and we drifted apart. Frazer was a splashy blur in the distance. "Come on," Alex said, and he set off swimming out to sea, and I caught him up and swam next to him. After a while he stopped and turned to face me and we kissed again, for longer, much longer, holding on to each other, treading water. His mouth felt really warm against the coldness of the sea. "Turn back?" he said, and I nodded, and we swam back to the rocks.

IT WAS GLORIOUSLY HOT once we'd climbed out, and I could feel my skin drying in the sun and the breeze. "Perfect spot for sunbathing, isn't it?" said Alex.

"Yeah, but I'm gonna have to get in the shade soon," I said. "Or I'll burn."

"Ah, you're reckoning without my planning and foresight," he said, and padded over to a couple of flat stones beside a great boulder. He shifted them, reached down, pulled out a liter bottle of water and a big bottle of sun cream, and turned to grin at me. "Foresight, see?"

"Brilliant. Chuck me the water."

Then Frazer heaved himself onto the rock and grinned at us. "S'OK, I'm not stopping," he said. "I'm off. See you later, Al, OK?"

"Yeah," said Alex, and we lay on our sides facing each other on the smooth flat rock, dripping and drying off. "Well, I'm impressed," he went on, "the way you got down here and in the water and everything. I thought you'd be a bit of a princess about it."

"Look, will you stop confusing me with Davinia? She's the princess, not me."

"Yeah, well, I bet you *played* princesses, when you were little. I bet you had all the frilly stuff, and handbags with little dogs on them."

"*In* them. Princesses carry little dogs *in* their bags."

"Not live dogs. I mean like a little Scotty dog picture with a real chain for a lead. . . ."

"God, *yeah*! I had one of those! God, I loved it, it had a little tartan coat on . . . hey, you—don't look like that."

"Like what?"

"Like all smug, like you've won a point. I never liked playing princesses, I preferred witches."

"Yeah? Did you prance around naked?"

"*Ooooh!* Been watching the Discovery Channel again?"

"Actually it was porn. Witch porn."

"I hate you."

"I hate you too. What did you do, when you were playing witches?"

"We dressed up in black and with hats, but that

wasn't a big part of it. The big thing was making spells. We cursed people. Especially boys."

He grinned. "I bet you did."

"We collected stuff like feathers and moss and stuff, and we put it in this big saucepan, and . . ."

"Chloe, I don't want to hear this."

"Scaring you, is it?"

"Just kind of turning me off a bit."

"Fine, *be* turned off." I laughed and sat up and started rubbing sun cream into my legs.

"I was joking," he said, "I'm not a bit turned off," and he put his hands on my shoulders, and nuzzled into my hair, and then we were kissing again, turning and twisting on the rock, not caring how hard it was. The little warning tick in my mind saying, *Careful, careful, don't trust him yet*, had grown very faint. It was just so fantastic, it was all I wanted, to be that girl on that rock in the sun, kissing Alex. He started to slide my bra straps down and the deal I'd made with myself, about being in charge and not going further than kissing, started to seem really weak. Soon my bra had slithered onto the rock and we were kissing again, and he had his hands on my breasts and then he pulled back. "What time have you got to be back at Hilly's?" he muttered.

"Shit. I forgot about Hilly's."

"It's being with me. All other thoughts are driven from your mind."

"Shut up. Bighead. Around five, I suppose. To get showered and stuff."

"Shall we go back up to the cottage? We could finish off those grapes you bought."

"That'd be great." I got to my feet and shucked my bra on again, fast, a bit self-consciously, and pulled on my shorts and T-shirt, and he put the sun cream and water back in the crevice in the rock and pulled the flat stones back over them. As we scrambled up the rocky path, I thought about why he'd pulled back from me and decided it was because he was just so turned on he was in pain.

Either that or he planned to jump me in the cottage, but I could deal with that.

But we didn't go in the cottage. We sat shaded from the sun with our backs against the fig tree, eating the warm grapes and figs we pulled from the branches above us, not wanting to go. The fig leaves smelled sweet, like vanilla, and lizards kept running from the cracks in a little ruined drystone wall nearby. One big brown lizard got so used to us it stayed on top of the wall sunning itself, lifting its feet up one by one to cool. "I love lizards," I said.

"Well, this is lizard city, up here." We were

talking lazily, mouths close.

"You know, if Frazer's uncle's turning these into holiday cottages, he wants to look after this fig tree. And those yellow flowers over there, and that frondy thing. People love plants."

"Yeah?"

"You could make it like a little oasis, use some of those rocks you're digging out from the floors to mend that little wall and build new ones round the plants—it would save you lugging them away. Hey—that's a brilliant idea!"

"Yeah, it is. Want a job?"

"And plant, like, a palm tree or something. And to make it all grow you need some of Saul's uncle's . . ."

"Shit, I know."

"*Pig* shit."

"Well, get us some, then!"

"I will," I said, and I leaned in and kissed him.

When we reemerged some time later, he said, "I'm serious, come up and help us do the garden. Can't promise Uncle Harry would pay you, but it would get him off our backs a bit about not working hard enough . . . and I'd take you out to eat, to say thank you. Lots."

"Lots of times or lots of food?"

"Both."

"Lovely. But you'd have to do something else, too."

"Yeah? What's that?"

I sat up. "Go and collect my suitcase from Davinia's," I said.

CHAPTER 44

**WE AGREED TO FETCH** my case the next afternoon, after Alex had finished his stint at the cottages. I'd text Davinia and ask her to have my suitcase ready. Alex wouldn't come into the flat with me because that would make it even more hideously embarrassing but he'd be there outside waiting and he'd rescue me if he heard all hell breaking loose. I was dreading it; all I could hope was they were as anxious to avoid me as I was them. The best possible scenario would be that they'd dump my case in the hall.

We got back on his motorbike and headed back to the harbor, but when Alex had stopped the bike neither of us wanted me to go in. "Shall I come and get you at the same time tomorrow?" he said. "When I've finished work?"

"What time d'you start?"

"Around eight. Before it gets too hot."

"Why don't you come and get me then? I can start doing some work on the garden."

"You sure? That'd be great."

"And I'll steal some breakfast for us, from the kitchen."

"Brilliant."

We kissed again, and I said, "Give me your mobile number. Just in case."

"I haven't got one. I forgot it was in my shorts and dived off the rocks and . . ."

"And now some big fish keeps *ringing*. Great."

"I don't need a mobile. I won't let you down," he said.

I smiled and got off the bike and he put both arms round me, keeping me close to him. "I don't want to wait till tomorrow to see you again," he murmured.

"Me neither."

"If I turn up at Hilly's tonight, will you think I'm stalking you?"

"Yes. But it's OK." And we kissed again, for about the millionth time.

I let myself into the convent and hurried down the long brick corridor and across the courtyard. I could hear someone in the kitchen but I didn't want to speak to them, I didn't want to speak to anyone, I felt like my mouth was still hot from all the kissing, I didn't want to use it for talking.

I raced into my room and across to the yard door and flung it open, letting the sun burst in. I raised my arms to it, just like Anthony and Deborah at their pretentious party; I laughed and spun off around the room, dancing in joy and triumph in among the piles of junk. I'd've died if anyone had seen me. Then I toppled sideways onto the sofa and stretched out till my muscles screamed. Alex's face floated up in front of me, I could feel his hands on my skin, his mouth on my mouth. . . . It had happened, it had *happened*!

I relaxed back, in bliss. I felt like I'd never be able to move again.

I felt too good to *move*.


"Soooo," purred Cora as I reported for bar duty an hour or so later, "what have you done to yourself? You look absolutely *gorgeous*."

I shrugged happily and thanked her. I was wearing my short nutmeg-colored skirt, a white spaghetti strap top and four wide silver bangles. And more eye makeup than I usually go for. I felt . . . I dunno . . . *bold*.

"It's your tan," she said. "That, and the enormous delight you're exuding." Then she laughed, and swam off.

I'd only been working an hour and a half before Alex turned up, but I was too busy to do much more than kiss him hello. He sat in the corner looking a bit lost and then on my second trip to check the Ladies' he followed me and we had a fantastic, passionate, illegal-feeling snog in the corridor. Then there was a huge influx of people into the place, and Cora had to help man the bar, so Alex helped me collecting glasses. He even started taking orders.

"You're a great hit with those *crones* over there," I said meanly—the women couldn't have been much more than thirty-five. "I expect they want to adopt you."

"You can talk," he said. "What about that fat loser in the nasty blue shirt—he was practically licking your hair."

"Yeah, but you should see the size of the tip I got."

"Chloe—that's called prostituting yourself."

"It's called good business sense."

We looked at each other, laughing—it was as hot as kissing. And then we were off again, weaving through all the punters, but they were like ghosts, they were like sheep, we were only aware of each other.

* * *

I finally got to sit down with him right before closing time, while Cora was charmingly herding the tourists toward Saul at the door. We sat knee to knee and practically nose to nose, and shared the last of the cocktail that I'd scrounged free from Zara. "You still up for gardening tomorrow, then?" he asked. "You won't be too knackered?"

"Yeah, I'm up for it," I said. "If I stay here on my own all I'll do is worry about going back to the flat to get my case."

He got hold of my hand across the table and squeezed it. "Hey, listen, don't feel weird about rowing with them. It happens all the time on holidays, people falling out."

"Yeah, but not *running* out."

"Yeah, they do. Holidays are meant to be all about pleasure, but they can turn you inside out. I saw this family a few days ago, at a café in one of the squares. They had this kind of . . . *fog* of misery round them, the two kids looked mute, the mum was all hunched and sad looking, and the *dad*—he just looked defeated. Like he'd never get up again."

"So they'd had a big row?"

"Maybe, maybe that's just how they are. And being together had brought it all home, how bloody awful their lives are. You see it with couples, too—they put everything on their big trip together and then they get away and it's shit. They sit there eating their meals and drinking their drinks and they're full of anger and misery and they don't know how to fix it. Holidays are like . . . I dunno, *ovens*—everything heats up and changes."

There was a beat or two of silence, then I said, "You can say that again," and we both burst out laughing and he trapped my leg between his underneath the table. I leaned across and kissed him hard on the mouth. Well, I was off duty now, wasn't I?

It almost scared me, the speed with which it was all happening. It was some acceleration. As if all the time we thought we hated each other, we'd been building up this head of steam and now we'd let go and everything was absolutely . . . well . . . *steamy.*

**THE NEXT DAY AT** 2:30 in the smoldering heat I left
Alex parked outside Belvedere Mansions and
walked on wobbly legs to the main entrance. I'd
deliberately knackered myself that morning at the
cottages, lugging rocks over to the broken-down
wall and trying to build it up again. I thought being
tired might make me feel calmer, but it didn't seem
to. Frazer had been there the whole time, and Alex
and I hadn't had a lot of privacy. But we'd had one
long kiss behind the cottage that had been so wonderful and promising of more that it was almost
enough.

I'd texted Davinia asking her if it was OK to
come at 2:30 and if she'd pack all my stuff in my
case. She'd texted back "OK." I spent some time
trying to analyze this "OK," work out if it was
accepting, or rejecting and harsh, decided I was an
idiot, and gave up on it. All I hoped was that it

would all be over quickly. I wanted to be back on Alex's bike, balancing my case precariously between us.

The main door was ajar when I got there, which somehow seemed ominous. I slipped inside, climbed the marble stairs, and walked slowly toward the Morgan-Harwoods' flat door. Then I stopped dead, because I could hear Davinia having a major tantrum on the other side of it. She was screaming, "OH, so I'm supposed to just be on this boring little island and not have a PENNY to spend, am I?" and then I could hear the quiet, reasonable voices of her parents, one after the other, and then she yelled, "Well, FORGET it then, I'm flying home!" and then more calm voices and then, "You DID NOT!" and then "How THE FUCK was I supposed to KNOW?" and then I heard Paul starting to shout too. And I was overcome with not wanting to see the three of them again. I was just turning round, about to creep back the way I'd come and admit defeat to Alex, when the flat door was suddenly wrenched open and Davinia's dad stormed out.

"*You!*" he spat. "I'd forgotten *you* were coming!"

"I've come for my case," I gasped. "I texted Davinia, she said OK. . . ."

"OK? *OK?* She most certainly is not OK! First

*you* run out on her and then that little *bastard* she was seeing dumps her with some half-baked excuse about his girlfriend trying to commit suicide and then she goes on an absolute drinking spree, steals money from us, has to be brought home by the island police catatonically drunk—"

"*Paul!*" shrieked Cassie from indoors. "Is that Chloe?"

Paul leaned toward me, teeth bared like he wanted to bite my face. "Why don't you come in?" he hissed.

It was like being a calf invited to the slaughter. But I couldn't say no, could I? I followed him in.

Davinia was crouched on the end of the sofa, face contorted with hideous self-pity, while Cassie fluttered and flustered behind her. Then Davinia looked up and saw me and she got off the sofa and *sprang* at me and just as I was about to protect my eyes or pass out in fear—or both—she threw her arms round my neck and I realized she was *hugging* me. She burst into noisy tears right into the side of my face and howled, "Oh, God, Chloe, it's been so awful, I can't tell you, I've never been dumped before in my *life*, how could he, how *dare* he, who cares if that stupid bitch dies, I *want* her to die." Then she made this sobbing noise that sounded like *weeuaaaauuurgh*—and over her head I saw

Alex walk through the still-open door of the flat.

"Who the *hell* are you?" raged Paul.

"Chloe's boyfriend," Alex said menacingly. "What's going on?"

Davinia let go of me. "Chloe's *boyfriend*?" she echoed, mouth all twisted in disgust.

"Yes, my boyfriend," I said. I liked repeating it.

"Don't be *insane*!" squawked Davinia, right in my face. "Have you forgotten what he *did* to us, the way he *behaved* to us? Anyway, look at him—he's so *crude*—you don't have to be this desperate, Chloe— you can move back here. *Tell* her, Mummy."

Alex and I exchanged an electric glance as Cassie tensely cleared her throat. I knew from his mouth that he'd burst out laughing any minute.

"We'd decided we'd talk to you, when you came to collect your case," said Cassie coldly. "We'd decided we'd forgive and forget. You were upset, you acted hastily. . . . It all got a bit heated but we can let bygones be bygones. . . . We're prepared to let you move back in."

"Be my *friend* again!" gushed Davinia, hanging on to my arm and twisting it a bit. "You don't want to hang about with *him*."

"And sleep in that dubious club, in the storeroom, or wherever Cora's dumped you," added Cassie.

"Come on," said Paul. "Be sensible."

There was a screaming silence, then I said, "Where's my case?"

"Now come on," said Paul, "you're being silly, you don't mean this—"

"I've never meant anything more in my life," I said. "Cora and Alex have been great to me. They *care* about me. *You*—you all knew what had happened, with my mum leaving and everything, but you still thought you could treat me like I didn't have feelings, like it was OK to push me onto this *creep* just to make a foursome with Davinia, and leave me stranded after the festa. . . . There's no *way* I'm moving back in here."

"You *ungrateful* little *bitch* . . ." breathed Paul. "We take you on holiday, we—"

"*WHAT ABOUT ME?*" wailed Davinia, completely drowning out his voice. "Don't you *CARE* what happened to *ME*?"

"No, I don't," I said, relishing every word. "You're snobbish and you're shallow and you're so utterly self-centered it's not even a joke."

"Don't you *dare* speak to my *daughter* like that!" shrieked Cassie.

"And worse than that, Davinia, you're boring," I went on. "You never want to do anything but sit around, you have no conversation that doesn't

**339**

revolve round *you*—you're unutterably, utterly *boring*."

Davinia gawped comically at me for a second, like a fish dragged from the sea gaping for life. Then she screamed, just like she'd screamed all that time ago when Frazer had smacked her across the face, on and on and on. And this time Alex did start laughing. I couldn't hear him, over Davinia's screaming, but I could see him. I grinned at him, and marched purposefully across the room. There was some kind of scuffling standoff between Alex and Paul that Alex seemed to win because soon he was at my side. Together we headed down the corridor to the bedroom I used to share with Davinia.

My case was open on the bed with a few of my clothes scattered round it. It looked like Davinia had started packing my stuff up, then decided she wanted me back. "I'll hold the door," said Alex, still laughing. "You pack, yeah?"

At top speed, I grabbed my clothes off their hangers, out of the drawers, swept up my stuff from the top of the dressing table.

"Gonna nick anything of hers while you're at it?" said Alex. "This belt's quite nice. . . ."

"Leave it!" I laughed. I was half expecting Davinia and her dad to try and push their way in the bedroom, and the way Alex had his arm braced against the door, he was expecting it too. But nothing happened. There was sudden eerie silence from the main room as Davinia shut up, then I heard Paul's voice and then Davinia started wailing and Cassie was bleating, "*Stop it,* stop it, darling, I can't *bear* it, I can't *bear* to see you so unhappy, stop it *please!*"

"Bloody hell," said Alex. "Shall we leg it out the window? We can drop your case. . . ."

It was tempting. And there was something fitting about using my escape route one last time. But . . .

"No," I said firmly. "Why the hell should we? I'm gonna leave by the front."

He grinned, took the case off me, and opened the bedroom door. We walked down the corridor and into the main room again, then out the front door. The Morgan-Harwoods hardly noticed us go.

Alex rode the bike very slowly and I held on to the case to keep it balanced between us, and we got back to Hilly's without mishap. When I got off the bike, I felt like my legs could give way. "I dunno, what's wrong with me?" I muttered. "I should feel great. I *did* feel great, when we walked out of the flat. But now . . ."

"It's 'cos you were pumping adrenaline," said

Alex. "You've come down. It's the same after a fight."

"Do a lot of fighting, do you?"

"Used to. You know, playground stuff. Hey . . . it's OK, it's OK." He put his arm all warm and heavy round my shoulders. "It's over, you can relax, you did it, you told them, nothing else is gonna happen."

"All that rock shifting at the cottages, then facing down Davinia . . . I'm *exhausted*." I sniffed. "I'm gonna have a nap. Or I'll be useless tonight."

"You do that," he said, "you have a sleep," and I knew he was thinking, like me, of my wide leather sofa, wide enough for the two of us to lie there in the breeze from the open door . . . He leaned down from his bike and we kissed, and he said, "I think I've done more kissing over the last few days than I've done in the rest of my life put together."

"Are you complaining?"

"No. Definitely not. You want me to come tonight?"

"Can you?"

"Uncle Harry's asked us for chow at his house, and you don't say no to Uncle Harry. But I can come along late if you want me to."

"Yes, please. If that's OK. If *you* want to."

"You know I do. Go on now, scarper. Get your head down, get some sleep."

I kissed him one last time, picked up my case, walked over to Hilly's, and went in. The door was unlocked, which meant Cora or someone was here already, getting ready for the night. I felt bone tired as I dragged my case down the corridor. I went into the courtyard, and there, at one of the far tables in the shade of the high wall, with a tall, cool drink in front of her, sat my mum.

I stood still in absolute shock for a minute.

Then I dropped my case and burst into tears.

CHAPTER 46

**MUM WAS OVER AND** in front of me in a second, gasping, *"Chloe . . . Chloe!"*

I didn't know if I wanted to throw myself on her and hug her or hit her very hard in the face. It felt like both so I did neither. I stood there and willed myself to stop blubbering. I glared at her through my hands and muttered, "What the fuck are you doing here?"

"Dad got in touch with me," she said. I didn't recognize her voice, it was breathless, breaking. "He'd heard from that Morgan-Harwood woman. She said you'd run out on them, moved in here."

"So why didn't he come?"

"Chloe, he has this *huge* thing on at work. He phoned me—I said I'd come. I wanted to. I've been in hell this last year, no contact with you. . . . Oh, God, it's so good to see you. Oh, you look beautiful. Oh . . ." Her whole body was shaking, convulsed with these huge sobs racking her body. Still I couldn't move. Then she sobbed *"Chloe"* again, and something broke in me, and I sprang at her, and we held each other as if we'd never be apart again.

IT TOOK AGES FOR us to come down, to let go of each other. And then it took ages for me to look at her because her burning eyes were always on my face. At some point during this furnace time Cora glided up with two tall cool fruit drinks, put them silently on a table near us, and glided off again. Finally, Mum and I stumbled apart and sat down opposite each other at the table and started to drink. "*Why* did you punish me like that, Chloe?" she whispered. "*Why* wouldn't you see me?"

"Because you hurt me too much," I muttered. It was like I was hauling each word up from the base of my being. It was like I was learning to speak for the first time.

She sighed, kept silent. "Where are you staying?" I asked.

"A tiny hotel near here. Cora found it for me. She's been incredibly helpful, she's—"

"She knew you were *coming*?"

"Yes. As soon as we heard from the Morgan-Harwoods, I got hold of her number and called her."

"She didn't tell me."

"I asked her not to. I thought if you knew I was coming . . . you might do another runner."

I felt flayed, absolutely flayed, sitting there. I knew we had to talk and part of me just wanted to escape but I couldn't move. I was shaking; my hand was jumping on the cold glass. "I hated what I did to you," she whispered. "I absolutely hated it. But I *had* to go. I fell in love, Chloe. Can you believe that?"

I shrugged. Of course I could believe it. "And that came before everything else?" I muttered.

"Oh, God. It tore me into shreds. But—I was alive again. I couldn't go back to my old life. For— *God*, at least five years before it happened I'd been . . . withering *away*, living with your dad. I was obsessed about getting older . . . plodding on in this dreary, half-depressed way, I felt I was dying, I felt I'd never see any more life."

"Thanks a lot," I croaked.

"God, darling, you know I don't mean *you*. You were the one good thing, the one happiness . . . but I couldn't live through you, could I? And I looked

347

ahead and saw you leaving home and me just . . ." She sat back and sighed. Then she took a sip of her drink and said, "Then Jack came along. It just happened, Chloe! Neither of us sought it out, we just fell for each other, and I felt . . . I felt like I'd come back to life. I just felt so incredibly blessed. I'd been given a second chance. Life was amazing again, sex was wonderful. . . ."

"Mum. Please."

"OK. OK. But it's important. You get older, you get stale. . . . We hid and met in secret for a year, but we wanted to live together. So . . . I made the decision to get you through your GCSEs and then I'd go. I knew Jack would wait, as long as it took, but . . . it got so I couldn't go on living a horrible lie. I just couldn't."

There was a silence, then I said, "Dad nearly had a breakdown, after you left."

"It wasn't me he missed. It was the routine, the safety."

"That is so bloody unfair," I erupted, "and crap, and not true, and you *know* it."

She looked at me, breathing fast, then she said, "I know."

"Mum, I *hated* you for leaving us. You did something that nearly destroyed him, and you left me there—alone—to clear up the mess."

"What else could I do? If I'd asked you to come with me you wouldn't, would you? You wouldn't leave Dad. You wouldn't live with a man who'd broken the family up, whom you'd never even met."

I felt this rage growing, swelling inside me. "What else could you do—you could've *stayed*. Oh, I'm not saying you *should* have stayed. I can see that maybe it was the right choice, even a *good* choice, to go. I can even see that going didn't mean . . . it didn't mean you didn't love me." Mum let out a kind of sob, when I said that, and I could see her love for me, all over her face. "But you went and that had *consequences*. It made me feel like I hated you. It made me cut you off."

"Yes, and if I'd known that—"

"What? *What*? Would it have made a difference? Would you have stayed?"

There was a long, long pause. Then she whispered, "I don't know. Probably. If I thought it meant you'd never see me again. But it would've half killed me."

"Well, you're a liar. If you felt that, you'd've moved back in with us."

"Is that why you cut me off? To blackmail me?"

"*No!* Yes. I don't know."

"D'you still hate me?" she whispered. "Will you see me from now on?"

"I'm seeing you now, aren't I?" I muttered.

This time it was Mum who burst into tears.

CHAPTER
48

WE SAT THERE, ON and on. We finished our drinks, and Cora brought us more. We went over and over what had happened, as though somehow, we were slowly mending it. We were hauling it out of the dark terrible place it had been in, we were making it part of us, we were accepting it. Then Cora swam up to me just before opening time, told me firmly that I had the night off, and suggested Mum and I meet up again later. I was very glad she did—Mum and I were kind of immobilized at the table. If Cora hadn't got us to move we might have just gone on sitting there, talking it all over and over and over until we faded away.

Mum got to her feet all shakily, and told me the name of her little hotel, and I agreed to meet her there in two hours so we could have dinner together. Then I picked up my huge case and dragged myself into my storeroom, opened the door to let the sea breezes in, fell on the sofa, and fell into a dead sleep.

I woke about an hour later with this burst of deep happiness, like something had broken inside me and flooded me with joy. . . . It was weird, it was unreal. I couldn't remember a single one of my dreams, but I knew they'd been blissful.

Somewhere, I knew this happiness was to do with Mum but I wouldn't let myself think about it. I was afraid of letting go of the strength I'd built up on my own, afraid of forgiving her too easily, getting hurt again.

There was just under an hour to go till I met her. I stripped off my clothes and went outside to shower. The sun was low and still hot; the trees in their tubs seemed to have doubled in size since they'd been getting watered daily—and since Saul's uncle's pig shit had been mulched in round their roots. They were the perfect screen. When I turned on the hose, there was a sudden burst of cicadas singing from the skinny tree on the other side of the wall, as though they loved the sound of the water.

I dried off in the sun and went back in. I had a whole suitcase of clothes to choose from now. I pulled out a flimsy red dress and high-heeled sandals. I put my hair up; I put on lipstick and earrings. I wanted to make myself look older.

I found Mum's hotel without any trouble. The table had been set for us at the end of the long terrace under great swathes of jasmine that sent its delicious smell into the night air. It was obvious she'd gone to a lot of trouble to make sure it was all perfect. We drank icy wine and ate delicious fish, and we talked again. Slowly, slowly I could see we were rebuilding who we were together. We were visiting that time when she'd left and it was like we were rewriting it, we were writing it with her side in now. I felt like this great wound I'd been carrying around with me was having balm spread on it, soothing it—it was starting to heal. She asked me all about what had happened with Davinia, about me doing a runner, and she asked about Alex. . . . She listened, she cared. But I was still scared, and whenever I felt how good it was to be with her again, to have her caring about me and listening to me, the hurt that she'd left would flare up, and I'd be sullen. But she'd be patient, she'd bring me round. We were getting there. Somewhere.

Then she said, "I've arranged to stay for two more days, Chloe. Are you going to fly back with me?"

"No," I said. I didn't even have to think.

"Oh, darling, think of Dad. He felt awful that he couldn't come out with me. . . . We've been so worried about you. That wretched Morgan-Harwood woman gave me the impression you were having a breakdown. Dad needs to see you. It would be so good, it would . . . Fly back with me. Please."

"I want to stay. I told you what's happening with Alex. And I love it, working with Cora—I want to stay on."

"OK," she said quietly, and I felt this rush of guilt, and then this incredible rush of anger. "Don't you look like that," I blurted out. "If I'm being hard or selfish or whatever you're thinking, I've had a good teacher."

*"What?"*

"You lie to me for nine months and then leave. . . . It's made me harder, Mum. It's made me put myself first. You said you thought I was having a breakdown—*I* thought I was, some of the time! And I was really scared, and alone, but I did it, I got away, I got something new started, and I love it, and . . . and I'll only do something if it's good for me, from now on. It's my life. I'm putting myself first. Like *you* did."

354

I expected her to look hurt, or angry, or both, but she didn't. She went a little pale and then she reached out and squeezed my hand. "That's my girl," she whispered. "That's my baby."

CHAPTER

49

I ENDED UP STAYING the night with her, in her room. There were twin beds, two feet apart. I thought of phoning Hilly's but I knew Cora wouldn't worry, she'd be half-expecting me to stay—and anyway, she could always phone the hotel if she was worried. Mum and I were exhausted, all talked out. We got ready for bed in silence, and it felt so weird and so right to be borrowing her face cleaner and stuff, hear her clean her teeth, not bother to shut the door when I went for a pee. . . .

In the night I thought I was dreaming, I thought she was really close to me, looking at me full of love, then I realized it wasn't a dream. "Mum?" I whispered, still foggy with sleep. "Mum, what're you doing?"

"I'm sorry," she breathed. She was kneeling beside my bed, kneeling beside me like she was praying. "Did I wake you? I couldn't sleep. And I just had to . . . I had to look at you again. You know. Go back to sleep now, darling. Go on." And as I dropped back into sleep she stroked my hair as if I was a tiny child again.

It wasn't until I woke up the next morning that I remembered I'd said I'd see Alex in Hilly's after he'd had dinner with Uncle Harry. I felt terrible for a few seconds, letting him down like that, then I told myself that he would've asked Cora where I was, and she'd tell him about Mum turning up, and he'd understand, we'd see each other soon . . . and it would all be all right.

I was longing to see him. I wanted to tell him what had happened but more than that I just wanted to be with him and kiss him and get lost in wanting him. . . . That was who I was now.

Mum and I were more awkward together in the morning. I didn't mention standing Alex up, I didn't want to talk about it with her. I was kind of brisk, saying I had to get back to work, and she was all matter-of-fact and laid-back. It was as if we'd said so much last night we were still digesting it all. "Don't worry about me, sweetheart," she said. "I know you've got things to do." Then she said it would be nice if we could meet for lunch but I said I'd already had the night off and lunches started, I didn't think I could, I was pretty sure Cora would need me on the lunchtime shift.

We kissed good-bye, and I promised to call the hotel, but I didn't promise to see her again that day. All I could think of was seeing Alex.

I let myself into Hilly's and legged it across the courtyard. There was a huge delivery of alcohol and soft drinks coming in at the door by the back of the bar, and Cora was looking harassed as she ticked everything off. "*There* you are, darling!" she called. "Are you OK?"

"I'm fine," I said. "We had dinner, we talked—"

"And I want to hear *all* about it," she cried, "but not now. Help me stack these, Chloe—Saul says he can't come in, he's herding goats or something, and Zara's gone off in search of some Galliano, there's none in this delivery and we have to have it for the Red Snappers—if we can't get it, I'll have to invent a new cocktail. . . . It's not like London here, with its trucks and its trains and its planes delivering goodies twenty-four-seven, I have to rely on my supplies coming in every week on the ferry and if they get it wrong, which they so often do, I have to adapt, I have to invent. . . ."

I'd never heard her moan like this before, it wasn't like her. I got stacking. I was longing to ask her about Alex—dying to find out if she'd spoken to him—but I didn't think it would be clever to interrupt. Not when she'd been so good about giving me time off and everything. She straightened up, wailed, "My *back*!" then said, "The cleaner's late. She's going to let us down again, I know it. . . . If she doesn't come in the next half hour you're going to have to do the toilets, angel. I'm so sorry, but you're going to *have to*!"

"That's OK. Really."

"Good. Keep stacking—keep stacking!"

I worked like a fury, hauling bottles out of boxes, lining them up on the shelves and folding up the cardboard boxes that had held them, while Cora moaned on. Then, when at last we'd cleared it all, I felt I'd earned the right to interrupt. "Cora," I said urgently, "did Alex come to the bar last night?"

"Who? Oh—your young man. I think so, I'm not sure. . . ."

I was dumbfounded. "You're not *sure*?"

"Darling," she snapped, "he might be the main star in your sky, but we were very busy last night! We were one down, remember—you weren't there!"

"I know, I know," I said, stung, "but—didn't he talk to you? I mean, ask you where I was?"

"No. As I said, I'm not even sure he was there. Why would he be, if you weren't? Now, Chloe, *please*—we have to get on. Those toilets need doing. We're opening for lunch. Or with all the drama in your life, had you forgotten?"

It was the first time Cora had even approached being bitchy to me, and I shouldn't have minded so much. But as I trudged over to the closet where the cleaning stuff was stored, I was near to tears. And then, as I drew out the toilet-cleaning box, with its bleach and brushes and day-glo rubber gloves, it hit me that I was really upset about Alex, not Cora. I *had* to know if he'd turned up last night and if he hadn't—*why not?*—and if he had—*why hadn't he asked Cora where I was?* He knew nothing about Mum turning up, so he must think I'd just stood him up, he must've been really upset. . . . God, if only he had a mobile. If only he didn't dive in the sea so much.

I set to, swilling out the mucky, hair-filled basins, cleaning off JT LOVES BH written in nasty pink lipstick on the mirror, and all I wanted to do was run out and find Alex and put things right, but I couldn't run out on Cora again, not after last night.

It was the first hitch in our relationship since Alex had jumped on me just outside the door over there and kissed me and I absolutely felt I couldn't deal with it. Now that we'd finally got together, I thought our problems were over, I thought we'd go on being magic and seamless forever. I didn't think I'd have to deal with feeling like this.

I finished the toilets, I got through the table-cloth ironing and table laying. I knew I should call Mum but I couldn't, I just couldn't summon up the energy. Everything in me was focused on Alex. As I waited on tables and cleared piles of plates, anxiety swelled in me because a big part of me was waiting for him just to walk in through the door and he wasn't, he *wasn't*. . . . *He's working*, I told myself, *he has to work*. Except it was now way past the time he'd knocked off when we'd gone swimming. . . . I wanted to cry when I thought of that swim, and kissing on the hot rock. . . . *Why isn't he here? He must know I can't get to him, why is he* doing *this?*

Maybe the cradle-snatcher had drawn up beside him in a sports car and carried him off. Or maybe he was hurt. Maybe he'd dived off a rock and killed himself. I couldn't carry on like this, I couldn't work here tonight watching the door, hoping he'd turn up, not knowing what had happened. . . . I managed to lurch on like a zombie till the last customer had gone and I'd cleared the last of the tables, then I went into the kitchen and said, "Cora, I've got to go out."

"*What?*" she squawked, straightening up from stacking the industrial dishwasher. "Look at the state of this place, we've barely started on it. . . ."

"I know, I know, and I'm sorry, look, you can dock my wages massively, you can not pay me for the whole *day*, you can fire me, I don't care, I have to go."

Then without giving her another glance, I went.

I felt terrible as I let myself out of Hilly's and started off in the direction of Uncle Harry's cottages. I'd treated Cora badly, she was mad at me. . . . Mum would be sitting alone in her hotel, waiting to hear from me. . . . She'd probably phone Hilly's, and Cora would be massively irritated at yet another interruption to do with me, and then she and Mum would compare notes on how crap I was. . . .

But none of that mattered. Nothing mattered besides seeing Alex again, feeling his body against mine, his arms round me, his mouth . . .

I set off on the little road winding up from the harbor to the cliffs. It was well after three in the afternoon, really hot, oppressive. I thought I knew exactly which direction to go in, but after half an hour's walking, the coastal path forked, and I wasn't sure which one to take. I took a gamble on the one farther in, because the cottages hadn't been right on the edge of the cliff. Only then the path seemed to veer off too far inland, and then it forked again . . . and I didn't recognize any of it. Panic started to beat in me.

I walked on, taking the left-hand path this time. The sun burned down on me and I cursed my lousy sense of direction and wished I'd brought my sun hat with me. I wanted to cry but I wouldn't let myself because I'd only brought along a small bottle of water and I didn't want to dehydrate. On top of everything else, I thought, dehydration would just about finish me off.

I trudged on another ten minutes, another twenty. I was at the top of the cliff now where I'd hoped the cottages would be and not only was there no sign of them but absolutely nothing looked familiar. The bay looked wrong, there was a clump of scrawny trees I could swear I'd never seen before. . . . I stopped, and let myself have a couple of mouthfuls out of my bottle. It was nearly empty. I was going to have to turn back. I was going to have to hope against hope I could remember the way back and make it down to the harbor again. . . . Heart like a stone, I turned round.

I'd been stumbling along for about five minutes trying not to cry, when I heard the moped. Getting louder, closer. I stood stock-still, praying, *Let it be Alex, let it be Alex.* Let it not just be a farmer who rides on by.

The bike stopped, and the rider pulled off his helmet. It was Frazer. "All right, Chloe?" he said deadpan.

**CHAPTER 50**

"NO," I CROAKED. "I'M not. I'm lost. I was trying to get to the cottages. . . ."

"Yeah? You've gone past them. Want me to give you a lift back?"

"Is . . . is Alex there?"

"Yes. Unless he's gone off for a swim. He's . . . *heeyy*, it's OK. Look, jump on, OK?"

I'd started crying, I couldn't help it, dehydration or not. Great fat tears were spooling down my face at the thought of seeing Alex soon. I swatted them away and jumped on the moped behind Frazer and we took off without another word.

We saw Alex heading to the edge of the cliff, where the swimming rocks were. Frazer kind of arced round in front of him, cutting across his route like a sheepdog rounding up a stray. Then he stopped the bike and I got off, and he roared away without a word.

"Hey," Alex said.

"Hi," I muttered.

"Where were you last night?"

"With my mum. Alex, I'm so sorry—I thought—"

"Your *mum*?"

"Davinia's mum phoned her, told her I'd done a runner to Hilly's. So she came out."

"Blimey. Couldn't she just phone?"

"Cassie told her she thought I was having a breakdown."

"Well, that was obviously crap."

"And . . . well . . . she thought I might not speak to her. We haven't seen each other for more than a year."

"*What?*"

"It was me . . . I wouldn't see her. She walked out on my dad last summer, to live with someone else, and I wouldn't see her, and . . ." The tears were starting again. I practically punched myself in both eyes, to try and stop them.

Alex must've seen them, but he didn't come closer, he didn't touch me.

"When you dropped me off with my case," I croaked, "I went into the courtyard, and Mum was there, just sitting there . . . we talked, and Cora gave me the night off, I went to dinner with her. . . . I should've left you a message, I'm so sorry, I was so blown away I just didn't *think*. . . ."

"So what . . . she flew out here, just to see you were OK? That's amazing. So you've made up now?"

"Yes. I spent the night at her hotel, I should be with her now but . . ."

There was something wrong, I could feel it. Something had happened to him. He was cut off, wary. Had the cradle-snatcher been at Hilly's again? Or someone else? I should've known.

It had been too good, too amazing, too powerful. . . . It couldn't have been real.

"I'm sorry I didn't leave you a message," I croaked, "but why didn't you ask Cora where I was, she'd've told you. . . ."

"She was busy."

There was a long, long silence. Then I decided I was too bone-weary, too wrung out, to pussyfoot around. "Alex, what's wrong?" I wailed.

"Nothing," he answered.

"You're all weird."

"No, I'm not."

"I've said I'm sorry."

"It's OK. I understand. You had to see your mum, of course you did."

"I should get back," I muttered. "I've walked

out on Cora, I need to call Mum. . . ."

"Why did you come out here?"

I felt like he'd hit me. This time I let the tears just pour. *"Because I had to see you,"* I sobbed, "I hoped you'd come to Hilly's at lunchtime, but when you *didn't come* I . . ."

I'm not sure which of us lurched forward first. Maybe it was absolutely instantaneous. But we collided in a great bear hug, I gripped his head like I was going to tear it off and we were kissing like we'd been starved of each other for a year. "What was it?" I gasped. "What was it? Why were you so weird?"

"Because," he breathed, "it scared me absolutely sodding shitless, the way I felt when you weren't there . . . just *not there* last night. . . . I didn't know what to do, I couldn't talk, I couldn't ask anyone. . . . I nearly smashed the bike getting back here, I was useless, you ask Frazer. . . ."

"But . . . but when I turned up today? I walked all this way just to see you?"

"It scares me, Chloe. Oh, fuck, it scares me what I feel for you." And he half pulled away from me. "We haven't even slept together, and I feel like this. It's not good."

"Yes, it is," I said. Inside me, I was cracking up,

breaking up with sheer joy. "Don't be such a coward."

And I took hold of his hand and towed him back from the cliff's edge, back toward the cottages.

## CHAPTER 51

THROUGH THE COTTAGE DOOR was a block of white-hot sun, his mattress on the floor was in dark shade beside it. We lay down on it and kissed and undressed each other, legs and arms and clothes all tangled, and when we were naked he said, "You sure, Chloe? You sure about this?"

"Yes," I said. "Stop talking."

He kissed me again, and then he pulled away and groaned, a real pitiful, heartbreaking groan, and said, "I haven't got anything. *You* know."

I didn't know what he meant at first, then I realized he meant a condom. It was so stupid, so silly, I giggled.

"Don't laugh!" he said, hurt.

"I'm not. I mean, I *am*, but it doesn't matter, *Alex*, it doesn't matter. . . ." A bit of me was relieved. I loved just being naked together, exploring each other, touching each other. . . .

"Thing is," he went on, brow all furrowed gorgeously, "after what we've been through—at the start—fighting and everything—I didn't want to rush things, screw things up with you. . . ."

"So, you don't just . . . have them, then. Condoms. In case you get lucky."

"The only person I wanted to get lucky with was you, Chloe." I laughed and climbed on top of him and he muttered, "Shall I see if Frazer's got some?"

"No. Don't move. Let's just stay here. Don't move."

It was so sexy, lying on him, looking down at his perfect face, bending to kiss him. It was like he was adoring my breasts with his hands. Then he groaned again and kind of shucked me off him, saying, "I need to cool off. Let's go for a swim. This is torture, Chloe."

"OK," I said. "And after the swim . . . oh, God. Yesterday I make you get my case from Davinia's place, and now I'm gonna make you have tea with my mother."

"And in between, you jump on me and torture me." He stood up, walked into the hot block of sun from the doorway while I ogled him, every inch of him. He grinned down at me. "Just as well I'm crazy about you."

We swam off the rocks like we were in a dream. Knowing we were going to make love together soon changed everything, colored everything.

## CHAPTER 52

**SO THEN FOR THE** next few hours I was walking in two realities. There was the reality where I went with Alex to see Mum at her little hotel, and sat down and had tea and enjoyed the strawberry tarts and was pleased she and Alex got on well, pleased she accepted that I was staying on in Caminos now.

And there was the reality where I was shaking with being so close to Alex all the time, aware of his every move, breath, every sense of him— where I had to ration how often I let myself look at him, just to keep on being able to function in the other reality.

When we'd seen Mum, we went back to Hilly's so I could throw myself on Cora's mercy. But before I could do that, though, Cora threw herself on me. "I was unsympathetic, darling—a beast!" she said, hugging me. "You were having dramas and traumas and all I could care about was the lunch menu!"

"Oh, Cora—I'm so sorry I left you in the lurch. . . . Did you manage?"

"Yes, of *course* we managed. We always manage. We're managing now, though we open in twenty minutes, and Saul is late again. . . ." She turned and looked at Alex appraisingly. "How d'you think you'd do on the door, young man? Hmm? Ever worked as a bouncer?"

That night, I was great on the floor, Alex was great on the door. He stayed on it even when Saul turned up. Saul didn't mind this—he said he liked being in where the action was. I checked on the toilets obsessively, so I could race along and see Alex, and if no one was coming in or going out, we'd kiss fast and frantically. All the time there was this energy like a force field or something between us, even when we were the whole long corridor apart.

Mum turned up for a couple of hours, like she'd promised to, to "see me in action." Cora made a fuss of her and bought her one of the best cocktails, and told me to go and sit with her for a bit: "We have three young men here tonight, darling! You're not so necessary!" Mum told me how much she liked Alex and Cora and Hilly's, how she understood why I wanted to stay on till the end of the summer. But all the time this drum was beating inside me, that that night I was going to sleep with Alex, and I was scared and excited, I could hardly concentrate on what she was talking about.

It didn't seem to matter, though. She looked so happy, just to be sitting across the table from me. When I said I thought I should get back to work, she stood up too, and said she'd make her way back to her hotel.

Then she reminded me she was flying back tomorrow. "Oh, *Mum*," I muttered. "I've hardly seen you. . . ."

"Look—you've *seen* me, and that's all that matters!" she said warmly, and she put her arms round me. "I can't tell you what that means to me, Chloe. And when you come home, we'll see each other then, won't we?"

"Yes," I whispered, throat tight. Going home— I hated to think about it. I *wouldn't* think about it. I kissed her good-bye and promised to go to her hotel for breakfast.

At closing time, I took Alex by the hand and led him into my storeroom. "Don't you have to ask Cora?" he asked.

"No," I said. "She won't mind." Somehow, I knew she wouldn't.

"And you're . . . you're sure? I mean—you've just met up with your mum again, you're shaken up, you're . . ."

"Emotionally vulnerable. I know I am and I *like* it, it feels pretty alive to me. I like not being timid and fearful and not-taking-risks anymore. Oh, God, this is gonna sound weird, and I don't know if I can explain it properly, but I just feel like I've come out of a box or something, and life is extreme and sweet and . . ."

"You sound like you've taken cocaine."

"Well, I haven't. I don't *need* to, trust me."

"Me neither," he said.

I took hold of his hand and pulled him over to the couch. Then I remembered something. "Oh, shit. Did you . . . ?"

"Don't worry. I just about cleaned out the machine in the men's room."

The first time you sleep with someone is meant to be pretty crap, isn't it? You don't know each other's bodies well enough, you're awkward, clumsy . . .

This wasn't crap. It was over much too soon and Alex kept saying sorry until I put my hand over his mouth, but it joined us and I knew it was only the start and I was so glad we'd made that start.

We lay afterward just holding each other, my head on his shoulder. The night was hot, oppressive, despite having the door to the yard open. "Want a shower?" he whispered, and we got up and walked naked outside, and sprayed each other with the hose, and it got colder and colder as the warm water from lying in the pipes was used up.

"God, that's better," said Alex. "That's brilliant. I've come back to life." And he grinned and towed me back to the couch.

The next morning, we woke as the first heat of the sun came through the open door, and made love for the third time. "If it keeps getting better and better, like this," Alex murmured, "my head's gonna blow off."

"Mine too."

"I won't fancy you without a head."

"You won't see me. You won't have a head either, remember."

"Yuck, gross. Making love without heads." We went outside for another blissful shower. Then we tore ourselves apart, and Alex went off to the cottages, and I went to meet Mum.

Why does life do this to you—why is it like that? It starves you for nearly a year, then it gives you a great big blob of candy floss (Davinia) and you're ecstatic for a while and then you realize how synthetic that is and you starve again and then . . . *then* . . . it feeds you real food, but twice as much as you can cope with. I had Mum back, and I had Alex, and I felt like I wanted to gorge on both of them and each alone was more than enough to fill me up. . . .

Mum and I had a big breakfast together, with the best coffee I've ever tasted. Although everything delighted me—the omelet, the toast, the perfect figs nestling on a fig leaf like a green hand. . . . I wanted to tell her about sleeping with Alex but it wasn't right, it was too fantastically shocking to me still, so I just sat there feeling amazing and very aware of my body and let her talk about how good it was going to be at home, now that she and I were friends again. And I agreed with her; I talked about coming to meet her new "partner" and staying at her new place in the spare room she'd always thought of as mine. But something inside me didn't think it was real. Something inside me couldn't admit I was ever going to leave the island.

Around eleven o'clock I walked with her to the ferry so she could go back to the mainland to get her plane, and it kind of flowered inside me that she was my mum again, but I had no regrets that I wasn't flying back with her. We hugged and kissed and she said, "Under three weeks till you're home, Chloe. I can't wait."

As I waved her off, *under three weeks* tolled in my head, like some kind of dark bell.

## CHAPTER 53

SO NOW LIFE WAS set in a kind of delirious, delicious pattern. Alex would turn up night after night at Hilly's and be the new doorman; business was great and Cora was paying him now. If I had to do the lunch session at Hilly's the next day, he'd stay the night with me and drive off on his bike the next morning to do his stint at the cottage. We'd always have the afternoon together. Swimming, making love, sleeping. If I didn't have to do lunches the next day, we'd both drive back together in the dark and spend the night in the cottage. I loved that. It felt like we were the only two in the world, with nothing but the sound of us moving against each other, and the sea.

Frazer had tactfully moved out and was staying in his uncle's garage; more and more, he'd work there and leave me and Alex up on the cliff on our own. I was really getting into my garden. I finished mending the old wall and laid out a new one that curved elegantly round the fig tree and collected any rain that might fall to slake its roots. I found some wild thyme growing under a mass of creepers, cleared the creepers away, and started an herb garden. Alex laughed at how pleased I was by all the lizards scooting about, wanted to know why I liked them so much.

"I dunno," I said, "I just do. I love the way they're not furry, they're smooth and green, they're like *tendrils* moving about. . . ."

"Tendrils?"

"Plants. You know. They're like plants made into animals."

"You're bonkers," he said, and kissed me.

We hadn't told each other we loved each other. But I loved him and I knew he loved me; he had to the way he looked at me when he laughed at something I'd said, the way he listened, the way he touched me, traveling every inch of me.

We hadn't talked about what would happen when we both went home again. I couldn't bear the thought of being on the same plane as the Morgan-Harwoods, so I'd changed my flight to fly home a week after them, which meant I missed the first three days of term. Alex said he was heading back a couple of weeks after me. It was like a taboo, talking about home life. Once, only once, I asked him what he'd do when the summer was over and his face went very dark and he muttered, "Re-sits." I didn't dare ask any more. And I didn't dare ask where he lived, back in England. Maybe it wasn't England. Maybe he just had the accent, but he actually lived in the Outer Hebrides and once we left Caminos we'd never, ever see each other again.

Neither of us wanted to break the spell, let the outside in.

One day as we sat in front of the cottage eating bread and tomatoes and cheese, waiting to go down to Hilly's for the evening shift, he said, "I wish we could stay here. I wish we could *live* like this."

But we both knew we couldn't. Even on this beautiful island, autumn would come, the summer would be over. Hilly's would close. . . . Everything would shut down. And we'd have to go home.

There were days off, of course, blissful long days when we spent every minute together. Alex took days off to match mine. Then, five days before my flight home, Alex announced he was taking me out for a special lunch. He told me he'd pick me up at midday and told me I had to get really tarted up.

The restaurant was on the coast, on a platform built on huge rocks. The sea shone unreal blue, the sky was almost as blue above it; waves crashed and sprayed onto the decking. A smooth waiter in white greeted us and showed us to the table Alex had booked under a canopy right at the edge, past all these tables with elegant people at them. I was awed at first, and I could see Alex was intimidated too, by the way he was scowling, so I took his hand and suddenly we were fine, we were loving it, we sailed through all the tables across to the edge and everyone seemed to be watching us and I thought of my gran's old saying, *All the world loves lovers*. Maybe what we felt was showing on us, maybe we were shining with it.

We drank cold perfect wine and ate fresh fish and wonderful green beans and tiny potatoes with herbs on them, and talked about how we wished we could live here forever, but we still didn't talk about going home.

Afterward, Alex drove along the coast road for a while and then stopped, saying he wanted to show me something. We scrambled down the side of the coast and walked along these long, sandstone platforms like moonscape, scoured flat and smooth by the sea. In front of us were these weird otherwordly sculptures, growing out of the rock—one looked like the face of an ancient giant, one was a foot, another a great, polished egg. "Who did them?" I asked, awed.

And Alex said, "The sea."

We walked on and on. The sun had started to drop into the sea. And we turned a corner and there ahead of me was the rock I'd sat on all that time ago, the rock that was like a pale disk in front of the huge red disk of the sun, that I'd sat on all that time ago when I'd let the grief about Mum pour out of me. I didn't say anything to Alex, I just towed him over to it and sat down, and he sat beside me.

And it was mythic, it was perfect, I couldn't contain it, I wanted to shout out loud or cry or at least tell Alex how I was feeling . . . and then I knew that that was just a way of ducking it, of not coping with it, and I knew if I didn't want to lose it I just had to sit there and be silent and *be*.

It was extraordinary, it felt like the sky and the rock and the heat . . . they were entering me, they were *breathing* me. That's what it felt like. It was overpowering but I didn't let it overpower me, I just sat there and took it, sat there and *was*.

Something in me knew Alex was feeling something like this too. Not the same maybe, but something special. And then his hand moved across the warm rock and covered mine. And I felt blessed, it was so perfect, I didn't want anything more.

If Davinia and I had turned out to be lesbians, I thought, would this have been enough for us then? Just sitting here in the sun and the silence? I knew it wouldn't have been for Davinia. Nothing was ever quite good enough for her, nothing was ever quite right. But it was right for us.

It was right for us.

After a while, I turned to him and said, "Five days to go till I go back again."

"Don't," he said. "I don't want to think about it. I want to make love to you."

"Me too. D'you think we can be seen?"

"No. If people look, they'll just look straight into the sun. They'll be *blinded*." He reached for the buttons on the fancy sundress I was wearing, undid the top one, then the next. I wrapped myself round him. It was just the two of us, there on that rock. All we had was the present, the now. We were scared to let the future in. If we let the future in, so much could go wrong.

I kissed him and thought: But it could also go *right*.

I took in another breath of the sky and the rock and the heat and said, "Alex—you've got to tell me. Alex—*where do you live*?"

# EPILOGUE

**YOU DIDN'T REALLY THINK** I'd just leave it there, did you?

When I asked Alex where he lived, first he swore, then he muttered the name of a town about thirty miles from Dad's new flat. So I laughed and told him my address and then, crazy with relief and hope, we made love on the hot rock, and he blurted out that he loved me, and I told him I loved him too, then we went back to the cottage for the night.

And that night the future was there with us too.

I thought I'd die of grief when he saw me off at the ferry. He wanted to come over to the mainland to see me onto my plane but I wouldn't let him. He gave me a tiny box wrapped in thin blue paper that he told me I could only open when the plane was in the air. I tore it open right after takeoff. Inside was a beautiful lizard brooch, filigree silver like the butterfly I'd wanted to buy in Victoria. I cried all over it—the poor little thing must have thought it was a newt.

Alex stayed on in Caminos for another couple of weeks, finishing off the cottage. We were in touch, of course—he got himself a new mobile and we texted every day. But it was a starvation diet after what we'd been used to. I went back to school to finish off my A levels. Davinia came up to me on my first day back and was all over me, very impressed I'd missed the first three days of term, bleating about letting bygones be bygones. The summer had knocked her confidence, the way she'd been trashed by Max and I'd walked out on her and everything. She kind of waved it all away, what had happened, telling me she *knew* she was an awful bitch but she really was trying to change. So we kind of picked up where we'd left off. You could still have a laugh with her. She took more notice of me now and I took less of her, so it balanced out.

Abby wouldn't speak to me at all. As if I cared.

Then Alex came home, and we met at a pub halfway between our hometowns because neither of us was prepared to meet the other one's family yet. Even though Alex had already met my mum, he felt mega-intimidated by the thought of my dad, no matter how often I texted what a softy he was.

It was awful at first when we met at the pub. I couldn't even look at him properly, his face seemed to sear into me, and we hugged all awkwardly but didn't kiss and we sat across from each other at this nasty pub table and everything seemed to be *brown* and dull and dreary and disappointing. Then we started to talk, and our eyes danced, and it was us again, making something new in England . . . and soon we were making plans, plans about next summer, and spending the whole of it in Caminos again. Well, Cora said I could have my job back, didn't she? And Uncle Harry would always need help.

Then we kissed for ages in the pub car park and agreed we'd go crazy if we couldn't sleep together soon.

So after that I made Dad agree to let Alex stay in my room and he'd ride down just about every weekend to see me. Sometimes I'd stay at Mum's, at the new room she'd made for me, but Alex wouldn't come there. I couldn't bring myself to like her new "partner," but we were civil to each other and he made himself scarce a lot when I was there, so Mum and I could spend time together.

We had a lot of catching up to do.

Alex and I were both working at our studies; no one could complain.

And all the time the next summer was getting closer.

We were too young, of course we were too young, and we had university and jobs and our futures to think of and . . . like I said before, so much could go wrong.

But it could also go *right*.

# The summer romance has only just gotten started—turn the page for more romantic holidays!

## The Boyfriend League

**By Rachel Hawthorne**

Dani's a tomboy, totally useless when it comes to romance. But this summer she and her best friend have a foolproof plan to change all that. Both of their families will be hosting summer league baseball players—a whole league of potential boyfriends!

## So Inn Love

**By Catherine Clark**

Liza has finally landed her dream job, living and working at a beautiful beach resort on the coast of Rhode Island. Now she just needs to figure out how to be part of the in (inn) crowd—and whether her hot coworker Hayden could be more than just a summer fling.

# The Boyfriend League

by RACHEL HAWTHORNE

*Families Needed to Provide Homes for Rattlers*

For anyone not familiar with Ragland, Texas, the front-page headline in that morning's *Ragland Tribune* may have seemed odd. But I'd lived in Ragland since the day I was born. I couldn't think of anything more exciting than living with a Rattler.

It was Thursday morning, and I'd grabbed the newspaper to check out my weekly column, "Runyon's Sideline Review," because it was always a rush to see my byline. But sitting at the breakfast table, before I'd turned to the sports section where my column usually appeared, the headline had snagged my attention and the possibilities bombarded me.

I absolutely couldn't believe I hadn't thought of it before. Having a Rattler in the house would be awesome!

1

Okay, I don't mean the slithering-along-the-ground-tail-rattling-in-ominous-warning rattler. I mean the sexy, hot, to-die-for players on our town's collegiate baseball team. As part of the Lonestar League, the Ragland Rattlers was one of nine city teams in the north Texas area made up of college players who wanted to play baseball during the summer. Local families hosted the team players.

Apparently this year, they were a few families short. And what better family than mine?

I heard a car honk and knew it was my ride to the softball field. My best friend and I both played on the high school softball team, but during the summer we just played whenever we had time to arrange a game with friends, which wasn't very often. Between attending the major- and minor-league games played in the area, plus being almost-groupies to the collegiate league, we didn't have a lot of time to commit to organized sports of our own.

I mean, if the choice was playing on a field with girls or watching a field of guys, Bird and I were going to choose the guys every time.

Her real name is Barbara Sawyer, but when she was a baby, her dad had thought she looked like a tiny bird, always chirping for food, and so he started calling her Birdie, which, over time, became Bird. Sometimes you gotta wonder what parents are thinking when they name or nickname their kids.

My own dad, I knew exactly what he'd been thinking when I was born. He wanted a boy. Instead he got me. Definitely a girl.

A year before I came along, my mom had given him another daughter, Tiffany, and Mom figured two kids were more than enough, especially since she wasn't a stay-at-home mom. We were a two-income family with a two-income lifestyle. Mom worked as a legal secretary in a prestigious Dallas law firm about thirty miles south of Ragland.

Anyway, Dad decided if he wasn't going to have a son, he could at least have a son-sounding name in the family. Hence, my parents named me Danielle, which of course, got shortened to Dani.

But it all worked out. I love my dad, and we're really close. Connecting with my dad has always meant connecting with sports. Over time, I've gained an appreciation for all sports. In fact, I plan to major in journalism when I go off to college in another year. I want to be a sports announcer.

Bird, however, insists that my desire for a career in sports reporting has nothing to do with my love of sports. "It's your other love: guys. You want to know what really goes on in the locker

3

room, and you want to get up close and personal with those towel-wrapped hotties."

Her theory is a lot closer to the truth than I like to admit, because it makes me seem less than noble in my pursuit of a higher education.

Bird honked again. She has her own car. I share one with Tiffany, but she'd already called it for the day. Actually, she'd called it pretty much for the entire summer, and since she had "obligations," I was used to her getting what she wanted. Especially guys. I basically carry a mop to clean up their drool whenever she's around.

Did I mention my sister is gorgeous? Gaggingly so.

I picked up my softball cap from the table, settled it on my head, and pulled my reddish-brown shoulder-length hair, which I was presently wearing in a ponytail, through the opening in the back. Tiffany has thick, lustrous, amazing hair that's more red than brown, but not red enough that anyone would call her Red. It's glorious.

While mine tends to just . . . hang. Which is the reason I usually wear it pulled back.

I grabbed my glove off the counter and headed out the door. It was the first official week of summer, the first week of no homework, no classes, no schedules, no bells. I was in heaven.

There are only two things I like as much as I like summer: baseball and boys.

Not necessarily in that order. But baseball has always been an important part of my life. Boys not nearly as much. I've never had a boyfriend, and I'm really starting to get bummed out by that fact. After all, next year I'll be a senior. As far as I'm concerned, it's long past time I had a boyfriend.

Oh, I've had a date now and then, but nothing long-term, nothing serious, nothing that's had my heart doing cartwheels inside my chest. Nothing that even hinted at any permanence.

I spotted the familiar white Grand Am waiting at the curb, idling, and sounding like it was shaking something loose beneath the hood. It's way older than I am, but I wasn't complaining. I was just grateful Bird could provide a ride.

I opened the car door, slid inside, and buckled up. "Did you see this morning's *Tribune*?"

Bird glanced in the rearview mirror before pulling out into the street. "Are you kidding? Mom took it for the Wed and Dead sections."

Bird's mom sells real estate. Newly married couples need places to live, newly dead people . . . well, their houses need to be sold, usually to the newly wed.

5

"Why? Did I miss something interesting?" Bird asked.

"They need extra families to host the Rattlers."

"And this concerns us because?"

"What is the one thing you want more than anything else?"

"You mean other than your autographed Babe Ruth baseball?"

In his youth, my granddad had watched Ruth play, and had gotten his autograph on a baseball. He'd given it to me the first time I hit a home run.

"Yeah, other than that," I said.

"A boyfriend."

I twisted around in my seat so I could look at her directly and accurately judge her reaction to what I was about to suggest. She so didn't look like a bird. Well, maybe she did a little. A ruffled bird. Her blonde hair was cut really short with different layers, so even when she styled it, it didn't look styled. It sorta poked out here and there, which she said made it easy to care for, because no one knew if she'd taken the time to fix it or not. Which in her case was usually not.

"How do you get a boyfriend?" I asked.

"If I knew that, I'd have one," Bird said.

"Hanging around guys. And where are there lots of guys during the summer?"

Bird pulled into the parking lot near the softball/baseball fields. She turned to me and arched a brow in question. She's one of the few people I know who actually have that whole Spock thing going and can make one eyebrow shoot way up. "Are you going somewhere with this?"

"There are lots of guys playing for the Ragland Rattlers," I explained. "It's a team of potential boyfriends."

"Not so far. Do we not traditionally hang out at the ball field during every practice and every game?"

"But we've always been no-name spectators. This year we could move into the realm of something more important. Let's talk our parents into letting us sponsor players for the summer. Then we'll hang out with them, and they'll hang out with the team. We'll have an in that we've never had. We'll be like ambassadors to Ragland, making them feel welcome, showing them around. Before we know it, instant summer boyfriends!"

# So Inn Love

### by CATHERINE CLARK

"Well, see you around, Beth," she interrupted me. Then she turned back to the group she'd been talking to when I first walked up to Zoe and her other friends.

*Wow,* I thought. If Caroline was part of the "in crowd," then maybe I didn't want to be. "It's *Liza,*" I said to her back.

"Hey, Liza. And don't mind her, she's not that nice to anyone."

I turned and saw Hayden—the guy who'd arrived right after me—standing beside me. "Seriously?"

He nodded. "Caroline's not exactly the person you send out on the welcome wagon."

"Okay, but here's the thing. Have you ever *seen* a welcome wagon? Like, what's in it?"

"And who pulls it? Horses?" Claire added.

We all laughed, that kind of nervous laughter when you first meet someone.

"So you're Liza. And you are?" Hayden asked.

"Claire. We're new hires," she explained. "You know, apparently the only two new people here?"

"Oh, come on, you're not the *only* new ones," Hayden said. "That guy, Josh, over there . . . and that other guy, what's his name. There're at least five or six of you."

"Someone over there just called us newbies," Claire said. "I hate that phrase, or term, or whatever it is."

"I know," I said. "We can't help it if we didn't work here before.

"So, non-newbies," Hayden said. "Don't get a complex. Hayden Overton. Nice to meet you."

"Same here," I said. At least one person in the so-called in crowd was being nice to us. And as I'd learned from moving, that was really all it took. If one person accepted you or decided you were cool—then everyone would.

"You know what? You want to get out of here?" Hayden said.

"Aren't we supposed to go to the dorm?" Claire asked.

"The dorm can wait. *Believe* me," Hayden said. "Especially since—" He stopped and looked at us for a second.

"Since what?" I wanted to know.

He shook his head. "Never mind. We've got half an hour before we need to meet up with Peach again. Come on, let's hit the water."

I looked at Claire. "I'm all for it. You?"

"Sure," Claire said. "Sounds good."

"You know what—I see someone I've got to say hi to. But I'll be right down, okay?" Hayden told us.

"He seems nice," Claire said as we walked outside onto the Inn's back porch, which stretched almost the entire length of the building. It had tables and chairs for guests, and standing on it, we looked straight out at the Atlantic Ocean.

"Very," I agreed. I stood on the steps for a few seconds, admiring the view. Then I stepped off onto the boardwalk and turned to look back up at the Inn. It was as gorgeous as I remembered. It was four stories tall, with white shutters and weather-beaten-looking blue-gray paint. Every room had two windows, and a few of them had small decks with big Adirondack chairs facing the ocean.

I loved the salty ocean smell that hit my nose as soon as I turned onto the road toward the beach. It's not as if we lived *so* far from the ocean, but I still didn't get there very much, especially not during the school year. Every summer's first trip to Rhode Island made my nose so happy.

My boyfriend back home had been really upset—no, mad—when I told him I was going away for the summer. He didn't understand, but that was because he'd never been here, never seen how gorgeous it was. Anyway, we were only talking about ten weeks. That whole time he'd be busy working the graveyard shift at his uncle's boat factory, and we wouldn't have seen each other even if I was around, working at my dad's law office.

Besides, it wasn't that kind of relationship. We went out when it was convenient, and we had a good time together—but I wouldn't die without him. I'd never had that kind of feeling for anyone. I didn't think I was the type of person to die for love, anyway. I wasn't into big drama.

"A private beach? This is incredible," Claire said as we stepped off the wooden boardwalk.

I slipped off my sandals before I jumped off into the warm sand. Since the Inn wasn't open for business yet, the beach was all ours. "I've never been on this part of the beach." I pointed to a public beach across the breakwater. "That's where we used to hang out. See how it's all crowded?"

Claire laughed. "You and Caroline hung out over there? Hard to believe."

"Why?"

"Oh, I don't know. You don't seem like . . . the same kind of people. To be friends, I mean."

"No. Not anymore, I guess."

While we were talking, I was digging my toes into the sand, watching the water roll over my feet, which were sinking a little deeper with each wave and the undertow that followed. I loved that feeling; it was so relaxing.

Suddenly I felt someone's hands on my shoulders.

"Are you ready for your initiation, newbies?"

I turned around and saw Hayden standing behind me. He squeezed my shoulders. "Initiation?" I asked. What was he talking about? This didn't sound good. And here I'd thought he was being so nice to us. "What's that?"

"It's a rite of passage," a guy named Richard said as he swooped up Claire in his arms, with one quick motion.

"Hey! Put me down!" Claire protested.

"You're not actually going to—" I started to say, as I struggled against Hayden. "You're not serious. You think you can—"

"Yeah, I do." He picked me up by the waist, sideways, as if I were a suitcase under his arm, and dragged me closer to the water.

"Since when is there initiation around here?" Claire demanded.

"Since now!" And Richard lifted her in the air and tossed her into the surf.

Before I could laugh at her, I found myself being lifted over Hayden's head—and the next thing I knew I was underwater. It was freezing cold and bubbling up all around me as a wave tumbled over my head. My feet were standing on sand and crushed shells. I surfaced and slicked back my hair, the salt water stinging my eyes. Around me I could hear a few other people complaining, and Claire was yelling at Richard. All the new people were in the water, including Josh. As he waded out, he looked at me and Claire and said, "So it's us against them, huh?"

"I guess so." I glanced back at shore and saw Hayden watching me.

What he didn't know was that I didn't really care if I got tossed in—I was dying for my first swim in the ocean, anyway. So it didn't have to be in my clothes, but I didn't care. What a great feeling.

I looked at my arm and saw my temporary tattoo dissolving in the choppy salt water, colors streaming off my arm. I felt something tugging at me and found a long thick piece of seaweed—the kelp kind that reminds me of lasagna noodles— wrapped around my right leg.

Hayden was smiling at me as I strode out of the surf. "You actually *liked* that, didn't you?"

I pulled the seaweed off my leg and threw it at him as I walked past. "Doesn't everyone like swimming?" I asked him with a smile.

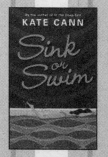